ANA TURNS

ALSO BY LISA GORNICK

The Peacock Feast
Louisa Meets Bear
Tinderbox
A Private Sorcery

ANA
TURNS

a novel

LISA
GORNICK

author of The Peacock Feast

+ KEYLIGHT
B O O K S
AN IMPRINT
OF TURNER
PUBLISHING

KEYLIGHT BOOKS
AN IMPRINT OF TURNER PUBLISHING COMPANY
Nashville, Tennessee
www.turnerpublishing.com

Ana Turns

Cover design by M.S. Corley
Book design by William Ruoto

Library of Congress Cataloging-in-Publication Data

Names: Gornick, Lisa, author.
Title: Ana turns / Lisa Gornick.
Description: Nashville, Tennessee : Keylight Books, [2023]
Identifiers: LCCN 2022061356 (print) | LCCN 2022061357 (ebook) | ISBN 9781684421398 (hardcover) | ISBN 9781684421404 (paperback) | ISBN 9781684421411 (epub)
Subjects: LCGFT: Novels.
Classification: LCC PS3607.O598 A84 2023 (print) | LCC PS3607.O598 (ebook) | DDC 813/.6—dc23/eng/20230113
LC record available at https://lccn.loc.gov/2022061356
LC ebook record available at https://lccn.loc.gov/2022061357

Printed in the United States of America

To Marian, who taught me to read,
opening the door to the infinite world—

To feel the present sliding over the depths of the past, peace is necessary.

—Virginia Woolf, "A Sketch of the Past," 1939

ANA
TURNS

MIDNIGHT

The second hand on the Museum of Modern Art desk clock
arrives at the twelve to align with the minute and hour arrows so that for
an instant the three form a vector pointed heavenward, shepherding in
my sixtieth birthday. The clock was a rare gift from my father, Rolf, dead
this past year, who never remembered my birthday. My mother, Jean,
never forgets. Of late, she's memorialized the day with an email sent
at midnight, more cyberattack—italicized and bolded fonts, hyperlinks,
·capitalized text—than Hallmark sentiments.

I peer out my seventh-floor window, across the dark moat of Central
Park, as if I could see my eighty-eight-year-old mother a mile to the east,
barricaded in the tower where she launches these missives. Last year's
had simply *Ana* in the subject line. My mother, who'd wanted *Anna*,
was disappointed when my father insisted on removing an *n* because
he deemed the double ungainly, and then disappointed again when I
more closely resembled an androgynous Giacometti, collarbones in lieu
of cleavage, than a stolid milkmaid like her Swedish forebears.

That email—last year's—included the pronouncement that having
been a better student of mathematics than my brother, *who suffered
from the ignorance of educators at the time of <u>attentional problems</u> in youth
(which his ENORMOUS SUCCESS proves he's outgrown)*, I should have
used my mathematical abilities. I would have made *a GREAT DEAL*

more money than I do as a psychological editor, **not** *listed as an occupation by the Bureau of Labor Statistics.* Without transition, my mother fired her final two bullets:

- Rolf Koehl is deceased, so I can tell you that HE DID NOT WANT ANY MORE CHILDREN after your brother and in protest he did **not** come to the hospital to meet you the night you were born.
- When I was *crying*, the nurses thought I was *overjoyed* by your arrival, but the truth is I was ***crushed*** by your father not being there.

Now my mother's latest birthday email sits atop my inbox with *Calculations* as the subject. Can I delete it unopened? For God's sake, I'm sixty years old. Am I not the sentry for my own mind?

I lean back in my desk chair. Yes, but tonight, at my birthday dinner, my mother will have radar tuned for my response. If she senses her communiqué unread, she'll retaliate with a cold shoulder that could last for months. I weigh the quantity of pain a season of iciness would cause against what the content of the email might produce.

I open it.

Ana:

On your 60ᵗʰ birthday, 04/28/2017, it seems appropriate to share the following CALCULATIONS that I made 20 years ago regarding the <u>inflation-adjusted</u> sum of money I spent on you.

- People *never* realize how VERY COSTLY it is to raise a child.
- If this information were more widely available, the <u>birth rate</u> would undoubtedly be lower and our economy *more* prosperous.
- I plan to write a letter to the <u>New York Times</u> on this subject.
- Twenty years ago, the number I calculated for the amount I spent raising you was **$56,000.00**.
- Adjusting for today's dollar value, this is equivalent to **$85,000.00**.

- Had I invested that money starting at your birth rather than spending it year by year on you, it would have grown with compound interest to nearly A QUARTER OF A MILLION DOLLARS.
- That would have been a *significant sum* for a single woman who now lives on her Social Security benefits and a small pension.

All of which is to say, being a parent is *a great sacrifice.*
Mom/Jean

I bury my head in my arms, the words detonating, my adult self imploding. *No*, I tell myself. *No, no, and no.* It's your day. You will not be wrecked by an old woman still ashamed of herself for believing at sixteen a catalog modeling agent's gravelly whisper that her Ingrid Bergman looks put the moon in reach. An old woman still angry at herself for at twenty spinning wildly out of her orbit with a man, my father, one of those magnetic bodies whose prodigious talent makes others feel charged by their presence.
No, no, and no.

ONLY ONCE DID I ASK MY FATHER WHY HIS MARRIAGE TO MY mother failed.

'Your mother had a tin ear. She pronounced *trompe l'oeil* "tramp doyle" and *Machu Picchu* "match-oh peeka." She bought vases at Pier 1 Imports and wore belted dresses long after she lost her model's waistline.'

What my father did not understand was that when he'd met my mother, she was already an old maid in the eyes of her parents, fifteen when they'd met on a boat from Rotterdam to New York. Both Swedes from villages a day's walk apart, my grandparents married in a Lutheran church just hours after clearing Ellis Island, their wedding night spent on a bench in Penn Station, waiting for the morning train to Baltimore, where an uncle would put them up with the pickle barrels in his cellar.

Nor did my father grasp that modeling had never been my mother's plan. It was an accident—the second mishap of her life, she claims, the first having been her birth, five years after her sister, Uma. Sweet, but too slow to add in her head the customers' orders at the bakery my grandparents had opened in a Jewish neighborhood, Uma had followed my grandmother's directive that she apply to be a file clerk at the Hutzler's department store. When, on the morning of an August back-to-school shoot, the teen model disappeared and a supervisor asked the clerks if they knew anyone to fill in, Uma's face lit up. Her fourteen-year-old sister, Jean, she said, was so beautiful, people couldn't help but stare on the bus. Two years later, a scout saw the catalog photos with my mother's wide-open face, her lake-blue eyes, her long, shapely legs. The week after she graduated from high school, he brought her to New York.

Not until I was married myself did I recognize that the dissolution of my parents' marriage had less to do with my father's displeasure at his wife's pronunciation or her inability to distinguish between machine-made and hand-blown glass than it did his awareness that with two young children, she'd ceased being impressed by his architectural genius or his having the private number of the *maître d'* at his favorite restaurant in Rome. Ceased being charmed by his pithy principles. Ceased caring about anything other than that the commissions she recorded in a quadrangle-ruled book, subtracting his expenses (the shoes bought at Crockett & Jones on trips to London, the bottles of Château Margaux ordered at client dinners), would cover the monthly household budget to which she assiduously abided.

In short, my mother had become a woman who would never again let anyone take anything from her, not even a letter in a daughter's name.

A TEXT ARRIVES AS I'M COUNTING THE BULLET POINTS IN MY mother's latest email: seven. Knowing my mother, deliberately a prime.

Fiona: *Still up? Can you talk?*

'Exceptionally intelligent people stay up late,' Fiona retorts whenever I lament during our wee hour calls that we should get to bed. 'Think about Emily Dickinson seeking her father's permission to write through the night. Or Obama at two a.m. in the Treaty Room of the White House with a Marilynne Robinson novel and his ration of seven almonds.'

Me: *Sure. Call my office line*

Henry says he knows it's a cliché that men who remain in love with their wives still see them, even decades later, as their girlish brides, but it's true for him with me. I could say the same about Fiona. I see her as she is now, but it's through the scrim of how she looked at twenty-four when we met in the English graduate program at Penn: her then glossy black hair now colored to hide the gray, her deep-set brown eyes now diminished by hooded lids, her dancer's high hips now welded with her thickened torso.

'Happy birthday,' Fiona sings when I pick up. 'How is it?'

'Surreal. I can hardly say the number aloud. I still think of myself as forty-six. Solidly middle-aged. Not someone entering the last chapter of life.'

'I'll be there in two years. And we are not entering the last chapter.'

'Realistically, the last third. But then there are moments when I feel thirteen. I just opened an email from my mother with a tally of what it cost her to raise me.'

'No . . .'

'Yes.'

'I'm sorry, love. That's low. Sorry, but not surprised. Did she include a spreadsheet?'

During the early years of our friendship, I recoiled each time Fiona called me *love*. Endearments from my mother or grandparents would have been as foreign as ancient Greek. 'Not *honey*, not *darling*, not *sweetie*?' Fiona asked when I admitted the jolt I experienced with her *love*. I shook my head, mortified that I was close to tears. 'Well, love, we'll have to get you used to it.'

'I've been telling myself I should feel grateful my mother still has the energy for that much hostility. The mental chops to do the math.'

'You know the saying that the opposite of love is indifference? Well, indifferent to you, Jean is not. But on your birthday—that's just mean.'

'She's still angry about my telling her I was upset by how my brother handled our father's will. Which was stupid of me. I should have known she couldn't tolerate any criticism of George.'

'I never thought I'd say this, but I kind of feel sorry for King George. Loving your kids means loving them, warts and all. Your mother loves the airbrushed version of your brother.'

With the banter, my adult self pieces back together. 'Her feelings about me are definitely not airbrushed. There's as much hate as love in the mix. In a perverse way, there's a kind of intimacy to it.'

'That's so twisted.'

'She'd push me in front of a bus if it meant she could keep George on his pedestal. And now George gets brownie points because he—or probably Catherine—made the arrangements with the restaurant for the dinner tonight, including a corking fee so he can supply the wine from his cellar.'

'He has a wine cellar? You never told me that.'

I want to say it just never came up, but the truth is I avoided mentioning my brother's wine cellar because of how ostentatious it would seem to Fiona, with her modest house half an hour north of the city. A house she and Charlie—when they first met, Fiona described him as brainy dorky; now she calls him *the people's on-the-spectrum poet*—saved for a decade to purchase. 'He rents a room in his building's basement. Catherine said he paid a fortune to put in wine racks and coolers.'

Fiona groans. 'We'll all be expected to stand up and cheer for King George and perfect wifey Catherine. Can't I whisk you off to a separate dinner? Leave your mother stewing with your brother over his precious bottles.'

I picture the scene: my mother, arrived pointedly early in one of her seven jelly bean–colored suits, pursing her mouth and repeatedly checking her watch while she demands that someone call my cell phone. Gemma, my pregnant molecular biologist niece stuffed into a business-style maternity outfit she relented and let Catherine buy, attempting to reason with her grandmother as Ella, her vegan baker older sister with her curls pinned helter-skelter, narrates a subway misadventure she and her fermented-foods-maker boyfriend had on the trip from their Queens apartment.

'We could go somewhere raucous with cheap house wine in carafes,' Fiona continues.

I hear drawers opening and closing: Fiona rummaging for her cigarette stash in the kitchen obsessively organized by Charlie.

'My goal for this decade is to follow Michelle. When they go low, we go high. To take seriously the compassion you and I are always talking about.'

'Bully for Michelle. But even if you believe in the turn-the-other-cheek bullshit, your mother has used up her quota of compassion received.'

'I have to give her credit for remaining essentially independent. And ditto with George. He's not a drug addict, he's never been in trouble with the law or been a burden to me. And he did give me two fabulous nieces.'

Fiona snorts. 'That's the logic of an abused wife whose husband just blackened her eye. *Well, at least he didn't smash my teeth.* What was it your brother said when your apartment was broken into? Call the police?'

'Call a locksmith.'

'You'd been in Philadelphia . . . What? Like a week? And he didn't come help you or offer for you to spend the night at his place?'

I feel a twinge of guilt that I've painted my brother too one-sidedly. Growing up as we did, crowded with our mother into our grandparents' row house, the five of us sharing a bathroom with a tank hanging over the toilet and a tub with no shower, the room permeated with the smells of old persons' bodies, our father's child support payments always in the mail but never arrived, George had survived by taking as his motto, *Me First.*

'In his defense, he'd already graduated from Wharton and moved downtown.'

'I wouldn't have been able to ever speak to him again.'

There's the sound of a match striking. Soon, Fiona will open the slider doors to let out the smoke, take Charlie's frayed barn jacket from a nearby hook, and step onto the cedar deck. Fiona won't comment on this—she officially stopped smoking decades ago when she was pregnant with Nick—nor will I, though each time it happens, I think about the summer when George, my mother, and I were all stealth smokers, stealing cigarettes from one another's hidden packs, unable to confront each other since that would have meant admitting our own use.

'I'll never forget you going white as a sheet,' Fiona says, 'at that stuffy English department cocktail party when I asked if walking home from the library at night creeped you out.'

'I couldn't believe you jumped in with that question—the first time we talked!—rather than the usual junk about where did you go to college or who's your advisor. I was afraid one of those old guys shuffling around the cheese table in their paisley bowties had overheard you tell me you hadn't started a paper due in the morning because you'd been working on your poems.'

'And you asked if you could read them! No one ever asks to read poems.'

In the morning, a brown envelope from Fiona was poking out of my mailbox in the English office. There was torrential rain that day, and I stood with my umbrella in front of the bank of cubbies, making a puddle on the floor, while I read the first line of the first poem—*A boy with hair slick as seaweed / a girl with molehill breasts*—and then, unable to stop, the rest of the packet. It was as though a stream of unarticulated experience had been run through a charcoal filter, rendering what's hazy crystal clear: the ideas, subtle yet precise; the observations, stripped of the usual adjectives, vivid and exact. I knew it was presumptuous to tell someone else, much less someone I'd just met, what to do with her life, but I was overcome with the certainty that I must urge Fiona to bag the English PhD and instead get an MFA in poetry.

To my amazement, Fiona responded by announcing that I was absolutely right and this was exactly what she was going to do. Two years later—Fiona by then in her last semester of the Hopkins writing program with her world turned inside out: her father exposed for running a Ponzi scheme on his Charleston jewelry customers, her mother, Fiona's best friend before me, diagnosed with ovarian cancer—I worried that I'd pointed Fiona, now penniless, down the wrong path. Going out on a limb, I asked my mother if Fiona could live for a few months in what had been my room. I planned to offer various compensations, but my mother immediately said yes. She felt sorry for Fiona. She, Jean, knew what it was like to scramble to find a roof.

'I can't promise I'll talk tonight to your brother, but I'll be nice to your mom.'

'She thinks you're buddies. She's always reminding me you had a symphony subscription together.'

'When she insisted we get the nosebleed seats, I thought it was because she knew how broke I was, but then she told me those were the seats she always got. What matters, she said, is to hear the music, not see the musicians. Once, there was a viola solo and I made a comment about your talent as a violist. She looked at me like she didn't even know you play the viola.'

The line sputters with an incoming call. Lance, the only other person who would phone at this hour. 'I'm not talented,' I say, ignoring the interruption. 'And I mostly practiced while my mother was at work.'

I expect Fiona to share some other story from her time living with my mother, maybe about Jean's driving—every passing car an emergency leading to pumping the brakes and honking the horn; getting pulled over for going so slowly it was a traffic hazard—but instead a pause settles between us.

'Okay, love,' Fiona says. 'We should get some sleep. 'Night.'

NOT UNTIL WE HANG UP DOES IT OCCUR TO ME THAT FIONA DIDN'T ask about Simon. I've told her that after six months of worrying—Is Simon in danger? Will Simon be harmed? Is my anxiety itself a harm?— I'm trying now to take worry breaks. Time off from adding to the list I keep with me always: topics to look up on the internet; questions to ask Henry. Fiona must have thought that today, my birthday, should be one of these breaks.

I sigh, my eyes resting on the park. When my father designed the apartment for Henry and me, he insisted I have the view from my office. During the day, the reservoir dominates: a blue egg sunk amidst the patches of trees, bushy as broccoli, and the wide swaths of lawn. At night, the lights from the Fifth Avenue buildings form a beaded chain on the far side.

With my elbows propped on my desk and my chin cradled in my

hands, I listen to Lance's voice mail: 'Hey babe, happy birthday. Call me. I'm not leaving my office until you do.'

I text my response: *It's nearly 2am . . . yoga early with my nieces so going to bed . . . will call in the morning*

Going to bed is a line in the sand Lance and I don't cross. We don't text or call with our partners at our sides. We don't slip under each other's marital sheets.

I turn off my desk lamp. *I can't go on like this*, I whisper into the dark. *I cannot.*

As always, I find Henry asleep on the floor of our little TV room, at the end of our long book-lined hall. There's a bolster tucked under his knees, and his T-shirt has ridden up from the waistband of his sweat pants, exposing the dark hair that fans out from his crotch and the fleshy roll that has accumulated now that he no longer exercises.

The television is on but silent because Henry, kind Henry, is wearing the headphones he purchased knowing I'd hated since childhood the sound of the television, blaring every minute my grandparents were home so I'd felt invaded, my very ability to think under siege. Then, before his back injury and the marijuana he discovered sufficiently blunted the pain to let him stop taking the prescribed opioids, his TV watching had been limited to intensive spurts during the World Series or March Madness, his evenings during the rest of the year occupied by baseball catches with Simon or planning our family travels or his ambitious reading of history and science.

A picture of a young blonde woman holding a toddler in her lap fills the screen. From the scrolling captions, I learn that she's Kayla Greenwood, whose father was killed when she was five by an escaped convict, Kenneth Williams, imprisoned for murdering an Arkansas cheerleader.

I study the young woman's face. Her expression is strangely serene. The screen splits to include a photograph of Williams, somber with wire-rimmed glasses and a neatly trimmed goatee. During Williams's escape, the captions say, he killed a man and crashed a stolen vehicle into Kayla's father's truck. Now the state of Arkansas is attempting to execute eight

men on death row in eleven days because the supply of midazolam, one
of the three drugs used in chemical executions, is set to expire. Williams,
the fourth of the eight, was executed an hour ago.

I stare at the dead man. As an anesthesiologist, Henry has testified
about the suffering experienced during chemical executions by death row
inmates, the majority of whom, like Williams, are Black men. I want to
ask Henry if he's been following the Arkansas story, but when I wake
him, he'll be too groggy.

I turn off the television and lift the headphones from Henry's ears.
He opens his eyes, alarm and confusion on his face.

'You fell asleep,' I say, as I do every night.

I take the bolster from under his knees and hold his arm as he stands.
Once on his feet, he looks at me. His eyes narrow. I hear my mother
screaming into the phone when my father had again not sent the child
support check: 'You're a cheat, Rolf Koehl. A cheat squared.'

Did I leave my phone in the kitchen? Forget to erase one of Lance's
texts?

No, I conclude, as I lead my stoned husband to our chaste bed. Unlike my father, I'm a careful cheat. A careful cheat squared.

1

ANA

HENRY IS LONG GONE BY THE TIME I WAKE. HOW HE DOES IT—rising every weekday at five with his mind clear, determined to make it through his shift at the gastroenterology procedures clinic with only the help of a brace and alternations of Motrin and Aleve—amazes but does not surprise me. This is Henry. Even-tempered, practical, hardworking Henry. The last person anyone would imagine spending his nights in a marijuana haze.

Next to the coffee pot is a note:

Happy Birthday Dear Ana,
 I love you more and more every year. To me, your wisdom and refinement at 60 make you even more beautiful than you were at 27 when we met.
 Your eternal admirer and husband,
 Henry

PS There is a glass of fresh-squeezed orange juice in the refrigerator.

I drink the juice, squeezed for me by a husband I've not had sex with since he cracked two vertebrae nine years ago. As good a man as I've ever known.

WHEN I OPEN MY PHONE, THERE'S AN EMOJI-DRIPPING TEXT:

Catherine: *Happy Birthday!!!* 🎂❤️🎉🎂🎊🎂🎊🎂🎊🎂❤️🎊🎂🎊
Don't worry, we'll bring your mom tonight XOXO

I've known my brother's wife for more than half my life, and we are in closer contact than I am with George. I credit Catherine, who set the tone shortly after her engagement by calling to invite me to lunch. Touched by the gesture, I was startled that Catherine seemed unaware that I was in my third semester of graduate school, making traveling from Philadelphia to New York on a weekday, as she initially proposed, impossible.

We settled on a Saturday. On reaching the restaurant, late on account of the train, I learned that Catherine had already ordered lobster salads for us both. The Tiffany solitaire George had given her glistened as she touched my arm. 'It's the signature dish,' she said with a sugary smile, as though soliciting my retroactive assent.

When the salads arrived, Catherine speared a chunk of lobster, and then rested her fork on her plate. She had a question. It had to do with my parents. She'd asked George how they met, and he claimed he didn't know. Did I know?

I bit my tongue to keep from laughing. Of course my brother knew. It crossed my mind that maybe he didn't want his bride-to-be to know. But he'd given her my phone number. If there was anything George objected to my telling Catherine, he would have called to deliver his instructions. Commands would have felt more like it.

'My parents agree that they met at a party. It was my mother's second year in New York. She was twenty, working as a catalog model, and he was twenty-two, in architecture school. After that, their stories differ.'

Catherine seemed to be holding her breath.

'In my mother's version, my father was a wickedly smart student who cornered her and insisted she take the subway with him up to Columbia so he could show her the balsam model he'd constructed for a class project. He says she was an astoundingly beautiful girl who looked more like a Swiss farmhand than a New York model, and that she drank too much and he gallantly escorted her back to her room at the Barbizon Hotel.'

Catherine clasped her French-manicured hands and wiggled her shoulders in a cultivated alternative to a shimmy. 'I love it! *Wickedly smart! Astoundingly beautiful!* It sounds like they swept each other off their feet!'

I no longer find the moniker 'Cutie Doll' Henry once had for Catherine amusing—the good mother Catherine has been having made me see her more generously. That day, though, at our lunch, *Cutie Doll* perfectly captured five-foot-two Catherine with her *café au lait* hair (requiring biweekly visits to her A-list colorist) and her purchased boobs (an embarrassment, I would have thought, for a Dartmouth grad, but apparently not in Catherine and George's set) and her four-inch Manolo Blahnik sling-backs (bringing the top of her head in line with my brows).

Catherine's expression darkened. Having met both of my parents, she'd surely heard Jean, who never missed an occasion to do so, call Rolf a liar and worm. 'But why did your mother marry your father? She must have known . . .' Catherine's voice trailed off. With parents who golfed together at their Greenwich country club, where they'd held her engagement party, she couldn't even utter the words that would complete her thought.

'My mother got pregnant. She wasn't religious, but abortion was out of the question. Somehow, she convinced my father that he had to do right by her and marry immediately at city hall.'

Despite having heard my mother tell what happened next for as long as I could remember, it still made me nauseous. 'She claims when she miscarried a week later, my father accused her of having faked the pregnancy and then pretending her period was a miscarriage.'

Catherine held her fork mid-air. 'My goodness,' she whispered. 'Truly, my goodness.' The gummy pink lobster dangling from the fork tines looked vaguely fetal. There was a long pause. 'So how did your parents' marriage end?'

'My mother says the beginning of the end was when my father won a prize for a boutique hotel renovation. There was a feature article about him in the *Wall Street Journal*. She says it went to his head and he was never the same.'

It was my mother who showed me the article, pasted into a scrapbook about my father she'd kept while they were married. The reporter described Rolf as having grown up in Sils Maria, not far from St. Moritz, in the staff quarters of an historic hotel, and how this led to his understanding of the romance of travel and his conviction that a great hotel should evoke a sweep of time that transports guests—and here, the reporter had quoted my father—'out of the specificities of their own circumstances into a more ethereal and perfect world while, at the same time, creating an environment with sufficient familiarity that guests feel entirely at home.'

'After the article, the commissions poured in. My mother suspected he slept with other women while on work trips, but by the time she was pregnant with me, he was sleeping with a draftsperson in his office. She caught him outright a few days after I was born.'

Catherine's lips parted.

'Not literally. A note or a receipt or something he couldn't deny.'

'She didn't leave him then?'

'She had a three-year-old and a newborn. She told him if it happened again, she would. Of course, it did. The timing was awful. Her sister had just died of a brain aneurysm. When she got back from the funeral, there was a letter from an associate in my father's firm with sordid details about the affair she'd been having with my father.'

I used to be mortified when my mother related this chapter of her history, which she wore like a red badge of courage. In my mother's account, she'd been so grief-stricken about her sister, she'd been numbed by that pain to the pain of leaving her husband.

'She packed us up—I was five and George was eight—and we moved in with her parents in Baltimore.'

Catherine waited for the server to clear our obscenely expensive salads, neither of us having eaten even half, before responding. 'George said he grew up with your grandparents—but I thought they'd moved in with you.'

Now my lips parted. Had my brother never told his fiancée about our grandparents' row house, with the cracked concrete in the backyard and the mousetrap under the dripping kitchen sink, the two of us sharing the room that had belonged to our aunt Uma, our mother sleeping in the one that was hers as a girl? That with the Baltimore public schools in turmoil, she'd enrolled us in Catholic ones, the least expensive private option, and it had been his job to deliver me to my classroom, a job he made clear he hated by walking so fast, I had to run to keep up with him? It seemed not. He must have assumed it would be impossible for Catherine, who'd grown up in a house with five sparkling bathrooms and a live-in housekeeper, to imagine our mornings—our grandfather banging on the bathroom door while we hurried to wash our faces and brush our teeth. Never cursing at us or our mother, but nearly every evening, after he'd had a few, shouting at our grandmother: *Shut up, you stupid bitch, you ugly hag.* Our grandmother's cheeks wet with tears as she shooed us away: 'Don't mind him. It's the whiskey talking.'

'My mother could never have afforded to stay in New York with us.'

Catherine patted her mouth with her napkin, and then softly asked, money a topic in her own family as taboo as sex, 'But didn't your father support you?'

If my brother hadn't told Catherine about our grandparents' house, perhaps he'd not talked either about our summers: how jarring it felt each time plane tickets arrived so we could join our father, at work on the renovation of a once-glorious hotel with crystal chandeliers in the dining room and a swimming pool where tall iced drinks were served by white-coated staff to guests on terrycloth-covered loungers. 'He paid for our trips to visit him and in theory he paid child support, but there was never any question that my mother had to work.'

'She was an actuary?' Catherine said brightly, pleased, it seemed, to know this.

I nodded. My mother had worked in my grandparents' bakery, I explained, until the clientele began decamping to the suburbs and there wasn't enough business to keep paying her a salary. 'Somehow, she came up with the idea of doing a night school program in actuarial science. It suited her perfectly—the doomsday computations of the likelihood of illnesses and deaths and other unfortunate events.'

Catherine twisted the diamond solitaire until it made a complete circle on her finger. It was hard to know which was more alarming for her: learning about her husband-to-be or realizing how little he'd told her.

I CARRY THE JUICE HENRY MADE INTO MY OFFICE. IT'S YOUR BIRTH-
day, I tell myself. You don't have to check the voice mail on your work
line.

If I don't, though, I'll regret it. At yoga with my nieces, at lunch with
Simon, the thought that there might be a message from a vulnerable
client that kindness dictates should receive a prompt response will niggle
like a bit of food caught in my teeth until I can't focus on anything else.
Had I realized I'd feel this level of obligation, would I have embarked
on the work I do, drawing as much from what I learned in social work
school as from my graduate studies in English? Maybe, but maybe not.

You're a manuscript therapist, Fiona says, plain and simple. I recoil
from the word *therapist*. The way I put it to prospective clients is that
in addition to helping clarify the content, narrative choices, and orga-
nization of a piece of work, I help writers understand how their texts
are constricted by conflicts about what to reveal and how to be seen. To
recognize the fingerprints of their inner lives on what's said and not, in
the tone employed, on the arc of a story. I've learned that it's too much—
too abstract, too overwhelming—to discuss during initial consultations
the most debilitating roadblock: re-creations in the writing itself of an
author's character traits.

With the time stamp on this morning's voice mail, five a.m., and the
pause before there are words, it can only be Bettina.

'I'm sorry for not giving you any notice, and I'll understand if you're
too busy . . . but is there any chance we could meet today?' It's hard
to hear the rest of the message because Bettina is mumbling and perhaps crying, but I make out *Teresa*, which is how Bettina refers to her
mother, and something about seeing Jack, her stepfather, and Carol, her
half-sister.

I exhale loudly. *Damn it.* I scheduled no client appointments for my
birthday, planned not to work at all. But there's an implied covenant
with my writers: I instruct them to dig deep, no matter how painful.
When they hit the shoals, I'll be at the shore to help them find their
way—which, from Bettina's message, means today.

In graduate school, we read a Marxist theorist on time as the truest
luxury and nirvana as the condition when work and play are one—though

having the good fortune of the two aligned, the author added, does not mean that at every moment our desires will match our obligations.

Buck up, I hear my mother saying.

I text Bettina: *Let's meet at 4:30.*

Never have I wavered in the belief that I learned everything important that I know about editing from Fiona. Instructors in college had scrawled illegible comments in the margins of my papers, comments that posed as penetrating but were slap-dash errant thoughts. Fiona, by contrast, was a surgeon zeroing in on the places where my writing was diseased.

My first experience of Fiona's scalpel was with a paper for our introductory graduate seminar that I sheepishly asked her to read.

'Do you want me to be frank or pat you on the back?'

My face burned.

'Hey—there's nothing wrong with wanting a pat on the back.'

We'd only recently become friends and already Fiona had discerned how insecure I felt. How worried I was that being a dogged workhorse wouldn't hide my scrappy academic background (community college classes followed by an undergraduate degree from a commuter branch of the state university, where my classmates read nothing aside from the assigned course materials, if even those) or, more devastatingly, my limited ability. How hungry I felt for praise. 'Completely frank, of course,' I said.

The paper, about Virginia Woolf's conception of time, came back with *dead wood, dead wood, dead wood* in red ink on page after page where I'd cited philosophers and physicists about the complexities and contradictions embedded in the notion of time and attempted, ineptly, to employ a deconstructionist analysis. Two years later, when I told Fiona, by then a year gone herself from Penn, that I was dropping out of the PhD program to move to New York with Henry, Fiona asked, 'Is it because of me? Have I been discouraging?'

'You are a hundred percent responsible. My decision has nothing to do with Henry having been offered his dream job. With our getting married.'

We were on the phone, so I couldn't see Fiona's face, read her silence. Had she taken my comment seriously?

'I'm joking. Truly, can you see me as a professor? I love novels and thinking about writing, but in my own loose way. You know I can't keep historical eras straight, and my mind turns to mush reading literary theory. I'd rather go before a firing squad than try to explain structuralism or Lacan's influence on post-modernism.'

'No one understands that shit. It's not meant to be understood. And yes, I can see you as a professor—with fantastic boots and an edgy haircut at a nice liberal arts college in New England. Half the students in your British lit seminar, the girls as much as the boys, in love with you.'

'I couldn't even confront the deli guy who put sugar in my tea after I said three times, *no sugar.* I'd never be able to toe the line with late papers and grades. I'm leaving with an MA in English. That should be good enough to get a decent job.' And it had led to a job, as a screen agent's assistant. A job that would have been decent had the screen agent, who expected me to do all his reading and once threw an ice bucket because his hotel room wasn't stocked with low-sodium V8, not fallen short of being decent himself.

Fiona says I'm the poster child for theories that posit the heavy hand of chance in every domain: evolution, history, love. Having quit the job with the screen agent, I stumbled into a blissful year as the nanny for my nieces, with their preschool chivalries of line up for the water fountain and share your baggie of Cheerios, after which I returned to graduate school, but in social work, not English.

I fell into editing in the same fluke way. Seven months pregnant when I graduated, I held off on searching for a social work job. Sitting home, though, with nothing to put my mind to aside from layette shopping and worrying if my baby would have a full complement of fingers and toes, I was miserable. When Fiona asked if I'd consider editing a novel by her former Hopkins classmate Nan, I told her I'd happily do it for free. But I wasn't an editor. Wouldn't Nan be better off working with an editor?

'Don't be ridiculous. You have a master's in literature and a social work degree. You spent three years deciding whether novels should become movies. You understand people. You'll be perfect.'

By fifty pages into Nan's manuscript, it was clear that the novel faltered from how Nan was trying both to develop and flee the central theme: the conflict the protagonist, the daughter of wealthy assimilated Jewish parents in nineteenth-century Vienna, felt between her longing for and disdain of religious practice. Terrified that a depiction of the full force of her character's ambivalence would offend her own parents, Nan was using vague contradictory metaphors, leaving the reader as confused as she felt herself.

'What you did with Nan,' Fiona proclaimed, 'was brilliant.' It was a bright Sunday afternoon, the following summer, and I'd taken the train with Simon, by then five months old, to visit Fiona. We were seated under an umbrella on the deck of Charlie's and her new house, sipping Charlie's concoction of iced red zinger tea mixed with lemonade and ginger while Nick played with a toy submarine in the wading pool and Simon napped in his stroller. 'You showed Nan the parts of the story she was afraid to tell.'

'It wasn't brilliant. In fact, it was pretty obvious.'

'You're underselling yourself. Most people can't think in two registers. You thought about the manuscript on its own terms, and you thought about Nan as both reflected in and existing beyond those pages. And then you put the pieces together. Which was exactly what you did for me that first time you read my poems.'

Nick let out a yelp. He'd thrown his submarine onto the grass, after which it dawned on him that if he climbed out of the pool to fetch it, the grass would, to his horror, stick to the bottoms of his feet. Fiona retrieved the submarine and held it over Nick's head as she firmly told him that she knew he did not like to walk barefoot on the grass, but he was four now and able to use self-control and she was not going to fetch the submarine for him a second time.

'You've got plenty of classmates who can work with the families of psychiatric patients,' Fiona said when she rejoined me. 'What you did for Nan is what you should be doing.'

The great paradox of our friendship is that while what I learned from Fiona about editing is key to the help I've given scores of people with their writing, I've not been able to help Fiona return to hers. To this day,

I wonder how Fiona's life would have unfolded had she stayed in the Penn English graduate program. Perhaps she would have become a professor and continued writing her poems. Instead, she responded to her father's bankruptcy falling atop her mother's cancer diagnosis by walking away from a writing fellowship and applying for the training program at a consulting firm like the one where my brother was working by then. *Money, honey, before art,* Fiona explained: Her sister's college fund was gone and her parents might lose their house. Having never taken a business class, not even Econ 101, Fiona figured she was offered the position because someone had looked at her summa cum laude from Harvard and the MFA from Hopkins and thought, well, the girl can write. She'd be value added to the math geeks with their modeling theories.

Now, no longer held back from writing her poems because she needs to pay for her sister's college or find a school for her calendrical-savant head banging son, the same woman who told me to forgo working with the families of psychiatric patients says she finds her grant-writing satisfying. Even if she could make ends meet as a poet, Fiona says it would seem wrong to direct whatever talents she has to finding the word with the particular meaning and rhythm and alliteration a poem requires rather than to securing funds for after-school programs for special needs children.

Still, I feel certain that Fiona suffers from the loss of her unwritten poems—that she wakes in the middle of the night with stanzas never put to paper on her mind. What took me longer to understand is that her father's chicanery and her mother's cancer and her son's neuroatypical brain had also been her protection from writing. Yes, there were practical forces at play, but in truth Fiona stopped writing because of what it did to her: how she felt that her writing ate her alive like a self-cannibalizing disease.

Remarkably, it was my mother, who I'd never thought of as observant of anyone, who recognized while Fiona was her boarder the agony Fiona experienced working on her poems—as though she were digging them out of herself. Not that my mother used those words. What she said was that Fiona had stretches during which she'd work until dawn, drinking at midnight a pot of black coffee and eating only vanilla wafers and boxes of raisins, sleeping no more than a few hours a day, followed by weeks on end when she was too exhausted to change out of pajamas or leave the house.

Most surprising was my mother's tone: Tolerant. Begrudgingly admiring.

LANCE: *WHERE'S THAT CALL YOU PROMISED? GOTTA SEE U*
Me: *tomorrow is better*
Lance: *nope wanna give you birthday present*
Lance: *TODAY*

I stare at my calendar, with Bettina's appointment now added to yoga with my nieces, lunch with Simon, and my birthday dinner. If I forgo walking home after lunch and take a cab to Lance's apartment . . .

Me: *2:30—but can't stay long.*
Lance: *we'll see*

I erase the texts from my lover. *Lover.* What a melodramatic word. *Mistress* at least has some heft and the allure of that *ess* falling somewhere between a sigh and a yes, but *Master* would be impossible. And, after seven years, is Lance less a lover than a second husband? If so, would that mean that I'm a bigamist, not a cheat?

Nope, Lance would say. We're cheats. Both of us.

When I first told Fiona—the only person I've told—about Lance, I burst into tears. We were on one of our reservoir walks, and Fiona wrapped her arms around me. 'Oh love,' she murmured as she rubbed my back.

'Listen to me,' she said. 'Henry's a fantastic person, especially for a man. But he's breached the marital contract by abdicating on sexual relations. I know that sounds legalistic, but your actions are a just amendment: You're committed to the marriage in every area save the one Henry by his actions, or lack thereof, excised from the contract.'

Fiona fished a tissue from her bag. She handed it to me. 'What matters in a marriage is the degree of authentic connection. Whether or not either party touches anyone else's genitals is irrelevant.'

Once, when I asked Fiona how she squared lying with an authentic connection, she countered that the very question was based on shaky assumptions. Much of what is true in fact, she's fond of saying, is a lie in truth. Honesty is a worthy aim, but as a virtue is inferior to kindness or respect.

It's been a revelation how easily truth can be sidestepped: with liberal elisions, my affair with Lance requires few lies. More troubling has been the awareness that I've abandoned Henry. Left him alone in our little TV room to vape himself each night into oblivion.

I CHECK THE CLOCK FROM MY FATHER: A QUARTER HOUR BEFORE I'll leave to meet my nieces. On the day my father gave me the clock, he called unexpectedly. It was after he'd moved upstate with Miko, his third wife, but before he got sick. He was in the city, he said. He'd just left the Museum of Modern Art and was hoping he could drop by. Tamping down the hurt that visiting me was clearly an afterthought and focusing instead on how nice it would be for Simon, I invited him for dinner. He placed the clock on my desk in what I'm sure he thought was the perfect position.

I'd always assumed that if my father became ill, I'd care for him in proportion to his limited parenting. When the day arrived, however, the equation dissolved: I was overtaken by what felt like a primal response, as though filial duty was encoded in my DNA. I made the weekly trips to see my father, which, as his end approached, became several-day visits, not out of obligation but out of desire: I wanted to be with him before he was gone. I wanted to help Miko keep him as comfortable as possible. I wanted to share what we could before it was too late.

'Talk to me,' Fiona said when we met in the park a few days after I'd learned that the count on my father's remaining days had shifted from months to weeks. 'Your dad, tell me what's up.' George was handling our father's legal and financial affairs, I explained, while I was on the front line arranging his care. I'd proposed the arrangement. George traveled so much, I had more flexibility to meet with doctors and home health aides. What I'd not said to my brother was that I feared he'd interact with our father's caregivers in the same transactional manner, with the same archived email threads, he used with his work underlings: he wouldn't realize that treating the women who changed our now bed-ridden father's soiled diapers as if they were medical appliances would impact how they'd treat our father.

Fiona stopped walking. She put a hand on my forearm. 'Guys like your brother, they lie five times before they've reached the bottom of their first cup of coffee. And I don't mean lie as in the truth in lies. I mean lie as in lie. They're not even aware of it.' Fiona added that I must insist that George give me, *in writing*, a summary of our father's assets and a copy of his will. 'Even the best of people can get squirrely in these circumstances. And let's be real: your brother is not the best of people.'

I took Fiona's advice and called George to ask for these items. A long pause followed my request, during which I imagined George conducting an analysis of the pros and cons of transparency.

'Miko has already decided that after Dad dies, she's going back to Nagasaki to be with her nephews. So, of course, we'll sell his house. Adding in those proceeds, Dad's entire estate will be worth about 2.8 million. Half of that will be put into a trust for Miko and the rest will be split between us. I still have to consult with an estates attorney about the taxes, but that's the basic plan.'

The number slipped off George's tongue as though it were of no more significance than the earnings from a Girl Scout cookie drive, but I was shocked. I'd known my father had been successful, but according to my mother, he'd made a lot of poor business decisions and was a spendthrift to boot.

For several days, I walked around in a fog, dazed at the prospect of so much money coming Henry's and my way. In the past, when I'd broached with Henry going to a drug rehab to kick his marijuana habit, he'd pointed out we'd not be able to make ends meet without his income. Oddly, the thought that I would now be able to disarm his financial concerns did not lift my spirits. Rather, the financial objection seemed like a weed. Once pulled, it would make room for a new rationale to keep everything the same.

USUALLY, I WEAR WHICHEVER YOGA PANTS ARE AT THE TOP OF THE pile, but today I take the time to make a choice. I peruse the T-shirts in my dresser drawer, settling on one Simon gave me last Mother's Day of a Matisse-like line drawing with the face of a man and woman composed such that their features are fused: the woman's nose forming the man's brow, his eye carved from her nostril. I cringe. How had I missed the message?

Outside, the April morning air is bright and cool. Heading south to meet my nieces, I drink in my city: the contrast of the trees across the street—elephantine trunks, arching branches, canopies that appear an arm's reach from cumulus clouds—with the building adornments— Juliet balconies, bas-relief friezes, scrolled iron entrances. Turning west, there are pristine brownstones with flower-filled pots lining the stairs to the parlor-level doors. A yet-to-be-renovated one wears a laggard Christmas wreath, now brittle and covered with soot.

It still amazes me that retrieving Ella at preschool when Catherine was on the way to the emergency room with severe abdominal pain led to my taking care of the girls for a year. I was thirty-two, three years married and beginning to think about getting pregnant—time still ample and life elastic, shaped by scaffolded *ifs*: *If* what turned out to be an appendicitis attack happened the Monday before. *If* George hadn't been on a business trip to Frankfurt. *If* the nanny hadn't called in sick, *if* I hadn't visited my nieces over the weekend and told Catherine I'd quit my job with the insane screen agent so she thought to call me because she knew I'd be free . . .

The nanny, it turned out, was not sick. She'd gone to Jamaica to settle a dispute over her mother's house, but she was too afraid of Catherine's response were she to reveal that she didn't know how long she'd be gone and too upset about being away from Ella and Gemma, who she loved like her own children, to say goodbye. By the time Catherine was back on her feet (she developed an infection and had to stay in the hospital an extra five days), I was into a routine with my nieces and they'd become so attached to me that Catherine jokingly asked if I wanted the nanny job. Why not, I thought. I'd do it for a year while I applied for social work graduate school.

What made it work was that Catherine was at peace with her daughters loving me while she was off to her tennis matches and luncheon fundraisers and visits to her mother and horse in Connecticut. She'd had a beloved nanny herself, and from this she understood that love is not a zero-sum game: the girls' love for me subtracted nothing from theirs for her. When I said that it would be easier to put Gemma in a baby carrier than taking the stroller on my trips to pick up Ella at preschool, Catherine immediately bought one even though she would never use it herself. When I suggested a Suzuki strings class for Ella and said I'd supervise the practices, Catherine rented a quarter-sized viola. When strangers assumed that the girls were mine (most of the Park Avenue nannies were from Nepal or the Philippines), Catherine simply smiled.

My mother was appalled, which she let me know on her first visit to her grandchildren after I'd become their nanny. We were in George's building's playroom, where Ella was hooting inside the teepee with two little boys while seven-month-old Gemma sat in my lap transfixed by the commotion. How could I go from an English PhD program at an Ivy League university, my mother asked, to an assistant's job (wasn't that enough of a demotion?) to— She broke off without saying *working as a servant*. Didn't Henry object?

'I like taking care of the girls,' I whispered. I nuzzled Gemma's scalp, angry at myself that my mother's words stung.

APPROACHING THE YOGA STUDIO, I SPOT ELLA WAITING OUTSIDE. She looks like a hip version of her mother: Ella's hair a curly mop and her laugh a snort, while Catherine never misses a blow-dry or shows teeth when she smiles, but with the same heart-shaped face and tiny nose. Catherine, who says she couldn't sleep otherwise, insists that Ella take an Uber on Catherine's account when she travels home at dawn from the vegan restaurant where she's the overnight baker to the Queens walk-up she shares with her boyfriend, Austen, and their poodle, Gertrude—the dog's name inspired by my mother's claim, which cracked Ella up, that this was my father's suggested name for me.

On Fridays, when Gemma works at home, Ella skips the dawn Uber ride and instead walks the few blocks from her job to her sister's apartment. Carrying two almond milk lattes, she arrives after Greg, Gemma's demography professor husband, up at 5:30 for his morning run, has showered and left. The sisters sip the lattes sprawled atop Gemma's bed. At nine, Ella washes her face and brushes her teeth with the toothbrush she keeps in Gemma's bathroom, and the two of them stroll arm in arm to the yoga studio for the class they take with me each week.

Usually my nieces wait together outside the studio, Ella sometimes jogging down the street to greet me, but today Ella is alone and standing still.

'Where's Gemma?'

'We came separately. But I think she's inside.'

'Is something the matter?'

Ella averts her gaze.

'Ella?'

'We're okay,' she whispers.

GEMMA IS LYING ON HER MAT WITH HER EYES CLOSED AS ELLA AND I enter the studio. I kneel to hug her. When Ella doesn't greet her sister and Gemma doesn't open her eyes, I know there is something the matter. Something between my nieces.

The weekend after Gemma learned she was pregnant, she came to see me. We sat on my couch, our backs to the park, a pot of tea and a platter of red grapes on the coffee table. Gemma reached for a clump of grapes. As a baby, she'd been an epic thumb sucker, a habit that turned into nail biting that led to a nasty infection and Catherine taking her to a behavioral psychologist. The cuticles around the fingers on her right hand were again red and puffy.

Gemma clutched the grapes. Her eyes filled with tears.

Alarmed, I retrieved the grapes, putting them back on the plate, and took my niece's hand. 'Gemma, what's wrong?' I hesitated but I had to ask. 'Is everything okay with the baby?'

Gemma touched her slightly bulging stomach. 'The baby's fine. It's me.' She brought her thumb to her mouth and chewed on the cuticle. 'I think I'm going to be a bad mother. My Facebook feed is filled with posts from women, some of them my college classmates, who make parenting sound like a spiritual practice. Women who studied linguistics or chemical engineering, and now they celebrate making brownies with their three-year-olds in chef's hats and their kitchens dusted in sugar.' She stared at the floor. 'If I posted that I'm grateful I can afford a nanny and go back to the lab, they'd unfriend me.'

'Oh, Gemma.' The mommy wars between women who work and women who don't, I told her, were in full vicious form when I had Simon—but they must be even more awful now with parents using their phones to document their children's every move. There's no one way to be a good parent, I tried to explain. And no one knows how they'll respond until they have their baby. 'I've known men who before they had kids wouldn't even come home for dinner on their wives' birthdays and then had complete turnarounds once their babies were born, racing home to give baths and read bedtime stories.'

'Greg wants to find out the sex. Did you and Uncle Henry do that?'

I paused before responding. I didn't want Gemma to think that what Henry and I'd done was what she should do. 'There's no right decision,' I said. 'Uncle Henry and I were agreed that we didn't want to know in advance. For Uncle Henry, it had to do with a mystical feeling he had delivering babies as a medical student. For me, it had to do with thinking I should be open to whatever the universe delivered.' Gemma and Greg would have to decide what was right for them. I didn't add that when the doctor identified our baby as a boy based on looking between the legs, neither of us had questioned, as I'd recently learned, that this might not be where the answer lay: that girls can have penises and boys vaginas.

Greg, Gemma said, viewed the decision through his demographer's eyes. The sex of their baby, he believed, was the most important predictor of their child's future. He'd rallied Nana's support. As a former actuary, Nana agreed one hundred percent with Greg. If she'd been able to know the sex of her children before they were born, she sternly told Gemma, she'd have jumped at the chance. She would have been able to override Gemma's grandfather painting what would be Gemma's father's room sunflower yellow—like a Van Gogh, he'd said. She hated yellow. Had she known, she would have been able to insist on blue.

Gemma plucked a grape. 'I agree with Greg that it's practical to know in advance. But I keep thinking it would be like having the data before you start an experiment. Ella says I'm carrying the baby, so it should be up to me. I kind of agree, but then I think that's not fair to Greg.'

A few weeks later, Gemma told me that Greg had relented, though more out of impatience than their reaching a meeting of minds. He was sick of arguing about it, he said. Last week at yoga, when Ella patted Gemma's belly and declared that she could not wait to meet her niecey-nephew—'I haven't been this excited about a baby since Simon was born!'—I wondered how much sway Ella had on Gemma's holding firm. Now, though, Ella, who usually places her mat between Gemma's and mine, positions herself between the wall and me.

OUR TEACHER, SUNI, STRIKES A CHIME TO SIGNAL THE START OF class. We're going to begin, Suni says, with a reflection on *lovingkindness*, which she visualizes as a single word. I glance at my nieces, flanking me in half-lotus pose. 'A challenge, dear yogis,' Suni continues with a Mona Lisa smile. 'Dedicate your practice to someone who has been unkind to you. Someone you can forgive and then treat with *lovingkindness*.'

Paranoia washes over me: Has one of my nieces told Suni it's my birthday and she's chosen this instruction for that reason?

'Imagine yourself immersed in a warm breeze of forgiveness,' Suni intones. 'You inhale the sweet nectar. You feel it tickling your nostrils, your chest rising with the taste of it.'

The class moves into a brisk progression of downward dogs and *chaturangas* and *utkatasanas*. Since Gemma has been pregnant, when Suni directs us to prepare for headstands, Ella has mouthed an exaggerated *No* to Gemma, who then sticks out her tongue. Today, without reminders, Gemma drags her mat to the side of the room and rests her feet on the wall.

Whatever is amiss between my nieces will surely resolve, but it's painful to observe. Their closeness has always filled me with awe. Awe and appreciation that since Simon was born, they've included him in their circle of love. They'd been so excited when he came home from the hospital, they insisted on spending the night the following weekend, arriving with their pillows and pink sleeping bags. Allowed to hold Simon only if she was sitting down, Gemma, not yet five, shed indignant tears as she watched Ella, then seven, prance with a cloth diaper on her shoulder while she made exaggerated circles on Simon's back and dramatically whispered, 'He burped! He burped!'

When the class moves into rest pose—*savasana*, Suni calls it, rather than the uglier corpse pose—I ward off the flip side of the awe: sadness that George and I will never be close. Will never think of each other with *lovingkindness*.

It took me a long time to recognize that our parents' divorce and the fall-out from it had landed more heavily on George than me. In my brother's mind, our father had shamed us by leaving our mother so strapped for money she had to choose in any month between dental checkups and replacing outgrown shoes. Even worse, George believed, our father had irreparably alienated him from the kids he knew by the summers he felt forced to spend with our father and whichever of his associates was in his bed at whatever hotel he was renovating at the time. George was certain that our travels were unimaginable and therefore weird and pitiable to the boys from our neighborhood, whose own vacations were invariably two weeks in an Ocean City bayside cottage. How could a kid who'd never been outside of Maryland conjure the pink and green macarons we ate at teatime at the Hôtel de Crillon in Paris? The wooden boat we took from a private dock behind St. Mark's Square to a convent-turned-hotel on an island in the Venice lagoon?

The rooms George and I shared, while in too great need of repair for paying guests, were for me still wondrous. Under the spell of our father—the renowned architect with his warm inquiries about wives and children, his outsized tips, his insistence that the renovations include updated employee quarters—the hotel staff treated us like royalty. Room service breakfasts would arrive on a wheeled table covered with a starched pink cloth: a basket of thickly cut slices from the breads baked at dawn, pats of white butter, jars of marmalade, silver pots of hot chocolate and cream. There were *gratuit* tennis lessons when the pro had cancellations, virgin drinks from the bartenders who would dream up new concoctions to amuse us.

Our last trip to visit our father was the summer after our grandparents, who'd soldiered on with their bakery until they were throwing out more challahs and rye breads than their dwindling customers purchased, died, both in their sleep—first, four months after the bakery closed, our grandmother, and then, just two months later, our grandfather. The following week, George and I flew to Marrakesh, where our father and his French girlfriend, Mathilde, a young architect, were redesigning the public spaces of a hotel, once a favorite retreat for Winston Churchill, who'd painted the gardens. Mathilde seemed not to know that our grandfather had just died. Instead, from the moment we arrived, she talked only about how it would be a crime—*un vrai crime!*—for Rolf not to take his children to the desert so they could witness the red ball of the sun rising over the mountains of sand. To my surprise, my father, who'd never altered his work schedule while we were visiting, agreed to Mathilde organizing a trip for the four of us to the Merzouga Dunes.

In the years since, I've wondered if no one had warned Mathilde that August was not a good time to go to the Sahara. Reaching the caravan camp at dusk, she seemed as bewildered as the rest of us that we were the only guests, a discovery that made George even more sullen and inspired Mathilde to drink so much wine, she decided it would be amusing to belly dance for the camel tenders. I can still see my father pouring a jug of water over Mathilde's head to try to sober her up. Mathilde screamed bloody murder, and then disappeared, leading to my father and the other men gathering lanterns and setting off to comb the dunes while George and I were instructed to go to sleep on the carpets spread out on the sand. Alone in the camp, George announced Mathilde was a cunt and never again would he travel to meet fuck-head Rolf.

Fiona once asked why George's refusal to go on any more summer trips with our father meant they halted for me too. Did Jean worry about my flying alone? No, my mother had not been a worrier. She'd expected me to be capable by four of waiting by myself in the children's room of the library while she went to check out her own books, and was so enraged when she returned to find me in full-blown panic, she locked me in my room for an hour while I screamed myself to unconsciousness.

A more likely explanation was that my mother thought it would be unfair for me to spend a month in Sardinia while George stocked shelves at a grocery store, even if this was his choice. In her eyes, the balance sheet between her children was already uneven, with greater leeway in the neighborhood—which she understood from having grown up there herself—for a girl than for a boy to be different from the other kids. If a girl was adequately pretty by schoolyard standards, she could be bookish or shy or dreamy without being branded an oddball or loser, which was how George, riddled with teenaged acne, had seen himself: snubbed (or worse, not even noticed) by the boys who gathered in parking lots, where they smoked pot and drank and made wisecracks about the girls who appeared in their own carloads, the nights ending with two or three couples in backseats while everyone else hid their envy by snickering as they finished the kegs of beer.

Not until he became a partner at his firm did George start to tell the stories about our childhood travels to visit our father in locations that now had currency in his social set. 'Is it true?' Ella once whispered after her father finished an amusing account of the prison her grandfather had helped convert into a hotel in Istanbul.

'Yes,' I whispered back. 'That and the hotel on Lake Sils where an old woman who claimed to be a princess would dine in her tiara and the chef prepared special meals for a rich American's dog.'

I squeezed Ella's hand. 'It's all true.'

THE CLASS ENDS WITH SUNI ASKING US TO RECALL THE PERSON WE want to forgive. I'd chosen my mother, but now my brother and father are also on my mind. I take a deep breath. It's my sixtieth birthday, I'll make it a triple-header—my mother, my father, my brother.

'With our last exhale of class, release all of your resentments so you can leave your mat filled with gratitude.'

I picture a triptych: Jean during her modeling days, her long legs, meatier than mine but still slender, with her feet in high-heeled mules; Rolf, with his garnet cravat and handmade shoes, under the chandelier in the lobby of the Swiss hotel where he'd grown up; George in his wine cellar selecting the quintessential pairings for the dinner tonight.

Outside the studio building, Gemma mumbles that she'll see me later and then, without saying goodbye to her sister, turns in the direction of her apartment. Ella and I walk together toward Central Park West, where Ella will catch the train to Queens and I'll continue on to meet Simon.

We're halfway down the block when Ella stops. She looks at the sidewalk, and then up at me. 'Gemma slapped me.'

I hold my face still, not wanting to betray my shock. Only once have I received a slap, and it's not something I've ever forgotten.

Holding Ella's elbow, I guide her to the steps of a nearby brownstone. She leans against a pillar, tears spilling. She went to Gemma's apartment this morning, she says, the way she always does on Fridays. They were lying on Gemma's bed, drinking the almond milk lattes she'd brought while she told Gemma about the night's calamities—mice in the flour, the assistant putting too much water in the dough so it turned to glue. 'Gemma slapped me so hard, my latte sloshed onto the quilt.'

Ella covers her face. I hold her shoulders, feel her trembling. I can't tell if she's aware that she's left out the why: why Gemma slapped her.

'I told her I couldn't slap her back since she's pregnant. Then I left. That's why we weren't together, waiting for you.'

I fish in my bag for tissues, hand the little packet to Ella. She blows her nose, and I smooth her hair back from her face. It's clear that she can't yet talk about the why. 'The two of you are so close. When you're ready, you'll work it out.'

I think, as I have so many times, how people say sons are easier than daughters. I would have loved to have both. A son and a daughter.

The little creature who sometimes alights atop my head to mock me cackles: *Ha ha, Ana. You got your wish.*

2

HENRY

HENRY IS AT HIS STANDING DESK AT SIX IN THE MORNING OF HIS wife's sixtieth birthday, looking over the day's schedule and listening to NPR's top of the hour newscast, when Sally, the gastroenterology clinic's office manager, bounds in holding the loaf pan she brings every Friday. Tufts of hair, the atomic orange that children find scary on clowns but funny on Sally, poke out from under her newsboy cap—tomato red to match her knit dress. As usual, she's left the tasks of getting her youngest son off to school in the hands of her cabinet-maker husband, Aziz, who built Henry's desk. By the time Gerry and the clinic's other gastroenterologist and two nurses come through the door, she will have put on a playlist of piano jazz, set the coffee brewing, and be seated in the registration area, ready to greet the patients who arrive before the receptionist with a *Morning, hon*. Dr. Henry, the clinic's anesthesiologist, she'll reassure them, is a wizard. They won't feel a thing.

According to the newscaster, the Supreme Court upheld the chemical execution of Kenneth Williams, the fourth of eight scheduled in Arkansas before one of the drugs expires. Williams's lawyers, having observed their client's convulsions following the lethal injection, are accusing the state of having tortured the inmate to death.

Sally shakes her head. 'Can you believe this? Racing to kill people because a drug is reaching its shelf life? In my house, we just toss the old cough syrup.'

She spreads a tissue on Henry's desk, sets down the loaf pan, and yanks at her dress, bunched a bit over her ample hips. 'I have a favor to ask. I told you Aziz and I have been collecting supplies to send to the clinic in Lebanon where his brother works?'

Henry nods. He unhappily remembers precisely when she told him: a Friday, nearly a year ago. 'A vaccination program.'

'Right. Mostly for Syrian refugees but also for local children.' Sally peels the tinfoil off her banana bread. 'I've been trying to get Aziz to ask your brother-in-law for a donation to cover shipping costs, but you know Aziz. He'd die of thirst before asking a client for a glass of water.' She looks sheepishly at Henry. 'I was wondering if you might mention it.'

For a moment, Henry is confused how Sally knows his brother-in-law. Then it comes back to him: after Catherine heard about the care Aziz had taken with Henry's standing desk, measuring his hip height and arm length to assure it was ergonomically optimal and then creating an object of beauty with bands of mahogany inlaid on the tiger oak, she hired Aziz to build George's wine cellar.

'Sure. I'll ask George tonight. It's Ana's birthday, and we're having a family dinner for her.'

Sally gives a wide smile. 'Oh, thank you!' The outlines of her thighs are visible through her dress. She looks like a soft lap. 'And say happy birthday to Ana from me.'

On the Friday when Sally first told him she was collect-ing supplies for her brother-in-law's clinic, Ana was visiting her by then very sick father. She'd driven upstate the day before. Henry wouldn't see her until Sunday.

Like today, Sally had come into his office carrying her banana bread. 'I didn't know you and Ana are friends with Dr. Felkowitz,' she said.

'Dr. Felkowitz?'

'Gerry's med school classmate.'

It took Henry a few seconds to recall Alice Felkowitz. Years be-fore, she'd emailed to ask about the school Simon attended. He'd put her in touch with Ana. 'Not really. I talked to her once on the phone, when she was researching kindergartens for her daughter.'

Sally looked at him quizzically. Dr. Felkowitz, she explained, was soliciting pediatric supplies from colleagues in private practice for Aziz's brother's vaccination program. Sally had gone to Dr. Felkowitz's house to pick up what she'd collected. Sally and the nanny were shuttling back and forth from the front door, loading the boxes into Sally's car, when she saw Ana dashing from Dr. Felkowitz's house. Sally called out to Ana, but Ana hadn't heard her.

Sally added she was sure it was Ana. 'She had that Ana cool look. Sort of sexy in her jeans and boots. Sort of not since she's a stick.'

Henry forced himself to smile. While Ana's angular shape suggested supreme self-control, it was in truth heritage of her mother's utilitarian approach to cooking, which had left her largely uninterested in food; when they'd met, she'd considered an apple and a package of cheese crackers adequate for dinner. Mother Time had treated him less kindly. Since his back injury, his stocky form had developed the sort of fat he trimmed off the tenderloins he prepared on special occasions. After-noons, when the pain escalated and he curled in on himself like a boiled shrimp, his belly overhung the drawstring of his medical pants.

'Maybe Ana and Dr. Felkowitz are friends?' Sally asked.

Arriving home that evening to the empty apartment, he plugged in his desktop vaping machine and ground the exact amount of weed he needed to stop his back from spasming. He'd resisted the new vaping devices, as though updating would signal resignation to the debilitation he'd experienced since cracking two vertebrae from bumping on his butt down a steep patch of a hiking trail near the Swiss hotel where Ana's grandfather had been the general manager.

With Ana away, he left the TV room door open. He inhaled the pungent vapor, three long hits, then turned off the machine and lay on the rug. Shoving a bolster under his knees, he pressed his lumbar spine against the floor. Alice Felkowitz. He remembered now that she'd contacted him not long after he came to work with Gerry. When they spoke, she'd mentioned she knew someone on the heart surgery team he'd recently quit, unable to make it through the lengthy operations without the Vicodin as a medical professional he'd been too liberally prescribed. It had been a difficult choice—between a job he loved and a path, he feared, that would lead to big trouble. It took him a month to wean himself off the opiates, after which he settled on a regimen of over-the-counter medications and marijuana: three Aleve in the morning with a Greek yogurt to coat his stomach, two Motrin at lunchtime with a glass of milk, and then vaping when he got home at five and again before bed. He was out of it at night, but his mind was thankfully clear during the day.

Drifting off, it came back to him that Alice Felkowitz and Ana had made a coffee date to discuss schools. When he asked Ana how it went, she told him Alice had an emergency with one of her child patients and sent her husband. The husband, Ana said, seemed indifferent to where their daughter went to kindergarten.

It was dark out when Henry woke. He pushed the bolster out from under his knees, reached for his phone, and googled Alice Felkowitz. She looked like an adult version of any of a dozen Jewish girls he'd known from his synagogue youth group: not the exotic long-necked ones, but the frizzy-haired ones with rectangular torsos, like Judy Feinstein, his Westinghouse science competition partner—the two of them so proud of their barometer and then mortified when they saw how amateurish it looked next to the telescopes and drosophila fly mutations other teams had submitted.

Scrolling, Henry learned that as a resident Alice Felkowitz had published an op-ed in the *Washington Post* about Palestinian children with stunted growth due to malnutrition living twenty kilometers from Israelis with childhood obesity. She'd written several papers on youth vaccination protocols, which must be why she was involved with the clinic where Sally's brother-in-law worked. The final entry was a *New York Times* wedding announcement from September of 2005: Alice Felkowitz, age thirty-nine, director of a pediatrics health center in Harlem, and Lance Lockley, age forty-three, journalist and author of a travel memoir made into a French film, were married in West Hartford at the home of the bride's parents.

Lance Lockley. The man Ana had said was indifferent to where his daughter went to kindergarten.

Since he was a teen, when his older brother, Aaron, had spied on him, and his younger one, Seth, shadowed him, Henry had hated snoops. He'd put a padlock on his bedroom closet door, not because he was hiding anything but because he couldn't stand the idea of his brothers going through his things. Once, he bought a pack of cigarettes simply to have something to hide. With Ana, though, he never kept secrets. Well, that was not entirely true. There was one thing. When they'd met, it seemed trivial, but it grew in import precisely from having been concealed. Fiona declared it was not a secret. What was the word she used? A discretion.

Moving slowly, he stood. He padded down the book-lined hall to Ana's office, where weekend mornings he brought her a freshly brewed mug of coffee. Otherwise, he was never in there. It was Ana's domain, the long table under the window, neatly stacked with piles of her clients' manuscripts, each labeled with a yellow sticky in Ana's precise hand.

From the doorway, he could see the expanse of Central Park, the lights on the eastern perimeter reflected like stalactites in the reservoir. His father-in-law, disdaining the design principles of home décor magazines, had carved Ana's office out of what was originally the apartment's dining room. A home, Rolf asserted, should be created for the people who live in it, not as a showpiece for their guests. The place where Ana would spend her days should have the view of trees and water.

The two walls of floor-to-ceiling bookshelves in Ana's office matched those in the hall, where there were bays for novels, histories, biographies, travel guides, cookbooks. Ana's shelves held essay collections, memoirs, volumes about writing—each subject alphabetized. Was a husband looking at his wife's books a snoop? Weren't book shelves different from drawers?

In the memoirs section, under the *L*'s, there was Lockley, *Adventures on the Hippie Caravan Trail*. He pulled the book from the shelf. On the front cover was a blurb from *Vanity Fair*: 'Cross Tom Wolfe with Ryszard Kapuscinski, and you have Lance Lockley.' On the back cover was a photograph of the author in a motorcycle jacket with hair falling over his forehead and a wry look on his sculpted face.

Inside, on the title page, in blue felt pen: *To Ana, For everything.*

HEARING ANA'S VOICE WHEN SHE CALLED AN HOUR LATER, HE
feared he might break down and sob.

'My father's not eating. Miko says he's never liked the Japanese food
she cooks, so she's trying to prepare Swiss dishes.'

Henry pictured tiny Miko, who made her own tofu and miso, studying the recipe for raclette.

'Since I arrived today, he's only had a few sips of tea.'

'That happens.' He did not say *at the end*. 'People stop eating as their
systems shut down. Digestion can be painful.'

'The hospice nurse said it's too bad we didn't get my father approval
for medical marijuana. It might have helped his appetite.'

When Ana paused, Henry knew that she did not want to ask him
directly.

'You'd like me to give him some pot?'

'Would there be any harm in trying?'

Henry had never told Ana how he got his own stash. Not wanting to
register as a medical marijuana user, he'd stayed with his dealer, a man
who was careful as a jewel thief and professional as a stock broker. Henry
placed his orders on a private messaging app and they met at a juice bar,
the dealer handing him a bag with a cucumber and kale concoction and
Henry's order tucked underneath.

'I was thinking,' Ana said, 'maybe you could take the train on
Sunday and we could see if it might help. We could drive back together.'

Ana said she would look up the train schedule and text him the
times. He was doubtful that a few puffs from a vaping machine would
make much difference to Rolf now, but trying apparently made a difference to Ana.

SATURDAY MORNING, HENRY SAT IN THE LIVING ROOM AND READ
Lance Lockley's book. It pained him that the guy was a good writer.
The book opened with Lockley's account of growing up in Atlantic City
with a fundamentalist Christian mother who wore pants with elasticized

waistbands and ran a daycare on the sunporch of their bungalow, and a bookie father with a slicked-back pompadour who had him running numbers by the time he was ten.

At sixteen, Lockley became a lifeguard and, not long after, a local celebrity for having saved a brother and sister caught in an ocean riptide. The Atlantic City Rotary group gave him a scholarship for his first year at NYU, with a promise of additional funding if he maintained a 3.2 GPA. He moved to the city with two hundred dollars and a duffel bag holding a sheet, a towel, and five changes of clothes. A black belt he'd earned at a street-front karate studio landed him a bouncer job at a club on the Lower East Side for some needed pocket money.

In May of his spring semester, his father forwarded a letter from the Rotary president informing him of 'unexpected fiscal complications.' Rumor, according to his father, was the group's treasurer had lost the club's savings at one of the newly opened casinos. Bottom line: no more money no matter his GPA. That's when, Lockley wrote, he learned that sometimes the worst thing that's ever happened to you can become the best. Moping on a bench in Washington Square Park about his futureless future, he met a girl—a dead ringer for Joni Mitchell, with teeth that verged on buck and blonde hair that skimmed her waist—who'd graduated the year before and was writing for a backpacker's travel series. She was fearless save for a spider phobia, which meant she wouldn't sleep until someone tore apart the bed to search for arachnids. Three weeks later, she left on an assignment to cover the hippie caravan trail—Amsterdam, Marrakesh, Crete, Afghanistan—with Lockley (she paid for his ticket) as her spider-hunter.

Henry finished the chapter on Afghanistan while he ate his lunch. Arriving in Kabul with the Joni Mitchell girl, Lockley settled her in a hostel, where he checked the bed and the cracks in the walls. Finding nothing aside from a handful of ants, he left for Bamiyan with a documentary filmmaker he'd met in a bar who wanted to film the ancient Buddhas carved into the cliffs. For a week, he and the filmmaker stayed with a Hazara family in a cave. When he got back to Kabul, the Joni Mitchell girl was near psychotic. While he'd been gone, she'd spent the nights in a chair in the hostel's kitchen, certain there was a spider in her bed. Two days later, after calling her parents, Lockley put her on a plane back to New York and took over her job.

AFTER HIS FIRST TWO PROCEDURES, HENRY EMAILS FIONA. *THERE'S something I'd like to talk with you about before Ana's party,* he writes. *I have a break between 11 and 12. Can I call you then?* It occurs to him that asking George with everyone around tonight to make a donation to Aziz's brother's vaccination program might seem off, so he emails him too.

A minute later, his cell phone rings. 'Henry!' Fiona says. She's coming into the city ahead of Ana's party—a work meeting, a doctor's appointment. How about an early lunch?

They arrange to meet at a café close to Henry's office. It crosses his mind that he should text Ana to let her know. She'd be tickled by Fiona and him getting together, but not telling her until afterward might rub her the wrong way: as though Henry was inserting himself into her friendship with Fiona, not acknowledging that his and Fiona's relationship is a satellite. But that's the point. The reason he wants to talk with Fiona.

To his surprise, there's already a reply from George. Only, Henry sees when he opens the email, it's not from George. He forgot that Ana has told him that Catherine acts like George's personal assistant, handling anything not related to his work. *Of course we'll make a contribution!!* ☺☺ *I'll run it by George, but I'm sure he'll sign off.*

There are three more patients on his morning docket—two colonoscopies and an endoscopy. The first two procedures go smoothly, but the last patient, a very elderly gentleman, is panicking about having an oxygen mask placed on his face. Seeing the numbers tattooed on the man's lower arm, Henry understands. It's been a while since he's had a patient who survived a concentration camp, but during his residency it was more common and they'd had what they called The Holocaust Protocol, which involved giving the patient an oral sedative a half an hour in advance. There's no time now for a sedative, but Henry talks softly to the elderly man, reassuring him that he'll have a bagel and a schmear in no time at all, holding his hand until he loses consciousness.

WALKING TO THE CAFÉ, HE THINKS ABOUT THE DAY HE MET FIONA. It was July, the beginning of his second year as an anesthesiology resident and Fiona's first weekend in Philadelphia, where she'd taken a job as a summer research assistant in advance of her graduate school classes. A guy he and Fiona each knew as undergraduates at Harvard (they'd overlapped for a year but never crossed paths) had invited them both to a luau, where he would be roasting a baby pig. Seeing the horror on Fiona's face when she walked into the backyard and found herself a foot from the rotating head—the shriveled pink ears, the lamentful eyes—Henry went to talk with her. 'Now I get it,' she said. 'Why Jews don't eat pork. Nothing to do with pigs not chewing their cud. They look too damn human.'

Henry laughed. He'd overcome his queasiness about bodies, human and animal, in medical school after they'd dissected everything from eyeballs to testicles.

'Did you grow up kosher?' he asked.

'Charleston kosher. We didn't eat pork, but that didn't mean you couldn't order a BLT if you were out. And no one asked if there was butter on the green beans my mother served with her pot roast.'

They slept together that night, both of them attributing their fumbling and decidedly non-erotic contact to having had too much to drink. But after a second attempt, Henry concluded they simply didn't have chemistry: their pheromones were mismatched. Or maybe they were too matched: their physiologies too similar, like the cousins they might have been. Fiona put it differently. 'Have you ever seen people who can't dance together? They might be fine dancers with other partners, but with each other they can't figure out who's leading or get into sync. We're like that.' She kissed him on the cheek. 'I think, Edelman, we'll have to be friends.'

They did not, however, become friends—not due to bad feelings, but because they settled into different social circles: Fiona into a group of English grad students, including Ana; Henry, on account of his Polish surgical resident roommate, into a loose network of Eastern Europeans. He didn't see Fiona until the following spring, when he bumped into her at a bar near campus. She was with her advisor, celebrating her acceptance to the Hopkins MFA program. He was with his roommate, Marek, who couldn't take his eyes off Fiona and later asked Henry for her number.

In the fall, Fiona came back to Philadelphia to visit Ana for a weekend. She'd had a brief but intense affair with Marek, which she broke off when she moved to Baltimore, though Marek, who still called her frequently, seemed not to have accepted that. Learning she'd be in town, Marek had made her promise she'd at least drop by the party he and Henry were throwing. Fiona twisted Ana's arm to come along.

When they arrived, Fiona pulled Henry into his bedroom. 'Talk to Ana, okay? She's shy and doesn't know anyone here but Marek and me.'

Henry had seen Ana when she walked in. He poked Fiona in the side. 'Come on . . .'

'I have an instinct about you two. What was it you said about us? Incompatible pheromones? That we could have been cousins? Well, she's definitely from a different gene pool.'

'Your friend certainly does not look like any of my cousins.'

'Her mother's family is from Sweden, her father's from Switzerland.'

'Does she know?'

'Know what?'

'That we had a thing?'

Fiona laughed. 'No offense, but it never came up. You and I were done by the time I met her. And then today, when I had the brilliant idea of introducing you two, it seemed like a jinx to mention it now. Less is more.'

'Mies van der Rohe.'

'Like you, Edelman, to know that. Okay, don't be a brainiac and recite the first nine digits of pi.'

'3.141592653. Actually, that's ten digits.'

'As my mother would say, it's of no matter.'

'Your mother thinks pi is of no matter?'

'No, dummy. That we slept together twice over a year ago.'

It made sense. Who opens a flirtation by announcing who in the room they've had sex with? Then, later, when Henry wanted to tell Ana, Fiona objected. It would be awkward for the three of them. Besides, she said, these things depend on timing, and the time for telling had passed.

FIONA IS AT A TABLE UNDER THE WINDOW DRINKING AN ESPRESSO. She waits for him to order his lunch before asking, 'What's up, Edelman? Something about Ana's party?'

Henry hesitates. Can he dive right in? As he says to Simon, best to just spit it out. 'I've been thinking I should tell Ana about us.'

Fiona's eyes open wide. 'Why? Why on earth now?'

Henry feels his armpits dampen as he realizes how little he's thought this through. Of course Fiona would want to know why now. And how has it never occurred to him that Fiona probably knows about Lockley? It's not a question he can ask her. She's had no problem not telling Ana about their fling—extraneous information, Fiona would say—but she'd never break Ana's confidence.

Fiona reaches across the table and touches his cheek. 'Henry. Dear Henry. You need to be a bit less *shtetl* and a bit more *français*. Haven't you heard the saying *discretion is the better part of valor*? Do you feel compelled to tell Ana if you don't like her blouse or the towels she bought? Or her new haircut?' Fiona shakes her head, answering for him. 'No. We withhold all the time. It would be sadistic not to.'

He cannot bring himself to say that Fiona's hypotheticals make no sense to him. He loves the way Ana dresses and what she purchases for their home. He loves how she wears her hair. Everything about her.

Everything . . .

To Ana, For everything.

ON THE TRAIN TO HIS FATHER-IN-LAW'S HOUSE, HE REALIZED THAT Lance Lockley reminded him of his younger brother, Seth, who as a kid had been obsessed with theories about Michael Rockefeller's disappearance after swimming away from a capsized boat on the Arafura Sea. Like

Lockley, Seth was enamored of the idea of travel as a way for a man to discover his mettle. It crossed Henry's mind to order a copy of Lockley's book for Seth, but then he thought how perverse it would be to give his brother a book by his wife's lover—the first time he let himself even think the word.

How could he have not worried that Ana would take a lover? It was the pot. It blunted his anxiety. Blinkered his view from beyond the immediate moment. From seeing how serious it was that aside from a single unsuccessful attempt a few months after his injury, he and Ana have not had sex since before his fall. Ana had initiated. When he yelped from a pang in his lower back, she sat up on the bed in alarm. Over breakfast the next day, he tentatively broached what had happened. They could find other ways of being together, *be creative*, he said. Ana smiled vaguely, but averted her gaze. He was relieved that she never brought it up again. If so, he would have had to explain that his own desire was so infiltrated by pain, he'd ceased thinking of his penis as more than an appendage through which he urinated.

Outside the train depot nearest to Rolf's house, Henry spotted Ana waiting behind the wheel of their old Volvo. She gave a little wave, and he waved back, struggling to remember that for him, there'd been an earthquake that left him in shambles, but for her, nothing had changed. His chest felt so heavy with grief, he feared he wouldn't make it across the parking lot to their car.

Before his back injury, he'd always driven. Now, she did. On the ride to her father's house, she talked about her father and then about Miko, who'd told Ana that she'd made arrangements to move, after Rolf died, to her late parents' country cottage thirty miles outside Nagasaki. She planned to grow the vegetables she'd eaten as a child. To spend time with her great-nieces and great-nephews. To visit the family grave where the cremated remains of her parents were buried. She'd shown Ana a photograph: a granite headstone shaded by a sakura tree.

He pressed his lower back against the seat.

'Are you okay?' Ana asked, touching his knee.

Could he say no, he was not okay? Not okay with another man attaching *for everything* to her name.

ON ENTERING THE HOUSE, HENRY SLIPPED INTO HIS DOCTOR persona. He went immediately to wash. Afterward, he found Miko, grating potatoes for a *rosti* she'd read Swiss families ate with a fried egg on top. He kissed her soft cheek and followed Ana to the room where her father's hospital bed overlooked a lawn, dotted with lingering patches of snow and stretching out to a gazebo with a grouping of Adirondack chairs. Rolf must have selected the placement for his hospital bed himself.

His father-in-law's hair, once thick and white, appeared brittle and stripped of color. His skin, once ruddy, seemed jaundiced.

'If I could have a few minutes,' Henry said to Ana. She looked at him curiously. He'd never before asked to talk privately with her father, but then he'd never before been in any medical role with him.

'Ana said you were going to bring some marijuana,' Rolf said once they were alone. 'She thinks it might make me feel like eating. I'm doubtful, but I told her I'd give it a shot.'

'Have you ever used it?'

'Twice. It didn't do much for me. Just made me sleepy. I prefer a good scotch.'

'Nowadays, there are so many strains. Some that ease muscle pain. Others that improve mood—which usually improves appetite too.' Henry paused. 'How has your mood been?'

'I'm dying. How's anyone's mood when they're dying?'

'As varied as when they're living.'

'Touché. My mood has been what you'd call reflective. Which is an interesting turn for me.'

Henry removed the vaporizer from his duffel bag. He set it on the table next to Rolf and plugged it into the nearby socket.

'When you're an architect,' Rolf continued, 'your mind is on creating things, not what's already built.'

For a man who was so weak, Rolf seemed surprisingly talkative. It sometimes happened, Henry knew, from his hospital days. People close to death could rally, as though to lighten their load before the journey.

'What have you been thinking about?'

'Nothing original. What I'm sure most old men think about when they're about to die. What I'll be remembered for.' Rolf's tone reminded Henry of the expression on Lance Lockley's face in the photograph on the back cover of his book. 'I get poor marks as a husband, and I wasn't much better as a father, but I take comfort in seeing how happily married George and Ana each are. Maybe my failed marriages—before Miko—were a lesson to them.'

Henry lowered his eyes so they wouldn't betray his no longer being able to agree with Rolf about the happy state of Ana's and his marriage.

'I feel lucky not to be worried about Miko. She looks like a sparrow, but she's made of steel. She survived the war, came to this country alone. When I met her, she was living in a cold-water loft with her drying undergarments hanging like pennants from the pipes and her seaweed and eggplants on the windowsill. It looked like a refugee camp.'

Rolf shifted in the hospital bed. It seemed that he wanted to sit up. Fearing his back spasming but unable to not help, Henry put his hands in the old man's armpits and lifted him gently.

'One of the strangest things about being so sick is how the past is like a Mobius strip. Things that happened more than half a century ago are as vivid as if they happened yesterday, and then there are things that happened yesterday that I can't recall at all. Since this morning, I've been stuck in a loop about my father's dying. I keep hearing my mother's scratchy voice on the line when she phoned to tell me to come.'

Rolf reached for the water glass on his bedside stand. 'I was still married to Ana's mother then. Jean had grown to hate me, but inside the hate there must have been a pocket of love. She'd heard that the airlines keep a few tickets for emergencies, and she called and got me a seat and then helped me pack.' Rolf smiled weakly. 'Trust me, not something she'd ever done before.'

He took a few sips of water. With his lips dampened, a little color returned. 'I flew overnight to Zurich and caught the train from there to St. Moritz. The driver, he'd been working at the hotel since I was a boy, met me at the station. He teared up when he saw me, and it hit me like a gale wind that my father was going to die very soon.'

When Henry and Ana and Simon had stayed at the same hotel, they too were met in St. Moritz by a driver—though surely a different man than had come for Rolf. It was Henry's first time in the Alps. He rolled down the car window, gulping the clean air, gazing at the green valleys dotted with wildflowers and tinkling with cowbells, the snowcapped peaks of the Engadin, the peacock blue lake adorned with the colorful parachutes of wind surfers. It looked like *Heidi*, Simon proclaimed, delighted when they later learned that the movie had been filmed nearby.

Rolf exhaled loudly. 'By the time we reached the hotel, I was so nervous, the driver gave me a swig of the brandy he kept in the car.'

'What were you nervous about?'

'It will sound strange to you. Spending time with my father. I hadn't been alone with him since I was a child and we'd gone on Sunday hikes into the mountains. But we'd never really talked on those treks. After a week tending to guests, my father wanted silence.'

How had it never occurred to Henry that the trail where he'd injured his back was probably one where his father-in-law had walked, even run, countless times as a boy?

'We always hiked single file, my father in front. I would count the coils of flesh between the bottom of his cap and the top of his oilskin jacket.'

What his father had wanted to talk about on his deathbed, Rolf said, was the war. Rolf had been a teenager then, aware of the outlines of what was going on, but not the details. 'As a student, I heard the Mies van der Rohe quote *God is in the details*. Nowadays, it seems to have been changed to *The devil is in the details*. That's what was haunting my father: his fear that the details pointed to his having consorted with the devil.'

Rolf's breathing was labored. Henry looked at the oxygen tank in the corner of the room. He wondered if he should set it up for Rolf. What it meant that he, too, often employed Mies maxims.

During the war, Rolf explained, Switzerland had been officially a neutral country, but in practice every interaction was marked by compromises. The hotel hosted many Austrian clients, enriched by their business dealings with the Germans. What was weighing on Rolf's father, however, was not the Austrians, but two Nazi generals who'd arrived with their mistresses to spend a week's holiday. His father had catered to their every whim—adjacent suites on the hotel's top floor, guides for their rambles, the best wines uncorked for their evening meals.

'After my father told me this,' Rolf said, 'he started to quietly cry. It was the first time I'd ever seen him cry. But, what could I have done, he asked me. What could I have done?'

Rolf looked at Henry. 'I'm not proud to admit it, but I felt disgusted. He sounded like a woman wanting reassurance.'

Rolf had slipped down again in the bed, his chin nearly touching his chest. 'I said all the expected things. If he'd refused to give the generals rooms, not treated them with kid gloves, there would have been repercussions for the hotel. He might have lost his job. He had my sisters and me to think of.'

For a moment, Rolf fell silent. 'If I'm honest with myself, nothing he said was really news. Since I was fifteen, I'd known he was a coward.'

Rolf was born in 1926. So 1941.

'That's when my closest boyhood friend, Hans, swore me to secrecy. His father and some of the other men in the village were helping Jewish refugees. Jews were entering the country on foot, carrying their babies and possessions through mountain passes because they feared being turned away at the border. My father, Hans said, had been asked to give jobs to some of the refugees. He'd refused.'

Rolf's gaze settled on his hands, folded atop the blanket. Not long ago, he said, he'd read a book about Gertrude Stein and Alice B. Toklas. The author asked how had two Jewish lesbians survived in occupied France without their artwork seized? Rolf had been furious at the author for the answer: Stein and Toklas had supported the Vichy regime. Then, Rolf added, he felt furious at the women. Later, he realized he'd felt the same way about his father. 'He protected us, like Stein and Toklas had their paintings, by his cooperation. It left me feeling dirty.'

Henry did not say the word that came to mind. *Collaborator*. Rolf thought his father had been a collaborator.

'I still remember Hans staring at the leftover breakfast pastries the hotel cook would leave for my sisters and me to eat after school and asking how we got the flour and sugar. His mother didn't have enough ration stamps for his family to have bread every day.'

Rolf paused, and for a moment Henry thought he'd finally run out of steam.

'I never told any of this to Ana or George. Ana, she's a forgiving soul, but George . . . He would hold it against me. More evidence of how morally deficient I am. And he would be right. I should have confronted my father at the time. I didn't know about the Nazi generals, but I knew the extra rations for the hotel were because of my father's relations with their proxies in the village.'

Rolf looked at Henry. 'Do you think I should tell Ana?'

Henry could not recall his father-in-law having ever asked his advice about anything. Not even how many Tylenol to take for a headache.

He glanced at the vaporizer. So much time had passed, it switched off. 'Let me think about it,' he said, 'and get back to you.'

HENRY FOUND ANA HAVING TEA WITH MIKO IN THE KITCHEN.

'How'd he make out?' Ana asked.

'After three puffs, he fell asleep. I checked his pulse, and it's as you'd expect. Hopefully he'll wake with some appetite.'

Ana stood. 'I'll go sit with him for a bit.'

Miko poured Henry a cup of her twig tea. It smelled pungent, like the deer's nest he and Simon had stumbled upon on a trip they'd made, just the two of them, before his back injury, to a Montana fly-fishing lodge. There'd been no magic for Simon in tying flies or scouring the surface of the river for tiny bubbles, and Simon seemed more horrified than pleased when they did catch a fish. The fawns, though, delighted him. Crouched next to Henry, Simon speechlessly watched the two sleeping babies, alone while their mother foraged for food.

Miko cradled her mug in her small hands. Her feet, in tatami slippers that exposed her bunions, barely touched the floor. She waited a bit before speaking. 'Your wife is kind to me. I must honor you for that. But she is still my enemy.'

Henry's eyebrows shot up.

'It's natural. She is the daughter. I am the wife. We are not on the same side.'

'What do you mean?'

Miko set down her mug. 'It is like with the war. The Americans were on the side of good, but they still killed my grandparents and three of my cousins. There were relatives who arrived at my parents' cottage with skin blackened like fish on a barbeque grill. They suffered terribly, clinging to life, and then died years later of cancer.'

Did Miko think of Rolf as an American? Was his father-in-law living with a wife who saw him as a foe? Had Rolf never explained to Miko that Switzerland had been officially neutral—even if, as Rolf had just told Henry, that neutrality had holes like Emmentaler cheese? He was tempted to say that Rolf's family had been more aligned with the Nazis than with the Allies, but of course, he could not. What Rolf had told Henry was not as his son-in-law but as his doctor. It would have to remain between them.

His mother-in-law, Jean—had she ever viewed herself as on Rolf's side? She must have. Otherwise, she wouldn't still harbor the hatred for him that she did. And George? Since Rolf got sick, George had been handling Rolf's financial and legal affairs but, according to Ana, he never phoned their father just to see how he was doing. For George, their father was firmly planted on the opposite bank of a rushing river. Were Rolf to call out to him, George would not hear his voice over the water's roar. It was Ana who always made the crossing. Ana, who when Rolf woke, would fry the egg to put on the rösti Miko had prepared.

OUTSIDE THE CAFÉ, FIONA KISSES HENRY GOODBYE. 'JUST LET IT go, Edelman,' she says. 'Telling Ana that we slept together before either of us met her would only hurt her. The important truth is we both love her, and she knows that.' She looks at her watch. 'I need to fly. See you tonight!'

Walking back to the clinic, Henry thinks about how he never got back to Rolf about whether to tell Ana that he'd not confronted his own father about his dealings during the war—Rolf's fear that this made him, like his father, a collaborator. Rolf was asleep when Henry and Ana left his house that afternoon. Henry had intended to call him that evening, but on arriving home, he saw Lance Lockley's book on their coffee table. How could he have forgotten to return it to the shelf in Ana's office? An hour later, the book was gone. That Ana didn't ask about it seemed as much a confirmation of the affair with Lockley as if he'd caught them in flagrante.

He told himself that he'd call Rolf during the week, but all he could think about was Lance Lockley. Twice, when Ana was out, he crept into her office and looked at the book: Lockley's photo, the *For everything*. Then, at the end of the week, Simon came home to go with Ella and Gemma to visit their grandfather and to attend a friend's twenty-first birthday party. When Henry caught a glimpse of Simon leaving for the party in flowered bell-bottoms, eyelids covered with shimmery powder, Simon, clearly embarrassed, mumbled something about a sixties theme. Henry reminded himself that lots of male rock stars wore extravagant makeup on stage— but it left him preoccupied with Simon in addition to Lockley.

After ten days passed without his calling Rolf, Henry decided some conversations are better in person. He would talk with his father-in-law when he saw him the Saturday after next. With Rolf's death the following week, there'd been no Saturday after next and Henry was left holding what Rolf had told him in confidence. In the year since, he's berated himself: he should have thought more carefully before acting, even for just an afternoon, as his father-in-law's physician. How shitty it would seem to Ana that he knows things about her father and grandfather that her father never told her himself.

Back at the clinic, Henry goes immediately to his office. In ten minutes, he'll need to change into scrubs for the afternoon procedures. He takes two Motrin with a milk box he keeps in his closet, adjusts his back brace, and stands at the desk Sally's husband made him, looking over the notes for his upcoming patient.

What he was really left holding this past year was what he'd learned from Sally: she'd seen Ana exiting Alice Felkowitz's house. For an instant, the crack in his marriage, so much deeper than that in his vertebrae, seems crystal clear. He's sidestepped his wife's breach of their vows because the problem is so much larger than intercourse causing his back to spasm. If it were only that, they would have found workarounds. The problem is that since his injury, he's retreated into himself. Eroticism has receded so far, he can no longer recall the last time he even fantasized about the silkiness of his wife's skin. Her still-firm small breasts. What he fantasizes about is marijuana smoke. The taste of it, the relief from pain.

He wonders if his secret about having slept with Fiona before he met Ana, trivial as it might seem, has been a wormhole in his marriage, insidiously weakening its foundation. Perhaps he should tell Ana. Maybe it would be like a nuclear arms agreement: we'll let you inspect our arsenals if you let us inspect yours. Maybe if he tells Ana about Fiona, she'll tell him about Lockley.

He clutches the lip of his standing desk. He feels like one of those inflatable air dancers flailing insanely in front of used car lots. How foolish, he thinks. As if there's an equivalency between his having had sex twice with Fiona before he knew Ana and Ana's affair. Apparently long affair.

How long? Since Alice Felkowitz emailed him—he counts backward to when he started working here—seven years ago?

PASSING SALLY'S OFFICE DOOR ON THE WAY TO THE STAFF LOCKER room, Henry catches a whiff of her banana bread. He imagines Sally's broad smile were he to ask for a piece. The contours of her generous bottom under her tight red dress as she leans to cut him a thick slice.

It crosses his mind that he'd like to ask Ana if she thinks George will make a donation to cover the shipping of supplies to Aziz's brother's clinic, but he's afraid that if he poses the question, Alice Felkowitz's name will slip out. Alice Felkowitz, whose house Sally saw Ana leaving. Alice Felkowitz, Ana's lover's wife.

In the staff locker room, he stuffs his street clothes in a cubby. Standing in his briefs as he takes the scrubs from their plastic covering, he can't tell if he is going to weep or laugh. Weep, not about Ana fucking someone else, awful as that is to envision, but because there is another man, a man whose name and story he knows, for whom Ana is everything. Laugh because he sees Ana's face, her clavicle, her hip bones, the pale hair between her legs. Laugh because for the first time, in a very long time, there's a stirring below.

3

ANA

WITH THE MAMMOTH ROCK OUTCROPPINGS AT THE ENTRANCE TO Central Park, I'm reminded that I live on an island, once a wild place without buildings or roads, without subway tracks and optic fiber lines. The only subterranean networks tree roots and animal burrows. As a child, Simon played on the rocks, fantasizing searches for berries and chestnuts in that before time: before Europeans arrived with guns and disease and humans in chains. Now, in the April sunshine, benches with brass placards identifying their donors are populated by nannies on cell phones, their stroller-bound charges asleep under pastel blankets.

I walk east, on a path that traverses the pine arboretum and the Great Lawn, where before his back injury, Henry would take Simon on summer evenings for baseball catches. Simon's attention was more often on a cardinal alit on a branch than the ball, but he obliged his father's love of baseball, and went along, too, with the fishing trips, despite never believing the hook didn't cause pain.

Save for Henry's gold-flecked hazel eyes, Simon takes after me physically: my narrow frame and light eyebrows; my height, which as a child yielded boy points. Boy points to counterbalance never having been bedazzled by the superpowers of action figures, never liking sports, always wanting to wear his hair long. A precocious math student (he'd inherited *her* mathematical abilities, my mother declared), Simon was doing three-digit multiplication problems in his head at nine. By sixth grade, he'd taught himself algebra, and by tenth had completed the most advanced math courses offered at his high school, after which he astonished the head of the math department by declining the offer for an independent study for the following year. Quitting the math and chess teams, Simon took to coming straight home from school. Worried that he was depressed, I asked if he might like to talk with someone, but Simon demurred. He wanted to spend his afternoons reading. Simon's okay, Henry said, sleeping and eating normally and doing fine in school. It's puberty. A lot of hormones flooding the system. Give him some time.

During Simon's first year at Brown, he reported liking the school and his dorm and his classes, but on our Sunday night calls, when I would inquire about the weekend, my heart would sink on hearing he'd spent the days in the library and the nights alone in his room. It was his choice, Simon said: he preferred it that way. By spring break, though, Simon seemed less isolated. He mentioned a few new friends and an occasional party and that he'd begun to see a therapist at the health center. He found a summer job in the sciences library so he could stay in therapy.

At the end of sophomore year, Simon announced that he'd selected Gender and Sexuality Studies as his concentration and would be spending his junior year in Copenhagen. It took every ounce of self-control not to tell Simon how anxious I felt about his being so far away. What if he got sick? How would I know if he was okay if I couldn't see him until winter break? When Henry and I visited, however, Simon seemed happier than I'd seen him in years. He had a wide circle of friends—both other Americans studying abroad and Danish college students—many of whom were openly gay or exploring what I'd come to understand from Simon was their gender identity. Simon's dress seemed more androgynous, and although he didn't say anything about romantic relationships, Henry and I assumed he must be experimenting with both boys and girls.

On Simon's return to New York a few weeks before his senior year, he surprised us with the news that he was writing a sci-fi novel. 'Wow,' Henry said, and I could see him trying to wrap his mind around how a sci-fi novel fit together with being a math whiz and having a Gender and

Sexuality concentration. On my end, I struggled to grasp the premise: a world in which sexual attributes are no more defining than hair color, shoe size, or ratio of limb length to torso.

When I responded as I do after clients' initial descriptions of their projects, 'Tell me more,' Simon flushed. Maybe it hadn't occurred to him that he was talking with someone who made a living helping writers with their books.

'I'm asking as your mom, not in my professional capacity.'

In the novel, Simon explained, gender was not even a concept, and reproduction, no longer connected to sexual acts, was a laboratory procedure involving the fusion of genetic materials from multiple ungendered persons. People received their names by algorithms. 'I could show you what I have so far,' he shyly offered.

Simon gave me the opening chapter. The rest, he said, was still too rough. 'I actually first had the idea when I was in high school.' Simon laughed. 'Then, I thought the idea of eliminating gender was so original. After I got to Brown and learned about nonbinary people, who are sort of living that way, I thought there's no point writing this. But when I was in Denmark, where the understanding of gender and sex are so much more evolved than here, I started thinking my novel might help people understand that masculine and feminine are ideas, not biological givens.'

Although Simon's novel wasn't the kind I work on or read myself, I was impressed by how well written it was. It felt taboo, though, to view Simon's writing as a window into his inner life the way I do with my clients. It was as though I'd drawn a curtain on that part of my brain.

'Of course you did,' Fiona said. 'You don't want to be a peeping Tom into your kid's unconscious. I'd love to read it!'

Simon gave me permission to share the pages with Fiona, who then suggested Simon talk to her college roommate, Inga, now a law school professor at work on a book about legal questions raised by reproductive technologies. 'I'm so happy, Mom,' Simon announced, after he interviewed with Inga and she offered him a job as her research assistant once he graduated. Simon kissed me on the cheek and grinned, and in that moment he looked more like Henry than me.

HAD ANYONE ASKED ME, EVEN A YEAR AGO, IF I BELIEVED FIONA'S aphorism—*There's a quota of angst every parent has to experience with each child. If you don't experience it when your kid is young, don't fool yourself: it's coming*—I would have nodded yes, while thinking, *Not for Simon.* Simon, so easy as a baby, as a toddler, as a child, was the exception. Yes, I'd worried if Simon was depressed during high school and his first year of college, but then he'd gone into therapy and seemed so much better. Fiona, though, was right. Six months ago—my father buried and Miko moved back to Japan, Simon graduated and settled into the job with Inga and an apartment with two college friends—my time to receive my quota of angst arrived.

It was a Sunday afternoon, a warm October day, when Simon called to ask if he could come to dinner. 'Of course,' I said, pushing away the stab of concern about the short notice. 'We'd love that.'

Henry made Simon's favorite meal of a kale and button mushroom lasagna with a Bibb lettuce salad, and after my park walk, I bought black-berries and lemon gelato for dessert. Over dinner, I studied Simon for signs of illness. He was skinny, but he'd always been skinny and if he seemed a bit more so, perhaps the way he was wearing his hair, pulled back in what I'd read was called a man bun, made it more noticeable. He talked about how well his living situation—an apartment with two female friends from Brown—was working out. There was a chores chart with a designated night for each to cook, and a Venmo system for managing collective expenses. 'You should organize Mom and me,' Henry joked.

Simon described his job. Inga was brilliant and he was learning so much: the intersection of feminist theory and law; the history of legislation concerning medical decisions; the philosophical debates about consciousness and the definition of what it means to be human that bear on these issues. I listened, filled with the gratitude Suni was always encouraging us to focus on during yoga class: a father who'd created the ideal proportions for my dining room, a husband who took pleasure in feeding his family, a friend who'd helped Simon find a job, a child who was now articulate and thoughtful and well launched and lived close enough that we could have these meals together. My cup runneth over, I thought.

We cleaned up in our habitual way, with Henry rinsing the dishes and Simon loading the dishwasher while I wiped the counters and put everything away. I filled the kettle for ginger tea and Henry dictated his lasagna recipe to Simon, who wrote it in a Moleskine notebook so he could make it on one of his designated cooking nights.

After the tea was brewed, I found Simon in the living room, kneeling on the couch and looking into the park. He twisted around, and I handed him a mug. 'It's still warm out,' I said. 'We could take a walk, if you'd like.'

Simon tipped his head slightly and squinted: an expression he'd had since childhood that meant there was something on his mind. 'Could we talk instead?'

The moment of anxiety I'd felt earlier when Simon asked to come to dinner returned. 'Of course. Dad, too?'

Simon nodded.

I found Henry on the floor of the TV room doing his back exercises. He'd vaped around five, before making dinner. It was now nearly eight. Usually, he would try to hold out until nine before vaping again, but I wondered if he was thinking about doing it earlier.

'Is your back hurting?'

'The norm.'

'Simon wants to talk to us.'

Henry looked at me quizzically.

'Just come in with me, okay?'

In the living room, Simon was now in the swivel chair, angled to face the corner of the room. Henry and I sat on the couch Simon had vacated. I passed Henry a pillow. He adjusted it behind his back, up and then down and then up again.

Slowly, Simon turned toward us. 'There's something I need to tell you.'

I froze as my mind leaped to medical problems, legal problems, financial ones.

'I've come to a realization . . .' Simon closed his eyes.

'Yes, son,' Henry said. 'Best to just spit it out.'

Simon took a deep breath. 'I've come to the realization . . .' His lids fluttered open. 'I've come to the realization that I'm transgender.'

I saw the word in my head: *trans-gen-der*. How could such an enormous idea have only three syllables?

'You're what?' Henry asked.

'Transgender,' Simon repeated so softly, I wasn't sure if Henry heard. 'You know what that means, Dad, don't you?'

Henry appeared to be in shock, and it flitted through my mind that this is how he would react were I to tell him I had a lover.

'I know it must seem to you like it's coming out of the blue, but knowing I'm a girl . . . I've been living with that for a long time.'

Simon looked at us sadly, suffering, it seemed, at the thought of causing us pain. 'Really, my whole life, though I didn't have the words for it when I was little and I didn't know anyone who was transgender until high school. One girl, but she left. Then, when I got to Brown, it felt like everyone was gender fluid. There were kids with identities I hadn't even known existed. That's when I began seeing a therapist.'

Simon was no longer looking directly at Henry and me. 'In Copenhagen, I felt liberated—or maybe it was just braver. I went to some parties dressed as a girl, began using gender-neutral pronouns. *They, them.* Played with calling myself Simona . . .'

I tried to say the name in my head, but the extra syllable wouldn't attach. All I heard was a stutter: *uh uh.*

'When I got back to Brown, my therapist explained that trans is thankfully no longer considered a psychiatric condition, but I met the diagnosis for gender dysphoria.'

I felt terrible asking. My question would make it seem as though this was about Henry and me, not Simon, but it was a boulder I couldn't get around. 'Why didn't you tell us?'

He— *No, oh my God, no...*Simon was now using *they/them*...immediately, that very minute, even in my thoughts, I needed to do the same— they, Simon, set their mug on the coffee table, still the considerate child who used a coaster. They rested their elbows on their thighs and cradled their chin in their hands. With their head lowered, I could see the elastic holding their hair in the man bun, but maybe that wasn't how they thought about it.

'I wanted to tell you, I really did. I was planning to, last year over winter break, but Pop was so sick, it didn't feel right. And then he died just weeks before graduation, and I couldn't see laying this on you then.'

I touched the corner of an eye to make sure I wasn't crying. Do not cry, do not cry, do not cry, I commanded myself.

'I'm sorry, Mom. I wish I'd been able to tell you sooner. Now that I have a job, I can start the hormones while I save up for electrolysis and then for the surgeries. I didn't want to begin without telling you first.'

I stared at Simon, my thoughts cycling through the book I'd read over forty years ago by Jan Morris, who'd undergone what was called then a sex-change operation, and to the movie *The Danish Girl* about a beautiful young man who became a beautiful young woman, only to die in the aftermath of one of the medical procedures, and to Caitlyn Jenner, whose *Vanity Fair* cover I found bold and brave but Fiona derided as a retrograde pinup pose.

Henry sat with his feet stiffly planted and the pillow now on the floor. Unable to speak, I listened while he asked about testosterone blockers and dosages of estrogen and progestin and the research on long-term effects and the training of the doctors at the clinic where Simon was going, questions for which Simon promised to try to find answers.

'Maybe you could come with me, Dad, when I go to my next appointment? Then you could ask your questions yourself.'

I glanced at Henry. Compared to my boorish brother and my prior boyfriends, I'd always thought of him as an ideal blend of traditional male and female traits: a damn good pitcher and campfire maker, legacy of Little League and Eagle Scouts, as nurturing and psychologically minded as a woman friend. Still, I could not imagine Henry at a transgender clinic.

'You don't have to tell me now, Dad. You could tell me when the time gets nearer.'

After Simon left with a plastic container of the lasagna and the Moleskine notebook with the recipe copied inside, I begged Henry to stay with me in the living room. With his shifting about, repositioning the pillow he'd retrieved and then abandoning the couch to lie on the floor, I knew his back was hurting and he must be thinking about vaping, but I couldn't stand to be alone with Simon's news.

Henry curled his knees into his chest and reached a hand out to hold my ankle while I cried with my face hidden in my hands. Cried because of my fears for Simon: the violence I'd read that trans persons experience; the rates of suicide. From my remorse that I'd not known something so central about my child. That I'd ignored the clues: the imaginary girl twin. My bra crumpled at the bottom of Simon's backpack, Simon mumbling something about a costume for a school play, but there was no play. The lipstick poking out of a jeans pocket one night in Copenhagen.

I cried from the avalanche of questions. Would Simon understand that after twenty-two years of thinking I had a son, I couldn't instantaneously let go of that idea? Or did Simon even want that now? They'd said they're using *they/them*. Did that mean that for now Simon was at an in-between place: neither my son nor my daughter? And what should I do about my memories? Should I try to transpose my memories of Simon as a boy to Simon as a girl misidentified as a boy? Would that even be possible?

Most of all, I cried from shame that I was weeping after my child had told me something so important about themself. Shame that I was worrying about myself and how I should or could respond.

I lay down next to Henry, the two of us stretched out in corpse pose. I despised myself for what I said next. Despised myself because it meant I harbored a wish that maybe this was a phase. Harbored that wish even though from everything Simon had told us, I knew it was not. 'At least there's some time before he—' I clapped my hand over my mouth. 'I mean they—they do anything irreversible. Simon said they'll start the hormones now, but they have to save up for the electrolysis and surgeries.' I paused. 'The hormones are reversible, right?'

Henry was staring at the ceiling. Was he not responding because he was trying to stop the spasming or because he didn't want to answer?

I felt a wave of panic, my words slipping out faster and louder. 'By having to wait to save up, it puts the brakes on the process. We'll have a chance to talk it over with Simon. To make sure this is something they are certain they want to do. If they change their mind, they can stop the hormones and they'll go back to . . .'

Henry tilted his pelvis so he was pressing the small of his back into the floor.

'Go,' I said. 'Do your thing.'

It came as a great relief when Simon told me that they didn't want me to scrub my memories of them as a male child. 'I haven't discarded my recollections of living as a boy, and I don't expect you to do that either. That would seem so unnatural—like we were papering over how we both knew me then.' Now, when I think about Simon as a child, as a teenager, as a college student, I let myself remember Simon as a he, a him. But when I think of Simon as they are now, they are a they. And soon, one day, not too long from now, they will be a she.

When my phone rings, I see it's Gemma. I look up at the pale mottled trunks of the London plane trees lining the path, take a deep breath, and answer.

'I did something terrible,' Gemma says. 'I slapped Ella.'

Unlike Ella, systematic Gemma tells the story step-by-step. She and Ella were drinking lattes, propped up with pillows on Gemma's bed while Ella chattered on about her job and the night's mishaps. Then, as though it was just another thing, Ella mentioned that Simon had called to say they were planning on having the bottom surgery in December to coincide with their boss being away for the holidays.

I stop walking: a crushing pain, as if someone hiding behind one of the nearby trees hurled a rock that landed on my breastbone. I've known Simon has been consulting with surgeons, but not that they set a date.

'When Ella told me she'd offered to help after Simon came home from the hospital, I saw red. It was like I was four again, watching Ella walk around carrying Simon while I had to sit with them on the couch.'

I recall Ella's stage whispers—'A burp! A burp!'—and Gemma's sobbing, her fury at her older sister made all the worse by not possessing the words—*smug, theatrics*—to explain why Ella's behavior seemed so provocative.

I can hear Gemma crying. 'She didn't even say I could help. I felt like she was hogging Simon. Shutting me out.'

I don't counter that Ella must have assumed that Gemma, with a five-month-old in December, would not be able to take care of Simon. 'But slapping her . . . I can't believe I did that.'

'Call Ella. Tell her how sorry you are and ask if you can talk it over.'

After I hang up, I hope that I've given Gemma the right advice. My own experiences talking things over with George or my mother have never gone well. Fiona says that's because George and Jean are charter members of the Never Say Sorry Club. They should wear pins on their coats, she says, identifying them as such.

Not that Fiona and I haven't had our own handful of bad times. The worst was the year I was trying to get pregnant when it felt like she was pooh-poohing my anxiety that it would never happen. I became so tense around her—afraid I'd say something that would elicit an upsetting remark, would seem like a hothouse flower if I confessed that I felt as if I were walking on eggshells—I made excuses to skip our weekly reservoir walks. I delayed returning her calls. Delayed a day, two days, a week, until one morning, I woke and realized a month had passed since we'd spoken.

It wasn't until I was pregnant with Simon, when Fiona and I tearfully tried to unravel how we'd become so estranged, that the picture came into focus. Having grown up with my mother's help essentially limited to providing food and shelter, Fiona understanding me so deeply had opened a floodgate: I'd wanted her guidance with everything. My fears that I couldn't conceive had unleashed a needy monster in me, and what had not been a problem between us suddenly was. With her grueling work schedule atop struggling to find a preschool for Nick after he'd been thrown out of two, Fiona was depleted. Like her sister, whose college Fiona had funded by taking a consulting job instead of a writing fellowship, I'd become a drain.

Ever since, I've tried my best to steer clear of that toxic dynamic. I remind myself Fiona loves me, but it's not her responsibility to take care of me. It's my responsibility to not expect that of her.

I WAITED FOR OUR WEEKLY RESERVOIR WALK TO TELL FIONA Simon's revelation. She listened with a curious expression while I circled the subject before finally sputtering the word *transgender*.

It was late October and the trees looked like they'd been painted with a child's tempuras. Fiona led me to a bench. She kept her arms around me while I hid my face on her shoulder.

When I finished crying, I wiped my eyes on my jacket sleeve. 'I feel like a compass that's wildly gyrating. If only I could settle on what I think, I'd know how to respond. Now, it's just chaos.'

I looked at Fiona, worried that I was going too far. Expecting too much. 'I don't want to burden you.'

'Of course I want to be there for you for this. The fact that there were times when your needs overwhelmed me doesn't mean that's usually the case.'

'I keep thinking I've been like one of those mothers who doesn't want to know her child is being molested: the evidence was there and I didn't want to see it.'

'You can't look at what you saw or knew twenty years ago through to-day's eyes. No one was thinking about this stuff when Simon was young.'

'I read Jan Morris's autobiography when it came out.'

'Back then, Jan Morris was seen as an anomaly. Now, transgender issues are everywhere—from preschools to the Olympics. A transgender woman spoke at the Democratic National Convention. It's a totally different context. If Simon were three today, you'd have figured it out.'

The reservoir looked different from the bench where we were sitting than from my office window seven floors above or from the southern rim where we always stopped to observe the ducks. I was too ashamed to tell Fiona how much time I'd spent watching YouTube videos that explained how a penis was turned into a vagina. Instead, I told her how intimidated I felt. Afraid of saying something wrong.

'You're not alone. Most cis people are ignorant about transgender people. And then, everything is changing so fast. It's impossible not to step in shit when you talk about the subject. Lots of trans people don't want it to be their job to educate us—which seems fair to me. I don't want to explain what it's like to have a kid and husband with neuroatypical brains. Go read about it, I always think.'

Fiona peered at me before continuing. 'Simon's twenty-two. At five, if they told you they were a girl, you and Henry would have had to figure out what to do. But now, the decision is theirs. Your only decision is how to respond to their decision.'

The reservoir was a murky gray in the late afternoon light. I couldn't control how I felt, I wanted to tell Fiona, but I knew this was not what Fiona was saying. For a moment, I hated Fiona for what she was saying: the only thing I could control was what I did.

In the half-year since, I've tried to educate myself. I've read memoirs of trans women. Watched interviews of parents who described their toddlers protesting the sex they'd been assigned at birth: small boys who screamed when forced to wear pants or pee standing up; small girls who refused to wear dresses or pee sitting down. Simon, though, had never been like that. Yes, there was the early resistance to haircuts, but I'd understood this as a fear of scissors—which seemed logical. Why should a two-year-old believe scissors could make a finger bleed but will not be felt on a strand of hair? What harm in letting Simon's hair remain uncut? Harm, that is, aside from other people's responses: George at Thanksgiving cornering Henry with *Dude, you can't let the kid walk around looking like a girl,* my mother pursing her lips as though Simon was smeared with feces rather than their then blond hair pulled back in a ponytail.

How, I reproach myself as I turn a bend on the path and catch a glimpse of the museum, could I have thought Simon, even at two, did not understand that hair and skin respond differently to scissors?

THE SLOPING GLASS WALL OF THE MUSEUM'S AMERICAN WING looms before me like a pyramid dropped into the park. When Simon was little, we'd walked here countless times. Approaching the façade, Simon would stare longingly. 'I wish I could climb to the top of the glass wall,' Simon would say. 'Then I could slide from the roof all the way down to the ground!'

It's been a relief to discover how many of my memories of Simon are ungendered: A child who on their walks would stop to gaze at the trees, which Simon thought of as friends. A child who loved a weeping willow, not far from here, with branches that grazed the ground so it would seem, ducking underneath together, that we'd entered a secret room. A child who would snuggle with me under the foliage ceiling and ask why anyone thought such a happy tree was weeping.

I have no memories of walking with my own mother or with my grandparents; for anywhere further than the corner, we would drive my grandfather's 1958 Chevrolet, the car he owned until he died. My memories of walking in Baltimore are all with LuAnn. Discovering, not long after we'd met in eighth grade at Our Lady of Providence, that the bus made us both nauseous, we'd taken to walking together the two miles from school to my house. With my grandparents both buried the prior year, my mother at work, and George, cut from the junior varsity football team and now miserably at track practice, the house was empty: heaven for two thirteen-year-old girls.

Nor do I have any memories of laughing with my mother or grandparents. My grandfather would mock my grandmother or make sarcastic remarks while he watched the evening news, but neither seemed funny. My mother on occasion repeated a joke she'd heard at work, but she always mangled the punchline. LuAnn, though, cracked me up. With her gap-tooth smile and wide forehead and plump legs, she got away with having a potty mouth and delivering incisive put-downs that captured what was pathetic in another person without seeming cruel. And she knew a million stupid jokes: 'Why did the can crusher quit his job? Because it was soda pressing!' 'What do you call an old snowman? Water!'

Sprawled on the rusted beach chairs in the cracked concrete yard of what I still thought of as my grandparents' house, LuAnn and I would smoke the pot provided by LuAnn's older sister's boyfriend while we analyzed the *Too Cool for School* girls. After a few tokes from a pipe, the *Too Cool* girls seemed hilarious: the brazen way they wore the required white blouses a size too small so their lace bras were visible in the gap between the buttons, the waistbands of their uniform skirts defiantly rolled once they'd passed morning inspection so as to show their thighs, their faces set in a rigor mortis intended to communicate that a teacher's enthusiasm for a poem or another girl's pride at solving a math equation merited only derision.

Now, at sixty (the number still strange on my tongue), it's hard to explain why LuAnn and I made it our project the year we both turned sixteen to become sexually experienced. Sexually experienced, not with the boys from our brother Catholic school—What did those boys know aside from the crude mechanics they boasted about employing with the girls they maneuvered into the backseats of cars?—but with married men we'd meet at a Hilton bar frequented by business travelers. Perhaps we thought sexual experience would be proof of our possessing some special quality (bravado? imagination?) that promised future exotic adventures. Perhaps we were bored. Perhaps, at bottom, it wasn't so different from how Catherine at the same age aimed for dressage awards with her horse.

One thing remains clear. There were no adults stopping us. On my end, I often didn't know what continent my father was on. As for my mother, by then, she'd moved into what had been my grandparents' bedroom, where she retreated each night by eight, leaving what had been her bedroom to George. Officially, I was to be home by midnight, but with my mother asleep and my brother and I no longer sharing a room so he wasn't privy to my comings and goings, I effectively had no curfew. LuAnn and I had fake IDs, also provided by LuAnn's older sister's boyfriend, though with the legal drinking age changed to eighteen earlier that year, we were rarely asked to show them.

LuAnn would get ready in my bedroom, where she kept a dress with a sweetheart neckline that showcased her D-cup boobs. I wore a sleeveless A-line dress that stopped a hand span above my knees and made me look like the still in-vogue Twiggy. We had matching three-inch-high beige platform shoes and brushed half-moons of glittery lavender powder over our eyes. In our purses were little pots of Yardley lip glosses that left sticky pink smears on the Virginia Slims we smoked and, in the zippered compartment, condoms we stole from LuAnn's sister's underwear drawer. I twisted my fine white-blonde hair into a French knot while LuAnn left her auburn curls, cut in a shag, loose so they framed her round face. Had there been a mother examining us, she would have thought we looked like little girls playing dress-up.

At the bar, LuAnn ordered rum and Coke with three maraschino cherries and introduced herself as Sugar. I drank Kahlua on ice, alternating with ginger ale. My name was Angel. The men claimed to be pharmaceutical reps attending annual conventions, car dealers at regional sales meetings, McDonald's franchise owners—which they probably were, though not from the cities they said. Married, some happily, some not. Children, some yes, some no. Paunches, hairy backs, balding pates. Bad breath. *Halitosis*, I told LuAnn, was the medical term, after which LuAnn would whisper in my ear about the guy next to her, *Hal's toes*.

After the first time LuAnn had sex with one of these men, she cried in my arms as we sat in a smelly taxi on our way back to my house. 'I'll never be a virgin again,' she wept. 'I'll have to tell the priest in confession tomorrow.' I stroked LuAnn's thick hair. 'What will happen when I get married?' LuAnn moaned. 'Won't my husband be able to tell?' My first time, I cried as it happened, less from shame than how much it hurt.

We never stayed the night and we never took money, aside from tens pressed into our palms for cab fare. Within a few months, we both had to admit that the evenings were sordid—*gross* was the word LuAnn used. (Neither of us said *slutty*, but that summed up how we felt.) Only a creep would have a one-night stand with a sixteen-year-old who said she was twenty-two and called herself Sugar or Angel. By the end of our junior year, we were done with the Hilton bar. We'd accomplished what we set out to do: We knew how to fake an orgasm, something neither of us had experienced but we'd both read about. We knew how to give a blow job, though neither of us would let it go far enough that we'd have to swallow. We knew how to put in the diaphragms we'd been fitted for because they were more reliable than condoms. We stopped, in fact, going out at all except to each other's houses, content to spend Saturday nights passing a joint (we'd moved on from pipes and could both proficiently fill and roll papers), listening to Fleetwood Mac and Tom Waits, and eating prodigious amounts of LuAnn's snack concoctions: pigs-in-a-blanket topped with Cheez Whiz, Lorna Doones smothered with chocolate sauce—all of which left me still struggling to fill out my jeans and LuAnn having to suck in her gut to zip hers.

I WAIT ON THE CIRCULAR BENCH TO THE RIGHT OF THE MUSEUM'S
main door, where Simon and I agreed to meet, with *Mrs. Dalloway* in my
lap. The first time I read the novel, shortly after I started English graduate
school, I was gobsmacked from the opening line and bereft at reaching
the end. Since then, I've reread the book on each of my decade birthdays.
On the last occasion, I was approaching Clarissa's age of fifty-one. Now,
long past, I still feel younger than Clarissa, drained of color since she had
the Spanish flu, who would find it unimaginable that a woman on her
sixtieth birthday would do a headstand or visit a lover or lunch with her
once son now en route to becoming her daughter.

The man next to me on the bench lowers his museum brochure
and glances at me. Balding with slumped shoulders under a ratty windbreaker, he smells of cigarettes. At first, it's unpleasant, almost turning
my stomach, but then I think of the pack of Virginia Slims LuAnn and I
each bought every Monday and remember the first long delicious inhale
as we sat after school on the beach chairs in the cracked concrete yard of
my grandparents' house, never smoking more than two cigarettes so the
rest could be saved for weekend nights.

Once we graduated and began working as clerks in a hospital billing
department and taking night classes at the nearby community college
and saving for a used car we planned to buy together, we cut back on
weekdays to a single cigarette we'd share in the parking lot after eating
our bag lunches. By then, we were going to bars again on Friday and Saturday nights—not the Hilton, but ones where there was a pool table or
dartboard in the back room and no one lied about who they were. It was
at one of these bars where LuAnn bummed a cigarette from a guy with
a red beard and a beer belly. A week later, she and Ron, a pipefitter, were
already a couple. I couldn't stand that his eyes were glued to LuAnn's
boobs and it worried me that the bartender, a woman with peroxided
hair, had warned me that my friend should be careful: Ron had a mean
streak wider than the Chesapeake Bay. When LuAnn wasn't looking,
he would give me the stink eye. I couldn't figure out if he didn't like
me because LuAnn had told him about the married men or because he
didn't like anyone who encroached on the corral he kept around LuAnn

and him. Mostly, though, what bothered me was that he never laughed at LuAnn's jokes.

On New Year's Day, LuAnn married Ron in Atlantic City. The ceremony, she told me two days later, had been performed by a blind justice of the peace. I tried to put on a happy face, but I knew that LuAnn knew I thought Ron was not a nice guy and not too bright either and that it had all happened too fast. A month later, LuAnn moved with Ron to Abingdon, where his family lived and he could work for his father's plumbing company. It was just twenty-five miles away, but too far, LuAnn claimed, to keep her job or attend the community college, both of which she quit.

For the first few weeks after LuAnn moved, I called her every day. Ron always answered. LuAnn's not home, he'd say. She's sleeping. She's in the can. I suspected he wasn't giving her the messages, but as the days passed and LuAnn never reached out herself, I began to worry that Ron had forbidden her from talking with me. After a month, I phoned LuAnn's mother and asked for LuAnn's address. Writing probably didn't make sense—if Ron was monitoring LuAnn's calls, he was likely monitoring her mail too—but I had to try. I can no longer recall how many letters I sent, only that there were no letters back.

Painful as the breach with Fiona while I tried to get pregnant was, it didn't touch how bereft I'd felt after LuAnn moved. Without LuAnn to confide in, my thoughts festered unspoken in my head. Without our laughter, my feelings stuck in my throat. I tried to distract myself by going on dates with boys I met in my classes. Sometimes, on one of these dates, I'd fantasize about calling LuAnn and our joking about the jock with arms bigger than my thighs who counted on his fingers to figure out the pizzeria tip or the guy who talked endlessly about his pet snakes and smelled like them too. I'd sometimes get so caught up in the imaginary conversation with LuAnn, I'd lose track of what my date was saying.

Still, there was a silver lining to the loss of LuAnn. It spurred my making an exit plan from my mother's home: I'd continue working full-time to build up my bank account, and ace my classes at the community college so I could get a merit scholarship to the University of Maryland.

Two years later, with my BA in hand, I'd find a job that would pay enough to rent my own place.

My last semester at the community college, I ran into LuAnn's older sister in a grocery store parking lot. LuAnn and Ron had had some problems. LuAnn had moved out for a few months, but she was back living with Ron, working nights as an aide at a nursing home. I asked LuAnn's sister for the name of the nursing home and wrote LuAnn again, sending the letter there. When there was still no response, I concluded that LuAnn herself had made the decision to cut me off.

THE MAN NEXT TO ME ON THE BENCH HAS STUFFED THE MUSEUM brochure in his windbreaker pocket. He seems to be trying to read the back cover of my copy of *Mrs. Dalloway*. With nearly everyone staring at their phones, my holding a book must register to him as a curiosity. I angle slightly away, a gesture I hope signals *Do not talk to me, we are here in parallel, two trees in a forest*, but the analogy crumbles as I recall Simon's interest in the new science about how trees communicate through fungal networks.

My exit plan from my mother's house worked: I aced my night classes, got a merit scholarship for a commuter branch of the University of Maryland, quit my job at the hospital, and bought a used Toyota (on my own, not with LuAnn). Worked, that is, until late fall when the transmission on the Toyota blew, leaving my bank account nearly depleted.

A classmate mentioned that a restaurant not far from the university was hiring waitresses, and I drove to the place. The owner, Dean, was just a few years older than me, with wavy blond hair and biceps that strained his pressed polo shirt; my first impression of him was that he looked like a Hitler youth. Interviewing me, he seemed less interested in my past waitressing experience (zero) than talking about himself: prep school in New Hampshire, then on to Duke, where he'd been on the rugby team until he was expelled for plagiarism, about which he did not seem embarrassed. He handed me a uniform—I was to start immediately—and fired the hostess when she made a scene because she saw that he intended to slot me into what had been her position as his on-site sex partner, a complement to his off-site roster.

Twenty and lonely and tired of boys who had nothing of interest to say, I let myself be seduced. With an elbow jutted out the window, Dean drove his BMW as though it were an extension of his body. He spoke passable Italian from the summers his family spent in Capri and gringo Spanish he'd picked up from their Guatemalan housekeeper. He read *Rolling Stone* and *Fortune* magazines. His parents had a condo in Vail and a time-share in Saint John, where he took me over spring break.

It was a relief that Dean had little curiosity about the details of my life. It sufficed, as far as he was concerned, to know I was living with my mother and brother, who was working at a savings and loan bank and applying to business schools ('Boring,' Dean announced. 'Path for a chump . . .'), and that my father was renovating a hotel in the Sacred Valley of Peru ('Been there. Food sucked . . .'). The only exception was my adventures at the Hilton bar, which I stupidly told Dean about one night when I'd had too much to drink. That, he wanted to know all about: How would LuAnn and I dress? Did we wear panties under our skirts? Push-up bras? Would the married men fuck us more than once?

'High school hotties,' he laughed.

My face burnt. I felt more ashamed that I'd told Dean about this interlude in my life and that it titillated him than about what I'd done.

'It was four years ago. I don't like to think about it.'

'Did you do threesomes?'

'Please stop.'

'I want to see you in the dress you wore.'

'Please, please stop.'

He pressed his crotch against me and whispered in my ear: 'Dirty little girl.'

I was ashamed, too, that I liked how aggressive Dean was in bed. It was the only time it seemed that I was fully on his mind. Liked it until he crossed a line and left a bruise on my upper arm and I realized that he not only didn't care, he found the line more arousing than he found me. After that, it was as though someone had given me corrective glasses and I could see him clearly for the first time: a spoiled kid who thought driving a BMW made him better than other people and, if no one were there as witness, wouldn't stop if he hit a dog.

What I felt the worst about was that I continued to have sex with Dean even after the bruise on my arm because stopping would mean quitting my job, which I needed for the repairs on my car and an unpaid dental bill. I could get another waitress job, but the new hostess treated me like a kid sister and worked my shifts out around my class schedule. The truth is I might have stayed even longer had the same classmate who'd told me that the restaurant was hiring not urged me the April before we graduated to come to a job fair. At the booth for a publishing company specialized in educational materials for Christian-based schools, a woman in a pussy-bow blouse and chartreuse suit gave me a proofreading test. When I got a perfect score, she offered me an assistant position on the spot.

'That's it? I don't have to interview with anyone else?'

The woman patted her helmet of hair. 'Tonight, you thank the good lord Jesus for sending you here. You start June first. And remember, no pants, no open-toed shoes, nylons year-round.'

Wary of Dean's vindictiveness were I to quit, much less break it off with him, I told him his sleeping with other women had become too painful. 'Girl, you know the rule book,' he said, 'no female pens me in,' after which I mumbled that if we weren't going to be together any longer, I guessed I should get another job. When I turned in my uniform at the end of the shift, he narrowed his eyes, as though suspecting there'd been a bait and switch, but then he smirked and swatted me on the butt. 'You better be on your hands and knees when you come crawling back.'

SIMON IS NOW TEN MINUTES LATE: LATE WITH A CAPITAL *L* BY both my mother's and Fiona's measure. For my mother, *Late* is anything after five minutes early. For Fiona, *Late* is a plank of the tough love policy she maintains with Nick. She'll wait fifteen minutes for Nick before she leaves; leniency, she believes, endorses irresponsibility.

To this day, *late* conjures for me the silver braid draped over the shoulder of the Planned Parenthood counselor who informed me a week before my start at the Christian publishing house that my period was *not late*. 'No, Miss Koehl. You are nine weeks pregnant.' The silver-haired woman's somber words fell like a judge's gavel: I was the pathetic object of the punishing gods egged on by my mother, angry because I'd said that with my new job I'd be able to move out by the end of the year.

Had LuAnn still been in my life, I would have gone to her for a loan for the abortion. Without LuAnn, I asked my brother. Having molted his once acne-blighted skin and graduated from the main branch of the University of Maryland with a grade point average sufficient to land his job at a local savings and loan with a boss who had connections at the Wharton business school where George was applying, I foolishly thought he might have a little goodwill to spare.

My brother was watching a baseball game, half-prone in what had been our grandfather's recliner, our mother upstairs in bed. My heart pounded when I asked if we could talk.

He didn't say okay, but he didn't tell me to beat it. His eyes never left the television as I told him I was pregnant and asked if I could borrow two hundred dollars. It would be just until the end of the month, I promised, until I got the first paycheck from my new job.

'No.'

I feared my knees might buckle. 'You can't loan me the money?'

'Not can't. Won't. You made your own bed, having sex with a sleaze-bag like Dean. Tell him to pay for the abortion.'

Desperate as I felt, I knew it was pointless to plead.

The following afternoon, I drove to Dean's restaurant. A look of surprise followed by a leer passed over his face when I walked into his office, where he'd probably had sex the night before with whichever of his female employees had been my replacement. I could see the gears spinning in his head as he tried to situate himself in the circumstances I was describing. He laughed when I said, 'I'll pay you back in three weeks.'

'Do you think I want your money?' He leaned back in his rolling desk chair so his pelvis was thrust out and pointed at his crotch. 'A blow job for an abortion.'

I breathed deeply to keep from puking.

'Good deal for a dirtly little girl like you.'

He was undoing his belt buckle as I left.

In the end, I asked my mother. We were in the kitchen, cleaning up after dinner. She turned off the water and rested her substantial backside against the edge of the sink. It was hard to envision that this same woman, with her now faded hair and chapped cheeks and mouth pinched with anger, had once bedazzled men with her Swedish beauty.

My mother folded the checked tea towel that had hung on the refrigerator door as long as we'd lived in the house. 'Why would you do such a stupid thing? Break it off with a young man who already owns a restaurant? From a wealthy family with two vacation homes? After you've seen what I've gone through to raise your brother and you? You think you're too good for Dean?' My mother shook her head. 'It's an insult to me.'

I stood stock-still, just two feet from my mother. I swallowed to stop the tears. The worst thing to do with my mother was to cry. Any sign of pain infuriated her and would only lead to an intensified attack.

'He's the father. You tell him to marry you.'

'Marry Dean?'

Never in a million years could I mention the bruise on my arm. But perhaps my mother would understand that Dean, like my father, was a man for whom fidelity was as impossible as sprouting wings and flying.

'It would be like your marriage,' I softly said. 'He'd never be faithful.'

My mother glared at me with the full force of her five feet ten inches. Besting me by an inch and fifty pounds, she looked like a rearing bear. She slapped my face.

In the morning, there was a check for two hundred dollars on the kitchen counter.

THE MAN IN THE WINDBREAKER HAS STOPPED HIDING THAT HE IS studying me. Is that a MAGA cap poking out of his pocket? Since the election, like everyone I know, I'm alert to clues as to whose camp others are in. I want to move, but this is where Simon and I agreed to meet. I bury my face again in my book.

The last time Simon was this late was also for one of our lunches, then at a Middle Eastern restaurant near Simon's workplace. It was a few weeks after Simon had told us they are trans, and I'd been glad they were late because it gave me a bit more time to prepare: to remind myself that they'd told me that for now, they were living in a nonbinary space.

'Sorry!' Simon said, dropping into one of the orange plastic chairs and unwinding a long color-block scarf. 'Ella kept texting she was stuck on the subway but it would only be another five minutes and Uncle George kept saying we should wait for her and we ended up starting super late.'

'You had a meeting with Uncle George?'

'He didn't tell you?'

'Didn't tell me what?'

'That he was giving Gemma and Ella and me the checks for our inheritance from Pops?'

'From my father?'

A look of alarm passed over Simon's face. 'You didn't know, Mom?'

I picked up a squeeze bottle of hot sauce and wiped a red glob from the side. Do not say, *No, my brother did not tell me. Did not tell me he went behind my back and changed our father's will so money was now going directly to the grandkids.*

Do not say, *I'm outraged he told you before he told me.*

'I'll call Uncle George. Let's order or you won't have time to eat.'

Simon, who Henry and I used to joke doesn't have a duplicitous bone in his body, who we'd once seriously discussed teaching how to lie should the need ever arise, ignored my attempt to change the subject. 'I'm afraid if I say the number, it will disappear. Let's just say it's enough for three women to have gender affirmation surgery.'

I tried to smile but it must have come off as a grimace.

'I'm sorry, Mom. I guess that's not funny to you. But, it's a good thing. Now I'll be able to do everything that will make my social transitioning go more smoothly. Have my Adam's apple reduced, start electrolysis. I can even do voice coaching.'

Simon looked down. I could feel them measuring their words. 'Not every trans woman aims to pass or wants to do surgeries, but I like the idea of not having to discuss that I'm trans in every situation—of being in control of who I tell my story. And the way I'm built, small-boned like you, passing is in reach for me.'

I nodded. I tried to smile, but I was sure Simon could see it was forced. I hoped they sensed how hard I was trying to respect their path. I hoped they'd forgive me for my emotions lagging behind.

'I feel guilty saying that because lots of trans women don't have the money to do what they wish they could.' Simon touched my wrist. 'I'm so lucky that with my inheritance, I won't have to wait years to save up or go to Thailand to do the surgery. And I'll still have money left for medical expenses that might come up later.'

I stared at the bottle of hot sauce, at a congealed drip I'd missed. So thoughtful, so organized. So Simon.

'You're acting like a moron,' George said when I called him later that afternoon. 'Families do generation skipping with their assets all the time. Half of what would have gone to us now goes directly to our kids. The estates attorney recommended it. It's a means of tax protection.'

For the first time in my life, I could feel my blood pressure sky-rocketing, as though a vessel strained by the absorption of my brother's treachery might burst. When George didn't help after my apartment had been broken into, when he refused to lend me money for an abortion, I told myself that his actions were impersonal: how he would behave with anyone. Still, I'd assumed he at least acknowledged we were siblings. That we shared a boundary with our parents and would not intrude on the one we each had with our spouse and children.

'I'm not questioning the soundness of what you did. I'm questioning why you didn't talk with me before you changed the will. Before you told Simon.'

'Dad agreed it was the right thing to do. I didn't need your permission.'

With the word permission, my anger swelled. 'This has an impact on my child. I would have liked to have a say.'

'It's financially advantageous for your child.'

'Simon is a lot younger than your girls. You may have no problem with them having access to that amount of money now, but I do for Simon.' My voice caught. 'You took the decision away from me.'

'Stop being so fucking melodramatic. There were papers that needed to be signed. Ella and Gemma were signing theirs and it made sense to have Simon do it at the same time.'

We'd reached, I saw, the end of the road. Nothing would change the way my brother thought. Nothing was going to change what had happened. I wanted to slam the phone down, but then the problem would be me—and besides, phones no longer have cradles.

When Henry got home, I was waiting for him at the dining room table. Seeing my face, he sank into a chair instead of immediately going to vape.

Never rushing me, never interrupting, Henry listened. After I finished, he took my hands in his. 'Ana, honey, I'm so sorry.'

I couldn't say aloud, even to Henry, what hurt most: George's actions contaminated the well of deep feeling I'd discovered for my father. I'd felt at peace with my father as I said my goodbyes to him, only to now be blindsided by the news that he'd been party (yes, unwittingly, but still...) to an arrangement that would allow Simon to proceed more quickly—shave his Adam's apple, fast-forward on having his penis turned into a vagina. Couldn't say because I knew that I might be wrong that this wasn't all for the best.

I crossed my arms atop the table, and buried my face in them. I loved Henry for saying nothing more. For just letting me cry.

'I can't believe my father wanted this change in his will,' I said when I sat up.

'My guess is he was so sick when George suggested it, he didn't think about Simon being so much younger than Gemma and Ella.'

As soon as Henry said it, I knew he was correct. In a way, it felt worse to imagine my father had simply been thoughtless. Had he acted from malice, at least I would have known he was considering Simon and me.

'My dad made a lot of mistakes, but unlike my mother and brother, he would admit when he'd done something wrong. A few days before he died, he told me he'd neglected George and me. He'd been so busy, he said, with so many commissions, in so many countries, he'd left it to our mother to handle everything.'

Henry passed me his handkerchief.

'My father never apologized—which felt right, as though he knew how he'd behaved was beyond apologies. Still, it was comforting to hear him acknowledge what he'd done.' I dabbed at my eyes. 'If George hadn't kept this from me, if I'd had a chance to talk it over with my father . . . He would have put in guardrails for Simon.'

I looked around the dining room. 'I don't think I'll ever be able to forgive him.'

Henry cocked his head.

'My brother. George.'

I'M ABSORBED IN CLARISSA DALLOWAY'S RESPONSE TO LADY Bruton having invited Clarissa's husband but not her to luncheon when Simon kisses my cheek. 'Happy birthday, Mom.'

The changes in Simon from the feminizing therapy have been gradual, but slowly a ravine has widened between the person who announced last October they know in their soul they're a woman and the graceful creature standing in front of me in a turtleneck sweater, with brows that look like they've been plucked and a chin with no sign of stubble. By the end of summer, they've told me, they'll change their name to Simona and begin using female pronouns. With this news have come new worries: Will Simona be safe? What if she's in an accident and the ambulance crew cut off her clothes and discover she's trans? What if one of them is transphobic? Will they still help her? Still perform mouth-to-mouth resuscitation? Apply tourniquets? Treat her gently?

Simon takes my arm as I stand. 'Sorry I'm late. Inga forgot I was taking you to lunch and scheduled a meeting with the book series editor.' They roll their eyes. 'I *had* to attend.'

While we walk through the Greek and Roman galleries to the restaurant, Simon tells me they'll be writing the footnotes and creating the bibliography for Inga's book. I listen, letting my eyes wander over the marble statues, for centuries considered the embodiment of an Aryan ideal, when, in fact, they'd originally been painted in a range of skin tones. Never before have I noticed the sheer quantity of male genitals in the galleries, depicted so sweetly and flowerlike. Smelling of stone, not man.

Look at these beautiful bodies, I want to say to Simon. *Bodies like yours. How can the problem be your perfect body?* Couldn't you take hormones, change your name, wear a dress, mascara, high heels—anything other than let a surgeon put a knife to your penis?

I hear Fiona's retort. *Your penis.* It's the first word here that matters. The *your.* It's Simon's penis. *His. Theirs. Hers.* Simon's decision. Simon's process. Simon's story.

I inhale deeply. We can only be as happy as our least happy child, Fiona is fond of saying. For both of us, our least happy child is our only child. With Simon, though, the saying isn't apt. Since declaring their intention to transition, Simon is not unhappy. Like Clarissa Dalloway's daughter who sees the horizon as infinite—she might be a doctor, a farmer, go into Parliament, or she might be indolent and do none of the above—Simon is excited about the changes ahead. Clarissa and I each occupy our unhappiness in solitude.

Simon pauses at a terra-cotta statue of a woman seated on a boulder. Belief, they've explained, has nothing to do with their experience: they don't *believe* they're a woman. They *are* a woman. What's most challenging for me is what I know in my bones: I must not turn a deaf ear to the essential difference between *believe*, which presumes other possibilities, and *is* or *are* with their full transitive equal-sign non-disputable force. I must not say anything to Simon that implies *I understand who you are more than you do yourself.*

AS WE APPROACH THE RESTAURANT WITH ITS FLOOR-TO-CEILING windows overlooking the park, I sense the hostess doing a double-take, uncertain whether to address Simon as *Miss* or *Sir.* She's a strikingly beautiful girl with red hair that grazes her waist and cream legs, a long swath of which are visible between the bottom of her flared very short skirt and her ballet flats. Simon, who's explained to Henry that they're not gay, that they are a heterosexual woman who desires men, seems unaffected by the girl and her lovely legs as she leads us to our table.

Simon insists I take the chair with the view of the 3,500-year-old Cleopatra's Needle, whose eventful journey from Heliopolis I learned about when I was a chaperone for the fifth grade's trip to see the hieroglyphs.

'You take after your grandfather,' I say, once we're seated. 'He was never much into things as gifts. But he loved giving views. Your uncle says it made him feel like God—controlling what others see. But I always felt grateful.'

Henry teases that I never read the menu, just give it a quick glance. It's true: the selection never seems important enough to spend time debating. When the server arrives, I ask for the endive salad with grilled shrimp and a green tea. Simon orders the chicken club and a diet cola.

'I really want the sausage terrine,' Simon says once we're alone, 'but I have to watch my weight with the hormones.'

'How's it going?' I ask, pushing away the thought that Fiona—with her ardent advocacy of the theory that menopause is a return to sanity after the insanity of the estrogen-saturated fertility years, when women eat the scraps off their toddlers' plates and drag themselves out of bed to offer their mammary glands to creatures who might bite or tug—would find it absurd for anyone to take feminizing hormones.

'It's going well, Mom. Truly. I'm starting to have breast buds. I've read that what I can expect is best predicted by my female relatives, just as it would be if I were cis gender. I told the doctor, my mom kind of has a boy's body, so I'm not expecting to look like Kim Kardashian.'

Simon smiles at me, and I think about the times with Lance when I've felt that I'm a stand-in for a boy. 'I don't mean that in an insulting way. You look totally great. The electrolysis—that's another story. It's no fun, but I'm getting used to it.'

A wave of sadness passes over me. Not so long ago, I knew every beauty mark and scratch on Simon's body. I can still hear the squeals from the kisses I would deliver on Simon's belly button, see the soap horns they'd make in the tub while I ran the washcloth between their legs and across their bum. Now I don't want to think about their body— where they're having hair removed.

When Simon tilts their head, I know there's something difficult they have to say. 'Mom, I didn't want to talk with you about this today, but I feel wrong that Ella knows and that means Gemma will probably know soon too.'

Simon looks at me as though asking permission to continue. I nod.

'I've scheduled my bottom surgery for December. I have a friend, Greer,' Simon glances shyly at me, 'she calls herself my trans-mom. Greer's been through the surgery, so she knows what it's like. She'll stay with me the first few days.'

My heart lurches: sadness at another mother—a trans-mom. Gladness that Simon has a guide.

'Ella wants to help me after Greer goes back to work.'

'I know, honey. Gemma told me.'

Simon's eyes open wide. 'That was fast. I just talked to Ella last night.' They pause. 'I hope you understand my not asking you. It wouldn't feel right to have you or Dad dealing with my bandages and baths.'

With *bandages*, the anger at George returns like a hot flash.

'Mom, it's not fair to be mad at Uncle George about this.'

Is Simon reading my mind?

No. Simon just knows me.

'I get it that Uncle George shouldn't have hidden what he was doing from you. That was wrong. None of us knew he hadn't told you about our inheritances or that he was giving us the checks then. Ella was pissed. She told Uncle George that he'd acted like an asshole. A control freak is what she said.'

Simon waits for the server to set down our plates and refill our waters before continuing. 'You have to remember—I decided to do the surgery before I knew about the inheritance from Pops. It just would have taken me longer. Aren't you glad that I don't need to work two jobs to save up the money? Or go to some other country to have the operation?'

I touch Simon's arm, hoping they believe I'm doing the best I can at this moment.

'I have to do this. I feel it in every cell of my body.' Simon leans forward. 'I've never forgotten something you said to me when I was at the end of eighth grade. I was on the fence about continuing Latin in high school, and I wanted you to make the decision for me. You told me it had to be my decision. That it was up to me to figure out not just what I wanted to do about Latin but what I wanted to do with my life.'

'I remember.' I see us from a bird's-eye view: a mother and child talking together. 'We were sitting on a bench in the park eating gelatos.'

A mother and child. As Fiona has said more than once: Simon, boy, girl, or neither, is still your child. I pick up my fork so Simon won't feel awkward about returning to their chicken club. They take a careful bite. It's the way Simon has always eaten: slowly, deliberately, with pleasure but never avarice.

What if you feel differently five years from now? I want to ask. *Aren't you afraid you might regret the surgery?* But the questions seem invasive, with their implied demand: *You must account for yourself to me. Your life is not really yours. It's mine.*

When the server inquires about dessert, I decline.

'Are you sure, Mom?' Simon asks after our plates are cleared. 'Not even on your birthday?'

'I'm good, honey.' I flush slightly because I could eat more but I'm sticking to the regimen (a salad with protein and a green tea for lunch) I've maintained since Simon was born when I was taken aback by the realization that returning to my pre-pregnancy size would require effort. I'd be the first to admit it's rigid, but I've accepted that feeling comfortable in my body makes me happier than any of the foods I avoid ever would.

Feeling comfortable in my body. Isn't that what Simon wants?

'But you'll have a piece of cake at the dinner tonight?'

'Of course.' Simon is smiling at me, and for a moment, it feels like everything is okay.

WE HUG AT THE MUSEUM EXIT. I INHALE SIMON'S SCENT, AS FAMILiar as my own. 'Sorry I have to race off. I promised Inga I'd get back to meet with her. But I'll see you in a few hours!'

Simon has not yet told my mother about their transitioning. Before Simon was born, I'd vowed to let my mother and child have their own relationship—to not pollute it with my own hurts and resentments. For the most part they have, first bonding over both being what Simon calls math people, and later, when Simon took sociology classes as part of the Gender and Sexuality concentration, over the intersection between actuarial and social science. Recently, though, Simon has become aware that their experience of their grandmother is different from mine with her. 'Nana is so supportive of Gemma and Ella and me. And she talks about Uncle George as though he's a god. But she can really be a bitch to you . . .'

When my mother learns that Simon is trans, she'll channel whatever discomfort she has onto me: She'll accuse me either overtly or by implication of having done something wrong. If that protects Simon, it's fine with me.

I sit again on the circular bench, the man in the windbreaker no longer there. With Simon having left earlier than I expected, I have a free half-hour before I'll leave for Lance's house. What do I want to do?

It takes a minute for an answer to bubble up.

The Storm. I'll go see *The Storm.*

FIONA SET UP HENRY AND ME. 'YOU HAVE TO COME!' SHE INSISTED about the party her ex-boyfriend Marek was throwing on a weekend she was visiting me. 'I need you as my out when he pressures me to sleep over.'

At the party, half the people were speaking what I assumed to be Polish, regaling one another, I imagined, with the sorts of stories I'd heard Marek tell about the hardships and absurdities of Soviet-era life: days spent in lines to purchase a kilo of flour and three tins of meat; suspended above a tub, a fifty-liter *bojler* that risked electrocution in the bath. I parked myself by a cooler and pretended to sip a beer (there was no wine) while I watched people wander in and out of the kitchen.

A guy with a scruffy beard approached. 'I can tell you're not a beer drinker.' He raised his thick eyebrows and I noticed his amazing eyes: hazel dotted with specks of gold. 'How about some orange juice?'

With the offer, I realized orange juice, not wine, was exactly what I wanted. As I'd done since ninth grade, when I'd reached my adult height and feared there might be truth to my brother's claim that boys don't like girls taller than themselves, I instinctively calculated our height difference. With the two-inch heels of my boots, I was about three inches taller, which meant that this guy offering orange juice was an inch shorter than me. An inch shorter but with a barrel chest and a goofy smile that suggested he didn't give a damn about my height.

I nodded and he thrust out a beefy hand. 'Henry.'

Henry, I learned, was Marek's roommate, and the juice would be made from oranges in a green mesh bag his mother had sent.

'You're from Florida?' I asked while he washed and cut the oranges.

Long Island, he explained, but his parents lived half the year in their condo in Boca Raton. His father was an accountant, retired save for tax season when he worked round the clock for two months. With her three sons grown—Henry was the middle child—his mother now occupied herself with mah-jongg and pickleball.

'I know. It sounds like a caricature of the kind of family whose son becomes a doctor. And it was. My mother kept a chart of our grade point averages, though she had to notate to the hundredth decimal point since none of us ever slipped below 3.8. We used to joke that all she ever wanted was HPYDBL.'

'HPY . . . what?'

'HPYDBL. Harvard, Princeton, Yale. Doctor, Banker, Lawyer. And what's disgustingly obnoxious is she got what she wanted.' His older brother had gone to Yale and become a banker. His younger brother, the lawyer, had gone to Princeton. And now Henry, having graduated from Harvard, was doing his anesthesiology residency at Penn.

'It's a boring story,' Henry said. He looked at my now empty glass. 'More?'

My mother always bought the frozen concentrate that tasted bitter and viscous. The juice Henry had made was the most delicious I'd ever had. I did want more. 'If it's not a bother . . .'

'I know you're an English graduate student,' Henry said as he washed another four oranges. I glanced at Fiona, seated on the couch, sleek as a ferret with her cap of dark hair and knees tucked under, a cigarette in her hand as she listened to Marek, whose mooning expression made plain he was still carrying a torch for her. Fiona flashed a mischievous smile.

'Don't be mad at Fiona. All she said was I should be sure to meet you. At the very least, she said, we could talk in English together.' He took my glass and refilled it. 'Tell me about your life before here.'

I looked over my orange juice at this man who seemed so genuinely curious about me, it made me nervous. I liked that most people have no interest in anyone aside from themselves, that dinners could pass where I heard an autobiographical recitation by the person seated next to me while never being asked a single question. Aside from Fiona, who'd approached getting to know me like a research project, no one at Penn knew anything about my life before here.

I thought about the opening lines of Graham Greene's *The End of the Affair*: 'A story has no beginning or end: arbitrarily one chooses that moment of experience from which to look back or from which to look ahead.' I'd play it safe, I decided, stick to the outlines of my education: a girls' Catholic high school, community college for two years, finishing my degree at one of the state university's satellite campuses, which had felt more like a vocational training school than an institution of higher learning, the students largely focused on preparation for the good jobs they hoped to get as marketing managers or probation officers or department store buyers. 'I still have moments here when the ivy-covered buildings seem like a movie set and the students discussing Nietzsche and George Eliot over coffee look like actors in a romantic comedy.'

I flushed at having referred to a *romantic comedy*.

Later, Fiona admitted that she instructed Henry to cook dinner for our first date. With any other man, I would never have gone to his apartment so soon, but Henry felt so safe, I didn't hesitate. 'My mother wanted me to be a surgeon,' he said as he untied the drumsticks and removed the bouquet of rosemary and thyme and the quartered lemons from the cavity of the chicken he'd roasted and was now about to carve. 'But this is the limit of my knife skills. I anesthetize the poor creature so it feels no pain. What you're tasting is the bird's appreciation.'

I must have looked confused because he let loose one of his goofy grins. He was teasing, he said. He could never start with a live chicken. He'd been so freaked out knowing that the mother of the family he'd boarded with during a high school summer program in the south of France would, on her return Sunday mornings from the village's twelfth-century church, twist the neck off a chicken from the garden coop and stew it for lunch, he'd had to beg off each week from the meal.

What I tasted was food flavored with the love it took to prepare. By the time my mother and brother and I came to live with my grandparents, my grandmother, after three decades working ten hours a day in her bakery, had lost interest in cooking. She made sure no one went to bed hungry, but dinner, peppered with ashes from her dangling cigarette, was usually sandwiches or French toast made with the day-old bread she'd brought home that night.

Following my grandmother's death, my mother approached meals as a chore like laundry and scrubbing the tub. She organized them according to the FDA food pyramid she affixed to the refrigerator door. Because she didn't get home from work until after six, preparation fell to me. Each Sunday, she wrote out her directions. *Monday: wash chicken breasts; pat dry and place in Pyrex dish; combine soy sauce and apricot jelly and spoon over top; cook for 45 minutes at 375. Tuesday: Chop onion; add with beaten egg yolk to ground beef; divide into 4 and make patties; fry 6 minutes on each side.* And so on . . .

Henry's meal was so delicious, my eyes filled with tears.

I CLIMB THE MARBLE STAIRCASE TO THE MUSEUM'S SECOND FLOOR, pass *The Horse Fair*, the gargantuan painting by Rosa Bonheur that looks more like a battle scene than a bazaar, and enter the room where Pierre Auguste Cot's *The Storm* is hung. 'It's my favorite piece in the museum,' Henry told me the afternoon he brought me here, our first trip together to the city, not long after we met. 'In high school, my younger brother and I took the train into Manhattan most Saturdays. Seth was infatuated with the rumors that Michael Rockefeller had been eaten by New Guinea natives who practice cannibalism. He'd spend hours studying the totem poles and the carved canoe and the other stuff Rockefeller had shipped back. I'd always come here, to look at this painting.'

Standing with Henry that day, I examined the canvas: a golden girl with the outline of her full breasts and the rose of her nipples visible under her diaphanous slip, and an Italianate boy with inky curls and a smooth chest naked save for some drapery over his middle. With one arm, the boy encircles the girl's waist, and with the other he joins her in holding aloft a swath of taffeta that might be her skirt or cape as they run from an impending storm. It struck me as a depiction of young love in a trite and clichéd way. A sign, I thought, that we were too mismatched: Henry too sweet and pure; me, too soiled by my ugly adventures.

'They're in sync,' Henry said, 'their strides perfectly aligned, but at the same time they're completely separate. The girl is absorbed in her alarm about the storm while the boy is absorbed in her. She's monitoring the blackening sky. He's monitoring her. She's light on the surface and dark on the interior. He's the reverse.'

I kept my eyes on the canvas, ashamed of my shallowness. Through Henry's eyes, I could now see the painting's complexity: Two distinct persons forming a single four-legged creature, each with one arm holding the fabric that billows above their melded bodies. The sand beneath their bare feet a glowing path.

I didn't tell Henry about my own not golden path—the married men at the Hilton bar, Dean, the abortion—until the night he proposed. I'd understand, I said, if he wanted to take back his proposal, but I didn't want to enter a marriage with secrets.

Henry's eyes dampened. He held my face, his beard scratchy as he kissed my forehead. 'I love you, Ana. I love you even more for telling me all of this. And if you grant me the privilege of being your husband, I will never let anything like that happen to you again.'

What was so intoxicating was not Henry's declaration of love or his generosity in forgiving my older self for the mistakes made by my younger self, but his recasting of those mistakes as something that had happened to me rather than something I'd done. Even more intoxicating, fitting hand to glove, was his claim that he would never let what I'd told him happen to me again. What I imagined Henry to be offering was the protection of me against myself. The one good that came from his back injury is it disabused me of that fantasy.

Outside the museum, I hail a cab. A cab to my lover's house. Why had Henry asked nothing of me in return? What did it say about me that I'd accepted that?

4

ROLF

On the last day Rolf saw Ana, just three days before he died, he woke thinking about her birth. He could no longer recall the face of the woman he'd slept with the night Jean went into labor with their second child—only that she smelled of cigarettes and perfume, which he'd never liked, and seeing her hands and teeth in the morning light, he realized she was older than he'd been aware when they left the bar together. At least forty.

Not until he arrived back at his own apartment, at dawn, and discovered his mother-in-law putting the finishing touches on what she told Rolf was a princess cake—a Swedish specialty iced with green marzipan and topped with a gold paper crown; she'd seen her Aunt Anna make the cake on the occasion of the birth of Princess Ingrid Victoria Sofia Louise Margareta—did he learn his daughter had been born.

At the hospital, an hour later, he found Jean propped up in bed, holding the unnamed baby. He leaned over to look at the child he'd not wanted. She was wrapped like a wonton in a blanket with pink and blue stripes, her face smashed against her mother's breast and her knees curled into her torso. The only part of her body he could see was a sliver of wrinkled neck between the bottom of the beanie cap covering her head and the top of the blanket. He was afraid if he touched her, he would love her, as had happened with their son three years before.

Jean's cheeks were tear-streaked. He would have preferred to be greeted with the torrent of curses her father spewed nightly at her mother, who'd nonetheless remained devoted to the man, her tepid protests limited to *Mr. Biggy seems to think the gutters will clean themselves* or *Wouldn't want to trouble Mr. Biggy to hang up his own coat.*

'How's George?' Jean asked.

Rolf felt a glimmer of hope. Answering honestly—that he hadn't seen their son—would give him courage to proceed with the rest of what he'd say, which would be entirely fabrication.

'I worked through the night. The plans for the Lisbon hotel had to be mailed this morning. George was still asleep when I got home.'

Rolf often used working through the night as an excuse. Most of those nights were spent with Cindy, the office draftsperson he'd slept with during Jean's pregnancy this past year. That he hadn't been with Cindy when his daughter was born but instead with a woman whose name he wasn't sure of—was it Belinda or Benilda?—made him feel a bit less slimy.

'Here.' Jean thrust the bundled baby into his arms. Instinctively, Rolf cradled her neck and drew her to him. It had astounded him when George was born and the nurse showed him how to hold the baby to learn that infants cannot support their own heads and arrive with their skulls partially open. Imagine delivering a hotel incapable of supporting its top floor or with a gap in the roof.

His eyes filled with tears as he inhaled the woodsy newborn scent. Warm and moist like wild mushrooms. He kissed the knit cap on his daughter's head. Goddamnit. Another one.

Two years after they met, when Jean informed him that she was pregnant, he told her he'd pay for an abortion.

'No, I'm not going to do that.'

Jean pulled back her shoulders. The first time he saw her, she'd reminded him with her square face and soft blonde curls of Ingrid Bergman in *Casablanca*. Not long after, her catalog modeling agent pronounced her too large. Rolf had encouraged her to look for a different agent, while dropping hints that she might have better luck were she to slim down a bit, but instead, she'd enrolled at CCNY, surprising him by becoming a math major.

About the abortion, he knew that there was no point arguing with Jean. She did not believe in God, but she did not question that abortion was a sin. Still, he felt obliged to try rather than sink down like a dog in the road and let her run over his future.

'How can there be sin without God?' Rolf asked.

Jean stared at him with disdain. Her no was final, she repeated. But, for the record, the existence of sin does not require the existence of God.

A woman today—and it had happened with the owner of a Vancouver boutique hotel, though with her, it had seemed a threat, and in the end, she'd not kept the baby—might say she'd raise the child on her own. For Jean, that idea did not exist even in the realm of imagination, which, in any case, was never her forte and undoubtedly why mathematics appealed to her. Numbers, as she knew them, did not require imagination. They aligned into formulas or did not. There was only one right answer. And for Jean, pregnant equaled married. Immediately, at city hall.

Faced with Jean's demand, Rolf thought of his father. His father viewed kindness expressed through courtesy as the highest virtue. As a child, Rolf had witnessed his father's devotion to the hotel's guests: A stooped descendant of the last Austrian emperor, whose pocket watch his father would wind each morning. Three German families who always arrived the afternoon of Boxing Day to find their skis, stored in the hotel's winter vestibule, freshly sharpened and waxed. An American gentleman who spent every June hiking in the surrounding Alps with his Jack Russell terrier, whose daily output of feces he insisted be weighed.

What would his father do were he in Rolf's situation?

His father would never have been in Rolf's situation. But if he were, he'd marry the pregnant girl. He would expect Rolf, his only son, to do the same.

Three weeks after they went to city hall, Rolf came home from his office to find Jean crying on the sofa. He'd only finished painting the apartment the weekend before and could not keep himself, before inquiring about her tears, from admiring how he'd made the room appear to soar by applying diminishing tones to the two phases of molding.

She was miscarrying, Jean said. She looked at him so mournfully, he felt repulsed. Did she expect him to comfort her? And then the thought flew into his mind that he'd been duped: she'd fabricated the pregnancy to get him to marry her and now she was faking the miscarriage. The thought so disturbed him, he turned his back to her so he would not see her face.

Later, she would claim he accused her of this while she was cramped and bleeding, but he had no memory of having done any such thing. Only of thinking it.

AFTER THE NURSE CAME INTO THE ROOM TO TAKE THE BABY, ROLF asked Jean if she had any ideas for names for their daughter.

'Anna,' Jean said. 'For my mother's aunt.'

He must have frowned because Jean then slowly, aggressively it seemed to him, spelled out A-N-N-A.

Rolf's mood sank even lower. The name struck him as suitable for a farm woman. He studied his wife's face. Jean had retained twenty pounds—purposefully, Rolf thought—after the birth of their son, settling at a weight she insisted was smack in the middle of normal according to the Metropolitan Life Insurance Company tables. She looked like a farm woman herself.

Having seen his mother-in-law just an hour before, icing the princess cake she'd learned to bake from this same Aunt Anna, the name seemed fated. When his in-laws had opened their bakery in a Jewish neighborhood of Baltimore, his mother-in-law transposed what she'd learned from her aunt about making semla buns and mandelkubb and vanilla hearts to baking the challah and honey cake and rugelach their clientele expected. Aunt Anna became Jean's family's patron saint. *Thank you to Aunt Anna,* his mother-in-law would respond when a customer would pronounce the bakery the best in Baltimore. *She's the one who schooled me.*

'Maybe Gertrude?' Rolf asked. Gertrude was his grandmother's name.

For the first time since he'd arrived in the hospital room, Jean laughed. A weak, mean laugh. She'd known a Gertrude, she said, in high school. A girl with wax in her ears and a nose dotted with blackheads.

'There's Gertrude Stein,' he countered.

'Gertrude who?'

'You've never heard of Gertrude Stein? She grew up in Baltimore like you.'

'I never met her.'

Rolf refrained from saying, Of course not, she was living in Paris by the time you were born. Nor did he mention that his father had shyly treasured having had a drink in the hotel's wood-paneled bar with Stein's mentee, Thornton Wilder, who talked about the play *Our Town*, which he was writing at the time, and how it was influenced by the work of Miss Stein, who he'd come from visiting in the south of France.

Later, when Ana had her own child and he related this story about Jean and Gertrude Stein, Ana informed him that her mother had already told it to her. Her mother claimed her father was wrong: she knew about Gertrude Stein long before she met him. Everyone in Baltimore did; Stein's friends, the Cone sisters, had donated half the paintings in the Baltimore Museum of Art. Rolf was quite certain, he told Ana, that her mother had never set foot inside the Baltimore Museum of Art. For God's sake, she'd never been to any museum in New York before he took her to the Museum of Modern Art, and aside from Van Gogh's *Starry Night*, she could not identify any of the artists whose works they saw.

'And why does that matter?' Ana asked.

The question gave him pause, but instinctively, he responded as though they were playing chess, deflection and diversion the goal. 'If it doesn't matter if you know *Le Déjeuner sur l'herbe* was painted by Manet, then maybe it doesn't matter if you know which countries were Allies or how many kids died in Vietnam.'

Ana smiled sadly. She would neither press nor indulge him. Behind her question, there must be a cascade of others: Did it matter that he'd missed her high school graduation? Her college graduation? Her wedding?

ROLF HAD THOUGHT ABOUT THIS CONVERSATION, FIVE YEARS BE-fore, when on a whim he went alone to the Museum of Modern Art. By then he was eighty-four, living upstate with Miko in a Dutch-style farmhouse he'd refurbished for them. Miko, seventeen years his junior, was the only wife to whom he'd been faithful, though in truth this was more because of his compromised sexual functioning and decreased libido than any increased commitment to fidelity. When he'd bought the farmhouse, he'd expected Miko to voice opinions and preferences about the renovation. He was surprised and a bit disappointed that her only request was that the kitchen open onto a garden where she could grow mustard spinach and daikon and dwarf eggplants and that there be casement windows with screens so she could listen to the birds while she made rice and pickled vegetables and brewed endless pots of kukicha tea.

At first, Rolf had assumed that his new wife's sole interest in the kitchen and kitchen garden was in response to her hurt that the foods she prepared did not appeal to him. On the increasingly rare occasions when he felt a longing for something in particular, it was for the rich dishes he'd eaten in his youth: the raclette and fondue and duck à l'orange prepared in the hotel's restaurant and served family-style to the staff before the dinner service, the veal risotto with morels and peas that one of the chefs from a village just across the nearby Italian border would make in the spring. Soon, though, Rolf came to understand that Miko's modest requests had nothing to do with resentments or enactments of hostility. Her desires had always been confined to a small terrain. She reminded him of the medieval miniaturists who depicted entire landscapes on surfaces the size of a dollar coin.

Since moving to the farmhouse, Rolf had found himself missing Manhattan: walking at night without fear of being hit by a driver on one of the ill-lit roads near his home; opening a newspaper to discover a handful of films that he'd like to see playing nearby. Knowing Miko would decline joining him—try as she did to enjoy Manhattan, she only grew tense and then distracted by the crowds and the noise—he'd not even asked her to join him on this short trip.

And so it was that he'd arrived alone late morning in the city, settled into a room at a small hotel for which he'd done the original design long ago, and set off on foot, without a destination until he reached Fifth Avenue, where it occurred to him that the Rothkos and Pollocks at the nearby museum would be welcome antidotes to the relentless green that colonized his visual field in the country.

AFTER AN HOUR WANDERING THROUGH THE GALLERIES OF AB-
stract art, Rolf's eyes itched and his ears buzzed. He was disappointed
in himself: he used to spend long stretches in these rooms. Wanting to
rest his mind on something identifiable, he asked a guard to direct him
to Cézanne's *Boy in a Red Vest*. It was a painting he'd visited often, the
subject's resigned expression and worn clothing a reminder of his closest childhood friend, Hans, from a dairy farm on the outskirts of Sils
Maria. Until high school, he and Hans had spent the after-school hours
together, either at the hotel where Rolf's father worked, Hans marvel-
ing at the remaining breakfast pastries to which they could freely help
themselves, or in Hans's parents' milking barn, where Rolf would plant
himself on a stool to sketch the triangles of light slipped between the
wide beams of the steeped roof, while Hans assisted the Romany milkers
with the afternoon chores.

Rolf was standing in front of the painting, his thoughts drifting from
the slumped boy in the red vest to his recollections of the barn floor
stippled with sun and shadow to a tune one of the milkers would whis-
tle to help the animals let down their milk, when someone tapped his
shoulder. Turning, he saw a short, compact woman with practical hair
the color of steel wool. An old person, like himself.

She looked at him curiously. He froze as he realized that he was supposed to know her. And she did look familiar in the uncomfortable way
that happened too often these days of a word lurking in his mind whose
meaning was clear but syllables he couldn't access.

'You don't remember me, do you?' she said.

'I'm sorry. I sometimes can't even remember the name of my first
wife.'

'Jean. Your first wife's name was Jean.'

Rolf's breath caught in his throat. For a moment, he felt fright-
ened, as though the angel of death had come to greet him here with
the boy in a red vest as witness. And then it dawned on him who the
woman was. She'd been his draftsperson. The woman he slept with
during Jean's pregnancy with Ana. Their affair ended shortly after Ana
was born. Strangely, although he could not recall the woman's name,

he remembered the note in her large back-slanted cursive that Jean had found in his pants pocket. *Darling*, it said, *the butcher has promised to save me his best tenderloin. I'll make my special twice-baked potatoes. Bring us a bottle of that Malbec you love.*

Rolf had expected Jean to make a scene and immediately throw him out, but instead she'd stared at him with a hatred too pure for impulsive action. She had a newborn and a three-year-old. His punishment was that he would have to live with her loathing and disdain. Four days later, he received in his office mail a typed memo from Jean stating that if Mrs. Jean Koehl ever discovered Mr. Rolf Koehl in an act of adultery again, she would commence divorce proceedings immediately—which is what she did, five years later, when she came home from her sister's funeral to be greeted by a letter from a Finnish associate at his firm detailing the sexual acts she and Rolf regularly enjoyed together.

To Rolf's horror, the name that came back to him was of the woman he'd been with the night Ana was born. Belinda. Or was it Benilda? The woman with whom he'd cheated on this woman, looking amusedly at him now.

'Cindy. Cindy Powers. I was Cindy Brach then.'

Not knowing what else to do, Rolf touched her arm. 'You look good, Cindy,' he said, but then he stopped himself as he recalled that one of the things he'd liked about Cindy was that he never had to lie to her: never had to pretend he loved her or was planning on leaving his wife.

Cindy peered at him, as though he'd said something lascivious. It was inconceivable that he'd had sex with her. Not once, perhaps a hundred times.

'Shall we have a coffee?' he asked.

'Sure. If you're buying.'

They took the escalator to the café and stood in line at the Italian-style bar to order: a cappuccino with skim milk for her, and an espresso for him. He led them to a table near the wall of windows and took the seat that would let her look out. In his memory, she'd been a good deal younger than him, but when she told him she'd turned eighty a month ago, he realized that it must have been their circumstances that made the age difference seem larger: he, the owner of the fledgling firm with a pregnant wife and toddler at home; she, the office draftsperson, a single girl, living alone—it came back to him now—in a brownstone apartment on Seventy-Eighth Street. She'd liked to cook for him and he'd tolerated it even though she was not a very good cook because it seemed to satisfy a fantasy of hers to be feeding a man.

She'd not married until she was forty-two, she told him, while she vigorously stirred two Splendas into her cappuccino. A man a good deal older than her with children, already in college, who'd become unexpectedly attached to her. When those children had their own children, they considered her a third grandmother, which she treasured. One of these grandchildren was now living here in the city—in architecture school, actually, she said, at Cooper Union. They would be having dinner tonight.

He asked what kind of work Cindy's granddaughter wanted to do.

'Oh, nothing like what you did. Or do?' She cocked her head.

'No, I'm largely retired. I'm emeritus at my firm and still consult on the larger projects, but I haven't been a lead architect for some time.'

'It's all political now. Houses for refugees that can be built from mud or recycled plastics. Sustainable materials. As my granddaughter has explained to me, it's immoral to put beauty first when there are people living without clean water or electricity.'

Cindy smiled in a way that suggested she both admired and was befuddled by her granddaughter. With the softening of her expression, he remembered what had been her trademark coyness. A quiet knowingness that signaled not only was she available, she could navigate these situations—a married man with a young child and another on the way. She'd intuited that he would enjoy sitting in front of the fireplace in her parlor-floor apartment—a one-bedroom with fourteen-foot ceilings and the original plaster molding, a Brahms cello sonata in the background rather than the ballistic cartoons George watched at night in his footed pajamas. Rolf flushed as he recalled Cindy running him a bath in the claw-foot tub. He'd loved that apartment, and his enjoyment had encompassed Cindy for having it.

'I need to buy my granddaughter a birthday present. That's why I came here. To find something for her at the gift shop. But I always feel intimidated in there—half the items seem like a joke that I don't get—so I decided to take a little stroll around first. Work up my courage.'

Her eyes twinkled. She'd had a good sense of humor, laughed at his descriptions of two-year-old George and his most difficult clients. Once, though, when he made a joke about Jean, she'd not laughed, and he'd admired her for that: for not wanting to mock a pregnant woman whose husband she was sleeping with.

After they finished their coffees, Cindy efficiently bussed their cups and saucers. At the café exit, she took his arm. 'Come with me to the store. You're an architect. You'll know what my granddaughter would like.'

She held his arm while she led them to the street level. To Rolf's surprise, the gesture felt pleasing. Companionable, without expectations. With one swoop of his eyes over the shelves in the home décor section, an object leapt out at him: a square clock with a black steel frame and an oyster-colored dial and clean numbers, no dangling serif tails. 'This,' he said.

Cindy squeezed his arm. She was not bad-looking for a woman of eighty. If his sexual functioning were not so delicate these days, requiring Cialis and some special techniques Miko had mastered, he would have considered inviting her back to his hotel room for a drink. Instead, he said, 'I think I'll get one for my daughter too.'

'Is it her birthday?'

Ana was born in April. It was now January. An uncomfortable feeling washed over him as he realized he wasn't sure when he'd last remembered her birthday. It hadn't occurred to him to tell either of his children he'd be in the city today. Like him, Ana loved looking at paintings. It was so unlikely, but what if he bumped into her? Once he left the museum, he would call to arrange a visit. She'd not be surprised at his having given her no notice. Unlike her brother, she was never vindictive. She'd invite him to dinner. He'd give her the clock then. Place it himself in the right spot on her desk.

He and Cindy were each holding a small shopping bag with a tissue plume as they said goodbye. Rolf leaned over to kiss her cheek. Her skin felt dry and she smelled of talcum powder. 'I'm glad to have seen you,' he said, confused to find himself on the verge of tears.

WHAT ROLF MOST CLEARLY REMEMBERED ABOUT THE DAY WHEN the oncologist had delivered his recommendation was the television playing in the waiting room and the man, renowned among architects as a developer fool and who now thought he should be president, bellowing about his hecklers, 'Knock the crap out of them,' the crowd chanting *USA! USA! USA!*, and the memories it brought back of a news clip of Nazi youth he and Hans had seen during a school trip to a movie theater in St. Moritz.

The oncologist was neither impatient nor abrupt, but there was no hand-holding or sad eyes. His professional advice was that Rolf commence hospice care.

Miko responded with calm acceptance. She did not press him to do another round of chemotherapy or radiation. We each have our time, was all she would say. Yes, he thought, like a dishwasher or vacuum cleaner: the body's tubing and surfaces inevitably degrade and the thing one day just stops.

When Rolf had met Miko, she was still working as a graphic designer. On his first visit to her apartment on the Lower East Side, he was amazed to see a rivulet of water running down an interior wall and the threads of rust in the sink that served both the makeshift bathroom and kitchen. Observing his eyes lingering on these places, she'd looked curiously at him, and for a brief moment, he saw the plaster and the porcelain through her wabi-sabi consciousness: the beauty in the aged walls and the spiderwebs of cracks. Days later, he traveled to Montreal for a meeting with the project manager for a hotel he was renovating in the old quarter. His team put 132 items on the contractor's punch list—chipped paint in seventeen locations, six doors hung slightly askew, eight bathroom floors with misaligned tiles—leaving him with a seeping despair about his life's work, which would inevitably be worn and outdated by the time his own grandchildren were parents, and then about his life itself. It was at that moment he decided to marry Miko, who struck him as having transcended the degrading physical plane.

Miko never spoke about her Buddhism or any guiding philosophy, but she operated with a duality of precise attention to her projects—her garden, her cooking, her calligraphy—and what appeared to be detachment from everything else, which he assumed was the result of her having grown up in the wake of the bombing of Nagasaki. When the bomb—the 'Fat Man,' she called it—dropped on the city, Miko and her parents and two brothers were at their country cottage thirty miles away. Her grandparents, an aunt and uncle, and three cousins were killed instantaneously. She did not know the English word to describe turned to vapor, and he did not want to say it aloud, afraid that the syllables, *va-por-ized*, would linger between them. For three years, she told him, her family had not returned to the city, their home in the countryside a sanctuary for countless relatives, friends, and acquaintances, many with oozing burns, all violently ill from radiation poisoning. Though only a small child at the time, Miko could still recall her mother, her hair wrapped turban-style in a white cloth, moving quietly among moaning bodies prone on tatami mats in a room that had become a makeshift infirmary: applying green tea compresses, massaging feet, sometimes simply holding a hand.

Accustomed to women crying when he was late or failed entirely to show up, Rolf was at first disturbed that Miko shed no tears at his impending death. His initial reaction was replaced by appreciation for Miko's imperturbable tranquility, which he realized was an extension of the distance she kept from him, a distance based not on coldness—she was gentle and attentive, making trips to the library for the books he requested, keeping the room where he lay in his hospital bed meticulously clean and scented with a citrus potpourri she fashioned herself—but on an acceptance of their essential separateness. Never would Jean have ignored, as Miko did, his turning his financial affairs over to George, who arrived in his Range Rover on a Saturday afternoon, leaving an hour later with a file box of Rolf's bank statements and bills. When George returned a few weeks later, with a copy of Rolf's will revised by an estate attorney George had hired, Miko did not even ask to see it despite Rolf being too ill to do more than pass his eyes over the pages and follow his son's instructions: Sign here and here and here.

The following week, Rolf seized a moment when his energy soared sufficiently for him to sit propped up in the hospital bed, drinking a cup of cream-doused coffee while he informed Miko that living alone in the farmhouse following his death would be too difficult for her. To others, his pronouncement might seem paternalistic and condescending, but he knew Miko's aversion to thinking beyond the present. She never purchased eggs until the carton was empty or bought new sheets until there was a hole in the old, the consequence, he presumed, of having grown up in the post-war years of Nagasaki, when the idea of a future seemed to have also vaporized. Planning for Miko's well-being after he died was, he thought, the most loving act he'd ever done. Miko astonished him, however, by having already made a plan: she would move back to Japan, where she would live in what had been her parents' country cottage, maintained all these years by her two nephews, one of whose wives had faithfully tended the garden.

THE LAST DAY HE SAW ANA (HE DIDN'T KNOW IT WOULD BE THE last day, though he did know that he would die soon), he astonished himself by telling Ana that he was sorry.

He hadn't planned to say this. Rather, it came to him as Ana sat by his bedside. A few weeks before, she'd had the idea that marijuana might help him, and she'd asked Henry to bring some. The marijuana hadn't done much for him. Mostly, the visit was memorable for his having told Henry about his father's dealings during the war. He'd asked Henry if he should tell Ana, but he could no longer remember what Henry said and it no longer seemed important. What seemed important was that Ana know he was not politely but truly sorry.

He didn't say what he was sorry for because it was larger than any one thing, but if he had to boil it down, it would be for not having made an effort to get to know her. He knew her, of course—but only what he'd observed. When his children were teenagers, he'd thought that not asking questions of them favorably distinguished him from their mother, who, he assumed (wrongly, he later came to understand), was intrusive. Much as having failed to inquire about a colleague's family in the first months of working together, it then seems impossible to ask two years later, not asking his children about themselves became a habit too awkward to change. He knew his daughter in the manner that a repeat guest to one of the hotels he'd renovated might recall the balustrades on the balconies fronting the lawn that spilled into the sea, all the while unaware that the electrical system was overloaded or the saline swimming pool pump was clogged with sludge. He knew that she worked as an independent editor, but could not say what she actually did. He knew that Henry liked to cook and fly-fish and had planned their travels before he injured his back on a trip to the hotel where Rolf had grown up, but not whether their marriage was intimate or companionable. Strangely, he knew the most about his grandchild, largely because Ana's reticence did not extend to sharing news concerning Simon: the mathematics prize in middle school, the early acceptance to a first-choice college, a major in something to do with sex.

'I should have paid more attention to you. I let myself get swept up in my work. There was always a crisis, always someone complaining. The owners, the contractors, my own employees . . .'

Ana, seated on a chair by his hospital bed, took his hand, but she did not say, as he realized he had been hoping she would, that it was okay. That he'd been a good father. What was the term the engineer, a divorced woman with fantastic legs and two young children, had used? *Good-enough.* The engineer aimed to be a good-enough mother. He could still see her elaborately made-up face, across from him at a restaurant table in New Orleans, as she explained that the good-enough mother failed to be there at times for her children. The mother's failure provided her children an opportunity to learn to handle disappointment and develop resilience. The engineer declared this with a certainty that suggested an optimal ratio of bad to good, then smiled brightly, delighted, it seemed, at the idea that being imperfect was better than being perfect. Eating shrimp gumbo and sharing with Rolf a bottle of an overpriced sauvignon blanc and then going back to his hotel room where she'd already decided to blow him but not to have intercourse, rather than sitting with her son while he did his science homework and reading the next chapter of *Charlotte's Web* to her daughter before she went to sleep, was a gift to her children.

No, Ana did not say that he'd been a good-enough father. No interpretation of his ratio of bad to good would yield that answer.

In the fifty-some years since his divorce, Rolf had come to see that even without the Finnish associate's letter, Jean would have left him. She told him as much that night, with the cream stationary pinched between her thumb and forefinger as though it were something she'd fished out of a toilet. Her sister's death had shown her the finitude of her days and the irreparable falseness of their marriage. The affair he'd had while she was pregnant with Ana could be explained as revenge that a second baby was arriving without his agreement—but this affair, this was an expression of something vile she could no longer ignore. Commencing immediately, Jean announced, their marriage was terminated. He'd not wanted the disruption of his domestic life and finances, not wanted his children three hours away by train, living in the decrepit house where their mother had grown up, but he admired Jean for doing what he knew was right.

'The projects always took longer than we anticipated, they always came in over budget. I was always so busy.' Rolf felt debased hearing himself. Debased by the self-deception: What did Sartre call it? *False consciousness.* The false consciousness buried in *always so busy*, as though the busyness had overpowered him rather than being the reflection of what he'd deemed important. 'It was foolish of me not to understand that there would be more hotels, but . . .' He stopped himself. Whatever he'd add—you'd never have another childhood, I'd never have another young daughter—would only sound sappy.

Was he imagining that Ana's eyes were damp? Was it cruel that it gratified him to think she felt deeply about him, even if what she felt was pain?

And where, he wondered, had his daughter gotten this tenderness? Certainly not from her mother, who prized being tough and resolute and, most importantly, right—which, in a perverse way, had made them a perfect match: with him always incontrovertibly in the wrong, there was never a question that Jean was incontrovertibly in the right. Ana, though, had seemed to understand from an early age that if she followed her mother's and brother's lead, responding to him only through grievances, it would be a bottomless well. Instead, she'd weathered his neglect lightly, as though it were a dusting of snow: all those years when he was remiss in sending money, either because his bank accounts were in a state of confusion or he succumbed to his dislike of writing the check and addressing the envelope. Misdemeanors, he told himself, outweighed by the beneficial impact on George and Ana of the month they spent with him each summer. Those visits were admittedly flawed, but could anyone deny that they enlarged his children's sensibilities beyond the artlessness of their grandparents' home?

Ana released his hand so she could give him the covered cup with the straw poking out.

He took a weak sip of the water. 'Do you remember when you performed with the quartet in Sils Maria?' he asked.

'At the hotel where you grew up.'

Rolf nodded. How old had Ana been then? Ten, eleven? Neither she nor George could have understood what it had meant to him to receive the contract for the interior renovations or the satisfaction he'd felt at converting the hotel's attic into generous apartments for the senior maître d' and chef, both of whom had worked at the hotel since before he was born. Ana, though, must have sensed his connection with the staff when the stooped cellist from the quartet that performed during the cocktail hour, having learned she played viola, offered to teach her the parts for a few of their pieces so she could join them under the lobby's Austrian chandelier.

Now, for a moment, he saw his daughter with her patent leather Mary Janes poking out below the floor-length black skirt the quartet's young violinist had taken Ana to St. Moritz to buy. Ana had shared a music stand with the cellist while they played Bach and Haydn. For Ana's last appearance with the quartet, the violinist made a program: Ana Koehl, *artiste invitée*. With his daughter's name in print, Rolf had congratulated himself for insisting on removing one of the *n*'s. How ungainly her name would have looked on the program with all of those humps—like the Van Gogh haystacks, *belle laide*, beautiful ugly, he'd told Jean the first time he showed her the painting, a term he'd come to think described Jean herself.

'Your mother had never been to the Museum of Modern Art.'

With the look of confusion on his daughter's face, Rolf saw that he'd lost track of the line between what he was thinking and what they were talking about. Which was? Something that had made Ana's eyes turn damp.

That he was sorry. Sorry for too many things to say.

'Henry took me to a museum, too, on one of our first dates.' Ana smiled. 'It's hard, though, to imagine my mother spending any time looking at a painting.'

That afternoon at the museum, Jean had been pure *belle* in his eyes, as perfectly proportioned as John Singer Sargent's *Madame X*, with the model's sloping shoulders and generous bosom and ample hips accentuating her slender waist. He'd been as cowed by Jean's beauty as she was by his knowledge. Cowed, but then charmed that she did not hide what she did not know: not simply the names of any of the painters, but how to look at a painting. What exactly was he seeing, she asked as they stood before Picasso's *Guernica*? There was something carnal about her innocence, as there must have been about his own when one of the farm girls who had worked on Sundays in the hotel kitchen, Adelheid, seventeen to his fifteen, brought him to a shed on the hotel property, where she cleared a space among the garden tools, spread her coat over the splintered floor, pulled up her dirndl skirt, and showed him step-by-step what to do with her.

He returned the covered cup to Ana, and rested his hand on her wrist. A prickly burning sensation moved across his cheeks. How could he have missed her wedding? Unlike him, her only wedding. He'd been in Jaipur and the municipal workers had gone on strike and a city sewer line burst, spewing fecal matter into the alley behind the hotel where he was working. *A genuine disaster*, he telegrammed three days before the wedding. He would make it up to her and Henry, he added.

It had taken the hotel operator half an hour to execute the international call to George, who Rolf would instruct to walk Ana down the aisle in his stead. But it had been Catherine who answered the phone. George was at the gym, she said in her honeyed voice. *Of course* he'd fill in for his father! On his return from India, Rolf learned that George had refused. If his father couldn't bother to make it to his only daughter's wedding, George had announced, then it should be his mother who substituted, a suggestion Jean rejected—spitefully, Rolf suspected: having no family member at all accompanying Ana would underscore his absence.

He closed his eyes. He could no longer remember if he'd ever talked with Ana about her wedding or if he'd only imagined her telling him that being given away was so antiquated, she'd preferred walking down the aisle on her own.

WHEN ROLF WOKE, HE WAS ALONE. FOR A MOMENT, HE PANICKED from the thought that Ana had gone back to New York and he would die before she returned. Die without having told her more. More of what? More of his regrets, he supposed.

He heard voices coming from the kitchen. It was then that it came back to him that Ana had said she would stay until the evening. She was probably with Miko, drinking tea and talking about whatever it was the two of them talked about. Miko's life in Nagasaki before she moved to New York? Miko's nephews, who she thought of as the children she never had?

If Ana knew, Jean had once written him, that he'd not wanted more children, she'd drop dead. It was true that he'd felt entrapped when Jean announced her pregnancy with Ana. George alone had transformed their apartment into a playpen with hideous plastic objects and an unbearable decibel level. But *drop dead*? That was excessive. Besides, he presumed that Ana knew. When they were kids, George would taunt her, calling her an unwanted child—something George could only have heard from his mother. Still, Rolf was relieved that he'd never told Jean he'd particularly not wanted a daughter. Outside of sexual relations, he'd had his fill of females by the time he was twelve: his invasive mother, insisting on examining the bowl before he flushed; his two older sisters, until he was old enough to protest, dressing him in girls' clothing and then drawing him to their flat chests so they could pretend they were nursing; his younger sister, not knocking before she entered the pantry that had been converted into his room after he was deemed too grown to share with the girls. Her shocked expression when she once saw him yanking on himself. Relieved because Jean would have surely told Ana, and because he'd been so wrong that a daughter would be the coup de grâce when, in fact, Ana had brought him more pleasure than his son.

Jean had never understood that he'd not wanted to be a father and yet, with each of his children, when faced with their tiny swaddled bodies, he loved them immediately. Granted, it was not in the way his Jewish partner, Saul, loved his sons such that he felt it his sacred duty to be involved in every corner of their lives, from coaching their Little League teams to doing their trigonometry problem sets himself over lunch so he could check their answers at night. Rolf was never that kind of father. He loved his children in his own way.

'You weren't even there when Ana was born,' Jean had never missed an occasion to remark.

Guilty as charged.

Guiltier than charged.

Now, though, he wondered if he would have felt differently about being a father had it not been with Jean. More powerful than his guilt the morning following Ana's birth had been his feeling of alienation from his wife: even with this new life in her and then his arms, this creation of a human being from an animal act, Jean had felt no awe. How could she? She did not believe in anything not reducible to an equation, which was why she'd had to ask him how to look at a painting.

He could not say where he'd gotten the idea that marriage should involve spiritual attunement. His mother had been chronically exhausted between her four children and the expectation that as the wife of the hotel's general manager, she would handle the difficulties of the female staff—pregnancies, desired and not; romances, broken and too quickly progressing; sick children and dying parents. By the time night fell, all she wanted was to put her feet up in front of the potbelly stove in the kitchen of their cottage on the hotel grounds and flip through a magazine left behind by one of the guests. As for his father, on Sundays, his only day off, all he wanted was to take silent rambles in the mountains without being asked to wind a watch or fetch a tiara or weigh a dog's feces.

At Rolf's retirement dinner, the young associates at the architecture firm he'd founded roasted him by presenting Rolf's Rules: Furnishings can be contemporary, but architectural details must be preserved. Guest rooms must be as close to square as possible and have a serene view and a claw-foot tub. Beds must be positioned in such a way that guests can see the door when they wake. Sheets and towels must always be white, flower arrangements with as much green as color. And God forbid anything was cutesy or kitsch. Design could be playful, but it must be serious at heart.

He laughed at his pet peeves along with everyone else. But in truth he was wounded that his associates, many of whom had been his students earlier in their careers, had missed the most important of his principles. Superficial mistakes could be fixed: the wrong light fixtures or the size of a shower head. But structural mistakes were irreparable. You couldn't post facto create an interior courtyard in a hotel. Without crippling expense, you couldn't change where a building sat on a hilltop. This, in a nutshell, had been the irresolvable crux of his marriage. Jean and his differences were structural. She saw numbers. He saw shapes. She believed that there was one and only one correct answer, whereas he viewed his principles as exactly that: his.

WHEN HE WOKE AGAIN, THE ROOM WAS DIM. SOMEONE HAD TAKEN the cup with the straw from his bedside table and placed a vase with peonies, two crimson and one orange, and leatherleaf ferns on a small table across the room. There was as much green as color.

Had Ana experienced his apology for his failures as a father as cheap words? 'Lies and more lies and more lies,' Jean would say. He'd never tried to defend himself, but he felt bruised by her proclamations. Yes, he'd told her countless lies, but he still thought of himself as a basically honest person. His father had taught him never to wrong a customer: If a room or a meal were not satisfactory, his father would without question void the charge. As an architect, it would have been easy to pad bills— How would a client know how many hours it took to do drawings or source materials or meet with the contractor? —but Rolf never charged a penny more than was fairly earned. His marital and sexual life existed in a separate universe where the very idea of a lie, he'd convinced himself, did not apply. In this separate universe, there were untruths that were kindnesses; deceptions required if he was to feel fully alive rather than like a caged rat.

Had Jean heard him say this, she would have pounced on *rat*. Rolf the Rat.

He'd been surprised by Ana's dedication to him these past months. Miko's too. He'd thanked them both, many times—but he wasn't able to bring himself to say that he was undeserving. How would one ever determine who deserved what? Had the princess with the albumen scalp deserved her tiara delivered every evening? Had the American's dog deserved specially prepared meals?

Now, again, he heard voices coming from the kitchen. He pictured Ana and Miko seated side by side at the round table in his square breakfast room—another of his rules: circular tables for square rooms—sipping Miko's kukicha tea. Ana would have drawn Miko out. Maybe Miko was telling Ana about the three years she and her parents had spent at their country cottage after the Fat Man dropped on their Nagasaki home. Or maybe she was telling Ana what she'd planted in the kitchen garden outside the window and what she would plant in the garden her nephew's wife was preserving at the country cottage. After he dies.

How many years had passed since that morning he saw Ana wrapped like a wonton on her mother's chest? Since he inhaled her woodsy smell, kissed the wrinkled skin between the bottom of her beanie cap and the top of the pink and blue blanket?

It took him a while to do the calculation in his head. When the answer arrived, it came as a shock. In eleven months, Ana would turn sixty. By then, he would surely be gone. He could write her a letter to read on her birthday. But how corny—cutesy and kitsch—would that be?

Was there anything more he could say? Anything more that would mean anything?

5

ANA

Usually, I walk from my apartment to Lance's brownstone. The route is uncannily direct: a straight path north on Central Park West, which becomes Frederick Douglass Boulevard, and then a single turn onto Lance's block. When the weather is unfriendly, I take the subway. Climbing the stairs to the street, I emerge into a neighborhood that's home to many West Africans. Women in twisted headdresses and long batik skirts mingle behind tables laden with yellow beads and metal cuff bracelets. Percussive music pours from open windows and cars, and men in dashikis seated outside a Senegalese bakery sip from miniature cups of coffee.

Today, though, in a cab from the museum, everything feels akilter—the route through the park, the uncertain timing, the duct tape on the partition between the seats—and there's a faint smell of smoke. I crack the window. The sounds of the acceleration and deceleration of nearby vehicles, the cacophony of car horns, the hum from people on the sidewalks fill the cab. And then the alert of a text.

Gemma: *Can you call me plz?*

I close my eyes. Would it be okay on my birthday—a Big One, as everyone keeps reminding me—to hold off responding? No, it would not. No more than it would have been okay to ignore Bettina's distress and not offer her a time to meet today.

When I was in social work school, first-year students were required to have ten therapy sessions so they'd get a taste of what it felt like to be in the patient chair. It was a ridiculous exercise, since the 'therapists' were the second-year students and the first-years were essentially their guinea pigs. My 'therapist' wore maxi-skirts and construction boots. She was always late and never showed up at all for what would have been our seventh meeting. A few days later, I heard that she'd been discovered leaning out a top-floor window. Her supervisor stepped in for the last four sessions.

Gordon—he told me to call him by his first name—was either well-preserved for past sixty, which in those days I thought of as old, or poorly preserved for someone younger. He was mostly bald, with a long fringe of hair on the bottom third of his scalp and a beatifically round face, and wore Birkenstock sandals with socks in November. But he had a way of listening that suggested not only did I have his full attention, he was considering everything I said from many angles. The maxi-skirt girl had taken notes, which she said she needed for her supervision sessions, and on occasion, she'd ask me to repeat something or slow up so she could get everything down. Gordon did not take notes, but at the end of our first meeting, I asked if he'd mind if I wrote down a few of the things he said. He studied me with an expression that might have been amusement but I feared was pity.

One of Gordon's comments that I wrote down was delivered after I described canceling a lunch with another student because I had a paper due and a dinner to attend with Henry that cut short my work time. My classmate had neither responded to the note I'd left in her mailbox or the message on her answering machine: Should I go to the lunch? But would she even be there?

Gordon said nothing until I'd sputtered the final details. 'Ana, let me tell you one of my basic rules.'

I felt a jolt of surprise. My father was famous for his design rules, but weren't therapists supposed to not give advice? Not impose their own values?

'Never cancel on anyone unless it's truly necessary—and I mean truly. You're on the way to the hospital with a broken leg or someone very close to you has died. You never know how much effort the other person has made to meet you. To cancel because you have a paper due is essentially saying my time, my projects, my feelings are more important than yours.'

I felt mortified. Mortified because I understood immediately what Gordon was saying. I'd experienced it countless times on the receiving end from my father, who canceled two out of three plans to meet. Even my wedding, he'd canceled attending. There was always something: drawings that had to be revised, a girlfriend who needed help purchasing a sofa. Sure, no problem, I'd say, but each time it would feel as though he'd let out the air from my tires, and for a day or two I'd drag myself from thing to thing with a lurching slowness, like driving on a flat.

WITH THE CAB CREEPING UP MADISON AVENUE, PAST THE BOU-tiques where Catherine has her personal shoppers, I call Gemma.

'Aunt Ana, thank you! I need to tell you what happened. As soon as we got off the phone this morning, I texted Ella. I told her I'd never been so sorry about anything in my entire life and begged her to come back so we could talk.'

And Ella did, Gemma says. She arrived with new almond milk lattes and they sat together on Gemma's couch. When Gemma explained that she'd been overwhelmed with jealousy that Ella would be helping Simona, Ella was stunned.

'I told Ella I felt the way I had when she lorded it over me that only she was allowed to carry Simon. She said she didn't remember that, but she was sure what I said was true. But since we were sweeping out the cobwebs, there was something she'd wanted to say for a while now.'

What Ella wanted to tell Gemma was she'd been feeling alienated from Gemma since Gemma married Greg. Gemma had ossified.

The cab turns west, toward the park transverse. Had Ella actually used that word, *ossified*? Or would she have said *hardened*?

'Ella said that for Greg and me, numbers are more real than what we experience ourselves. She said I'd begun to remind her of Nana. We both flatten people, turn them into data points. No matter what she tells me, she said, I respond robotically. She said she could tell me she'd just been hit by a car and I'd say, Oh, that's good.'

I imagine myself in Gemma's shoes: hearing what to me would feel like a barrage of accusations. Sucked into a vortex of anger and confusion. Yet my nieces seem so open, neither accusing the other of remembering wrong or lying.

'Once, when we were on a family vacation, we went to an ancient fountain where visitors throw coins and make a wish. My wish was that I could solve the Poincaré conjecture. I thought that was a perfect wish since Poincaré was French and we were in France. Ella couldn't believe I hadn't wished for something human: that Mom or Dad or Nana stay healthy or there be no more war or starving children.'

I remember my brother's France trip. Catherine had organized for him to attend a wine course. It was after the class that he built his wine cellar and my nieces began their imitations of his sommelier commentary every time he opened a bottle.

'On the card I gave Ella for her thirtieth birthday, I wrote that she'd reached the mean age for American women in the eighteenth century. She said that felt awful. So impersonal. Even worse, she said everything is scheduled with me. If she asks for my help, my first response is always I have to check my calendar. She feels like an item crossed off my *to-do* list.'

Gemma is softly crying. 'I was afraid she was going to say she couldn't see me getting up in the middle of the night to take care of a crying baby. A baby who'd not made an appointment with me.'

I can hear my niece blowing her nose. 'Ella should be the mother. I haven't held a baby since Simon. I don't even really like babies.'

'Oh, Gemma, you'll love your baby. Everyone does. It's biological. You, more than anyone, should know that.'

Gemma is quiet for so long, I wonder if we've lost our connection.

'I don't know that. What I study is cortisol mechanisms in rats. Yesterday, two of the rats in my lab died. It was one thousand percent my fault. I forgot to put the heat on in their cages.'

I want to tell Gemma she shouldn't blame herself, there are always accidents in labs, but it would sound like pablum.

'Ella claims I never pick up the phone just to say hi. Just because I miss her or I'm thinking about her. She said that's why Nana and I use email so much. The communication is one-way. A monologue.'

And then, finally, I see a glimmer of light. 'But you did, Gemma. You called Ella. It was you who did that.'

AFTER GEMMA HANGS UP, I SINK INTO THE SMOKY BACKSEAT. SINCE moving to New York, my mother has refused to take a cab. With the driver now loudly talking on his phone, I think she's right. I should have taken a bus from the museum.

When George and I agreed to work together to convince our mother to move from Baltimore to New York, we told her it would be good for her not to need to climb stairs, leaving unspoken the most important reason: we would be able to keep a closer eye on her as she edged toward ninety. I hoped my mother might take pleasure in the city, as it seemed she did during her modeling years. She has not. My father's complaints about my mother centered on her insensitivity to aesthetic distinctions, but they captured something essential about her—a lack of imagination that, to use Ella's word, flattens experience. For my mother, there are no centuries of ghosts hovering over the trees in the park, behind the stoops of brownstones.

George's plan for moving our mother, I discovered, boiled down to his paying the security deposit and first and last month's rent on an apartment, leaving it to me over three weekend trips from New York to Baltimore to help my mother weed through decades of accumulations: The powder-blue dishes my grandmother had brought from Sundsvall that my mother carted to the basement after her parents' death so as to make room for the footed soup bowls and gold-rimmed dessert plates she bought at thrift stores—dishes she must have thought would ameliorate the pity her neighbors felt for her because she had no man to shovel the walk and two teenagers to raise on her own. The needlepoint her sister had been working on the day she died. The file cabinet with George's consistently terrible report cards (Conduct: *Poor*; Homework: *Poor*; Attitude: *Poor*) and my invariably excellent ones, which had seemed like a worse failing, as though I lacked the gumption to misbehave. Even more challenging, moving our mother meant that it fell to me to inform her that a one-bedroom apartment in a post-war building with postage-stamp closets would not accommodate the twenty-two footed soup bowls or the six afghans my grandmother had crocheted or every coat purchased from the Hutzler's department store basement discount racks over the past fifty-five years.

'You can't say you're surprised,' Fiona said, when I told her it felt like a slap in the face that the weekends going through the Baltimore house from attic to cellar seemed to have only lessened my mother's regard for me—who of any worth would have time for such a task? —and enlarged her idealization of George: too important with his work trips for sealing boxes with packaging tape. 'George, he's so busy all the time,' my mother would sigh, while I sorted clothing and linens and books and kitchen contents into piles labeled *Discard* (the bra elastic too frayed for even a woman in a shelter), *Donate* (thirty years of my grandparents' *Life* magazines), and *Pack* (the gold-rimmed dessert plates my mother refused to return to their thrift store home, so they live now in stacks on the back burners of her galley kitchen's stove).

Looking back, I find it laughable that I thought because I'd done the packing for my mother, my brother would handle the unpacking. Instead, days before my mother's arrival in New York, George announced he was off on one of his family's fire and ice vacations—a week of skiing in Vail followed by a week recuperating in Anguilla. 'Catherine and I will give a hand when we get back,' George said, as though I could leave our mother for two weeks surrounded by boxes and unable to find her coffee maker or checkbook or blood pressure monitor.

Not until I was summoned in a snowstorm to fix my mother's printer did I grasp that the consequence of being the sole person to help set up her new home was that in my mother's mind, her possessions and apartment were now my responsibility. When I suggested over the phone she look to see if the printer was unplugged, she dismissed this as impossible. I trekked across the park to my mother's apartment to discover the dangling cord.

Standing at her front door as we said goodbye, my mother—who'd kept the furnace at the Baltimore house so low, I spent my childhood winters wearing a wool cap inside—proclaimed that the coats she'd brought from Baltimore, *perfectly adequate there*, were inadequate here. Her tone suggested this was my fault. At the same time, there was a pathetic note to her plaint: *I'm cold. I'm cold. I'm cold.*

It crossed my mind that perhaps my mother was reacting to my spending time upstate with my father: reacting both to her ex-husband having entered the anteroom to his death, which must remind her that she couldn't be far behind, and to sharing my attentions with him.

'Where did you buy this?' she demanded, fingering the sleeve of my microfiber coat.

I hesitated before answering. Most of the time, my mother regarded Henry and me as the poor relations in comparison to George and Catherine, which was absurd, since we lived very well. Sometimes, though, my mother's view flipped and she saw me as a pampered doctor's wife.

I'd bought the coat at Saks, I said. During the winter sale when everything is deeply discounted.

After my mother asked that I write out the bus directions to the store—'Not in your tiny cursive but printed clearly'—it dawned on me that she expected I would accompany her there.

'It has to be tomorrow,' she said. On Wednesday she was getting her hair cut and on Thursday the handyman was coming to fix her broken blind. She did not like having more than one thing on her calendar for any day.

'Okay, Mom. We can go tomorrow. I'll meet you in the coat department at two o'clock.'

BY THE TIME THE CAB REACHES THE NORTHERN PORTION OF THE park, the smell of smoke has dissipated. When Simon was young, we would often picnic here: Simon in a striped T-shirt and red sneakers somersaulting down one of the grassy slopes of the Great Hill while Henry stretched out with his head propped on a backpack and a book in his hands.

On the afternoon of the Saks shopping trip, I walked to the store, crossing for a second day in a row the park blanketed with snow. I arrived early, with the hope of intercepting my mother before she began harassing the salespersons. My mother, though, was already there.

'I've been here since one thirty.' She patted her box-blonde hair, which drove Catherine crazy: my mother refusing to go to Catherine's colorist. The Clairol kit she'd been using for over forty years, my mother insisted, gave excellent results. 'There's nothing I like.'

I pointed to a nearby circular rack. 'Those are the same make as mine. Why don't you try one on?'

'I would never wear anything so ugly.'

Something in my chest—a heart valve? a trap door?—slammed shut as I realized that more than coat shopping was afoot. 'You said you're cold in your wool coat. I thought you wanted one like mine.'

'I'm not wearing a sleeping bag.'

To my relief, my mother was polite to the salesperson—Florencia, her badge said—who offered assistance. I did my best not to roll my eyes when my mother inquired where Florencia was from and if Saks provided its employees with health insurance.

'I read in the *New York Times*,' my mother said after Florencia left to look in the stockroom for a different size of the one coat she'd consented to try on, 'service industry employees appreciate customers expressing interest in them.'

My mother dropped her friendly manner once Florencia returned with the coat. 'If I purchase this now, and it's marked down further next month, can I bring it back for the lower price?'

'As long as you've not worn the item or removed the tags, Madam, you can return anything you've purchased at any time.'

'I wouldn't be returning it. I'd keep the coat but get the lower price.'

Florencia knit her brows. 'I've never heard of that, but if you'll kindly allow me a few minutes, I'll ask my manager.'

With Florencia gone again, my mother looked defiantly at me. 'If she says no, I'm going to request an extra twenty percent off if I pay in cash.'

I inhaled slowly, the way we did in yoga class. 'Mom, a salesperson in a department store doesn't have the authority to set prices.'

On her return, Florencia apologized. She was very sorry, but she'd been informed that the store does not have this price-matching policy. Madam, however, could return the coat if she was dissatisfied.

My mother raised her chin. She was dissatisfied, she said. Very dissatisfied.

The following morning, an email arrived outlining my mother's coat purchase battle plan:

Ana:

1. You might have the means to not care about prices, but I *DO CARE.*
2. I telephoned the <u>Macy's</u> here in New York and spoke with a **very knowledgeable** woman named Mrs. Morris, who I believe is African American.
3. Mrs. Morris has *guaranteed* me that if I purchase my coat at Macy's, they will give me the *lower price* if they discount it further. I WOULD NOT BE REQUIRED TO UNDERGO THE INCONVENIENCE OF BRINGING BACK THE COAT. Only the receipt.

Mom

In the evening, Gemma called. It was hard to tell if she was more confused or frustrated. Nana had reached her as she was leaving for work. She'd actually telephoned rather than emailing. The purpose of her call, she informed Gemma, was to ask how close Gemma's lab was to Macy's. Nana, Gemma reported, had remained silent for so long after Gemma said 'not very close,' Gemma had made up a story that she needed to buy some tights and could meet there during her lunch hour. Macy's didn't have the same coat that Nana had tried on at Saks, but they had a similar one. Nana was planning a trip to the library so she could look up the brand in *Consumer Reports.*

My mother's second coat email arrived with the subject line *Update on Purchase of Winter Outerwear.* This one was addressed to Gemma, Ella, George, Catherine, and me.

- The coat at Macy's was manufactured by <u>S.P.Q. Clothing</u>. There are **no reviews** on the Internet of their products.
- I found a *toll-free* number for <u>S.P.Q. Clothing</u> online. I reached a polite woman named Amita. She was speaking to me from Bangladesh.
- Amita is not aware of any reviews for the coat I am interested in purchasing, but **she will ask her supervisor**.
- MY PLAN IS TO GIVE HER 48 HOURS TO RESPOND.

Using REPLY ALL, Catherine wrote back: *Let me know if I can help!* ❤️❤️ George's response, to me alone, was: *WTF is Mom talking about?*

I imagined having a good laugh with Fiona when I told her the coat saga. But in the telling, on our reservoir walk the following day, the story didn't seem funny. My jaw clenched. Was I acting with Fiona like my mother did with me? Whining about something trivial, ignoring that Fiona would have given a pinky finger to have her own mother alive to annoy her?

Fiona sipped from the hot chocolate she had in a carry cup. A haze hovered over the water and the sky was not so much white as drained of color. A few birds moved from spindly tree to spindly tree looking for early buds or a tender bit left from the summer.

'You get caught with your mother in that bind you told me about when you were in social work school,' Fiona said. 'The psychotic something or other . . .'

'The psychotic knot.'

We were nearing the south side of the reservoir, where the water spurted through a blow hole and ducks congregated. 'Each step in isolation seems sane,' Fiona continued, 'but the whole is insane. Your mother is like a car rolling out of control down a hill. She can't stop to reflect on what she's doing. And you're the kid in the backseat of that car.'

I welled with tears. Tears of appreciation for Fiona putting into words what I could not. I squeezed Fiona's free hand, snug in a red woolen mitten made by Nick, who she'd taught to knit while he was in high school and suffering from the long weekends when he'd never had any invitations or anywhere to go.

'My poor mother. She's managed to live all these years without gaining any wisdom. She develops these convictions and there's no budging her from them. And what's always been so confusing to me is that some of them are good ones.'

'Remember that paradox you said one of your professors talked about: intermittent reinforcement is more powerful than predictable reinforcement? That's what happens with you and your mom. On rare occasions, she acts like a sensible or even sensitive person. And that's just enough to reinforce your belief that the rest of the time there must be a good reason for what she's doing.' Fiona held up her carry cup. 'Want a sip?'

I shook my head no. The smell of the chocolate brought back the chalky days-old babkas my grandparents would cart home from their bakery and my mother would refuse to discard until they turned so hard, they'd crumble into shards if anyone tried to cut a piece.

'I feel sad for you, love,' Fiona said. 'To grow up with a parent without wisdom is like navigating without a map. You can find your way, but it's so much harder . . .'

THE CAB APPROACHES THE CIRCLE AT THE TOP OF THE PARK, WITH the Frederick Douglass statue in the center of the plaza. It's the halfway point between Lance's house and my apartment, a spot where we sometimes meet since it's so unlikely anyone we know would be there.

Thinking back over the lunch with Simon, a wave of anxiety washes over me. With Simon having asked Ella to help after their surgery, that step is now concrete. I know the real dangers to Simon are not the surgeries, but other people. The thought loop about my brother is a distraction: If George hadn't changed our father's will, Simon would have to proceed more slowly. And if Simon had to proceed more slowly, they might have second thoughts before doing anything irreversible . . . Round and round and round my mind goes.

'Asshole,' Fiona said when I told her about the change. 'Your brother could have had it both ways—released the money for his daughters and made you the trustee for Simon's portion. And that he told Simon before you? That's just low. A fucking diss. He wanted to be the bagman handing out the cash.'

'I already couldn't stand my mother's endless talk about George and Catherine and their marvelous lives. Now, when we're together, all I can think about is, does she know what her perfect son did?'

'Maybe you should tell her.'

I laughed. 'I can't imagine that going well. The way she sees it, George being wealthy means he's above reproach. She reveres rich people, as though the universe wouldn't grant that much money to someone who isn't deserving.'

After Fiona voiced it, the idea that I should talk with my mother about how my brother had handled our father's will wouldn't go away. How would I feel if she died and I'd never tried? Wouldn't I regret not having tried more than I would having tried and failed? My mother loved breakfast. I'd invite her to breakfast at her favorite coffee shop, two blocks from her apartment, and give it a try.

When I arrived, my mother was standing outside. It was a bitter December morning, but she was dressed in only a blazer, with a look on her face as though daring me to ask why she wasn't wearing the coat she'd bought the previous winter at Macy's, the one she called Bangladesh to research, sparking an argument about who was correct about the current temperature and the appropriate clothing for it.

I kissed her cheek, still, after all these years, startled by the strange way she retracted her chest, a deep concave that assured only our lips and cheeks would touch.

'There's something I want to tell you,' I began once our food arrived.

She looked at me suspiciously.

'It has to do with George. Something happened with him that's been very painful for me. It's making it even harder that you don't know what I'm going through.'

A speck of onion from the hash browns that came with my mother's sunny-side-down eggs had stuck to the red lipstick on her lower lip. 'If this is about your father's will, you can stop there. Your brother did nothing wrong. He was acting responsibly to protect all of you.'

'He told you about it?'

'Yes. That you attacked him and were so unappreciative about what he arranged for your family.'

My mouth turned dry. 'I didn't attack him. I told him I wished he'd discussed the change with me first so we could have decided together. And that he'd not told Simon before he told me.'

'George would never do that.'

I stared at my mother, at first not understanding what she meant.

'That's not what happened,' she continued. She opened a packet of blueberry jam, and slathered it on her toast. 'You're wrong.'

'But it is, Mom. I don't think George would claim otherwise.'

'You're lying. Making up a nasty story about your brother.'

My face stung. I felt my breath turn shallow and a sense of impending panic.

My mother bit into her toast. 'Your brother worked extremely hard to get your father's finances in order. From what I knew of them years ago, I'm certain they were in terrible disarray. You should be thanking George.' She wiped the remnants of jam from her mouth and sat up taller in the booth. 'If there was anything improper about your father's will, it's that he didn't leave *me* any money. I gave him all the savings from my modeling career—it was nearly five thousand dollars—when he set up his architecture office. There were thirteen child support payments he never made and the rest were always late.'

I focused on the smears of lipstick and jam streaking the napkin my mother was twisting. She was putting on a good show, but the conversation was agitating her too. My eyes welled and I feared dissolving into tears. I stood. 'I'm sorry, I have to go.'

I fished two twenties from my wallet, dropped them on the table, grabbed my coat and scarf, and bolted for the door. With my gaze locked on the floor, I hoped the hostess wouldn't register the pathetic image of a woman just months short of her sixtieth birthday crushed by what her eighty-eight-year-old mother had said.

A few days later an email arrived from my mother at seven thirty in the morning with IMPORTANT RESPOND IMMEDIATELY in the subject line.

- My **Kelly green cardigan** is missing.
- It has black buttons. I am certain that you remember it.

- Come **ASAP.**
- THIS MORNING would be best.

Even for my mother, the demand of THIS MORNING seemed extreme. Was she sending a smoke signal that she was ready now to talk about what had happened with George and the will? Perhaps she'd had a poor night's sleep before the coffee shop breakfast. Perhaps it would go better if she was at home, in her own apartment.

The cardigan, as I expected, was at the top of my mother's closet in a stack of pilled and moth-eaten ones she'd insisted on putting in the *Pack* rather than *Donate* pile. When I handed it to her, she waved it triumphantly. 'See, I told you I would use this sweater.'

I refrained from the retort that she hadn't been able to find the sweater because she hadn't worn it, not once since I'd packed and unpacked it. Instead, I took the sweater from my mother and sat with it on my lap atop the bed. I patted the spot beside me.

My mother situated herself on the edge of the mattress so her feet were stamped flat on the carpet. The hope that she might today be open to listening was quickly evaporating. I took a deep breath. 'Mom, I'd like to try again to explain to you how I feel about what happened with my father's inheritance. George is your son. It's good that you love him and want to defend him, but it would be a comfort to me to know that you understand how I feel about what he did, even if you think I'm wrong to feel that way.'

'I don't want to know how you feel about it. I want you to stop falsely accusing your brother. He was acting in the best interest of all of my grandchildren. Of my family.' With the word *family*, she raised the pitch of her voice and slowly enunciated, as though she were saying a holy word.

From there, it went like the Freud story I'd once read about the man accused of returning a borrowed kettle with a hole in it whose response morphs from *I never borrowed the kettle* to *The kettle had a hole in it when I borrowed it*, and then, finally, *The kettle was undamaged when I returned it*. My father's will was never changed. It was not George who'd advised our father to change his will. George did nothing wrong by advising our father to change his will.

I turned the Kelly green cardigan over and examined it. Not only was it pilled, there was a hole in the sleeve. 'I think I'm just going to have to live with this,' I said.

My mother paused before she responded, and for a moment, I thought maybe now something would soften and she would allow what I'd told her to penetrate her carapace.

'Yes, Ana. You just have to live with this.'

WITH THE CAB ROUNDING THE FREDERICK DOUGLASS CIRCLE, I'M able to see the face of the statue. The eyes and mouth are cast in un-flinching resolve. From what Lance has told me about Alice, I imagine her face set in the same expression.

When it came to searching for the right kindergarten for their daughter, Lance said, Alice's affluent suburban heritage reared its head. The right school, Alice quickly determined, meant a private one. She approached the search with what Lance describes as her characteristic *Leave no stone unturned modus operandi*. Henry was one of Alice's early stones in the research phase of her mission. After he suggested to Alice that she talk to me—I was on the front line with all things school re-lated, he explained—Alice emailed to ask if we could meet for a coffee. Could I pick somewhere convenient for me?

I suggested the diner where I had my initial consultations with cli-ents. Thirty minutes beyond the arranged time, with still no Alice and my tea finished, I was debating leaving when a lanky man with longish hair and a motorcycle helmet tucked under his arm came through the door. He caught my eye, smiling slightly, the situation strangely flipped from the margin of acceptable New York lateness having been exceeded to his having rescued me from an uncomfortable decision.

'Ana?' He slid into the booth without waiting for me to answer, and put the helmet beside him. 'Lance. Alice's husband. There was an emer-gency with one of her patients. Al didn't have your phone number, so she sent me.'

It was apparent that the man took for granted what came his way from his quiet movie star looks—the high forehead, the straight, narrow nose, the grayish-green eyes—but that unlike my mother, who'd once had that caliber of looks, he didn't think they were important. There was a male smell about him, a bit like the burger he said he hoped I wouldn't mind if he ordered. 'I was playing racquetball when Al reached me, and didn't get a chance to eat.'

Lance took off his bomber jacket. In his black T-shirt, his gym biceps and a jagged scar on the soft inside of his forearm were visible. I flushed when he put down the menu and caught me looking at the scar. He looked back with what seemed like a challenge—I'll tell you if you ask—but then the waiter returned to take his order and bring more hot water for me, after which I launched into a description of Simon's school and our experience there since Simon, then in ninth grade, had enrolled as a kindergartner.

When his burger arrived, Lance ate slowly, an amused expression on his face while I walked him through the admissions process. Was he mocking me for thinking the steps merited discussion?

'Sounds like a lot of hoops to jump through. I'm for public school or if it's going to be private, at least one with both sexes, but Al went to an all-girls school, and she's into it in that Wellesley-Hillary kind of way.'

I considered saying that I'd also gone to an all-girls school, but there'd been no Wellesley-Hillary vibe at Our Lady of Providence.

Lance wiped a film of grease from his mouth. Two of his bottom teeth were a bit crooked, an imperfection that made him seem genuinely attractive rather than like a picture from a magazine.

'Al is compromising by looking at some co-ed places, but since she'll be the one filling out all those forms and taking Zena to all those interviews—she'd never trust me to do any of that to her perfectionist standards—she'll end up deciding.'

That evening, Alice sent me an apology email. She'd had to arrange a hospital admission for a two-year-old with a punctured lung. She thanked me for having met with Lance. I wrote back that I was happy to help and she should reach out with any questions she might have. I didn't hear from Alice again, though I found myself thinking about Lance on occasion, sometimes with a flash of anger at what had seemed like his condescension and sometimes with curiosity about the scar on his inner arm and the motorcycle helmet and what he did that he could play rac-quetball on a weekday afternoon.

The traffic slows at the top of the plaza, not far from the granite block where Lance and I were sitting, just a week after my father died, when Lance told me that Alice, habitual obituary reader, had shown him my father's obit in the *Times*. It was a warm day in late May, and I was wearing a loose sleeveless dress with sneakers and a hoodie tied round my waist. Thinking about Alice reading my father's obituary, a chill passed through me. I untied the hoodie and pulled it over my head.

Alice had recognized my name in the list of family members as the person she'd emailed when she was researching schools for Zena. That, though, was not the detail in the obit that had caught Alice's attention. What had caught her attention, she told Lance, was that the renowned architect's father had been the general manager of a hotel in the same Swiss village where her grandparents sought refuge during the war. Alice thought the architect's father could have been the man who denied her grandfather work because he was a Jew.

My father's death still felt raw. We were in public—not a place where I could hide my face in Lance's shoulder.

'I'm sorry. I shouldn't have told you that.'

'No. I'm glad you did.' I'd never met my father's father, but my mother had once told me he was a decent sort and that he'd written her a letter, asking her to be patient with his son: 'He described your father as a young man who, if there was a line, had to cross it, as though not crossing it made him a coward. He wrote that he blamed himself. He'd been weak during the war—not a good example for his son.'

'You have to take what Alice said with a grain of salt. She worshipped her grandfather. He believed that everyone in the Swiss village where they stayed during the war were to some degree collaborators.'

'I visited the hotel where my father grew up. Twice—once as a girl, and then later with Henry. It looked like a drawing from a children's picture book: perched over a lake, with a glass-ceilinged atrium and a wood-paneled library. The guests included all of these eccentric people, some of whom returned year after year.'

The cab is moving again. The pattern in the paving of the circle,

Lanec once told me, was based on traditional designs by Black quilters and is now being marred by skateboarders.

Whether or not Alice is right about my grandfather having harmed hers, the man must have made a lot of compromises to keep that hotel afloat.

'I'LL GET OUT HERE,' I SAY AT LANCE'S CORNER. IT'S NOT A PRECAU-tion Lance ever suggested: the buzzer to the fourth floor studio apart-ment he uses as his writing office is at the top of the exterior stairs, along with the buzzers for the studio adjacent to his where a flutist lives and the third-floor apartment occupied by medical students. Were Alice to spot me, she would have no reason to think I was visiting Lance rather than one of these other persons, any of whose mother or aunt I might be.

My concern is about myself. Unlike Lance, I can't think about our affair as separate from our marriages, though I am able to think about his office as not part of his house. But were I to see Alice (I insisted Lance show me pictures of Zena and Wally and her) coming or going from the brownstone, the room where Lance and I spend afternoons together would become part of Alice's home. Alice's home, where she wakes her children every morning and gives them breakfast and checks their back-packs and writes a note for the nanny about after-school schedules and errands to be done and dinner food prep.

Were I to see Alice, I would never be able to enter her home again.

6

LANCE

LANCE IS WRAPPING A PHOTOGRAPH OF ONE OF THE BAMIYAN BUD-
dhas, before they were destroyed, when Neil calls from the airport in Mel-
bourne. He's about to get on a plane to LA, where he'll connect to New
York. 'Sorry, mate,' he says. He meant to call last week. He got caught up
in meetings with the Australian partners for the documentary he's working on about the parallels between the experiences of indigenous peoples
in New South Wales and Native Americans in the Dakotas. He'll be at the
Soho Grand for four days, meeting with the American partners, before he
heads to the Pine Ridge Reservation. Maybe they can have a meal?

'Don't be a dope. You'll stay with me. The kids love having you here.
Alice too.'

Lance wonders if he should tell Neil that it's Ana's sixtieth birthday,
that she'll be here soon, but before he has a chance, Neil tells him he has
to jump. His plane is boarding.

'REALLY?' ANA SAID WHEN HE TOLD HER THAT FOR HIM, THEIR
affair began at the diner, the afternoon they met. 'Not at the Rubin
Museum?'

At the museum, three months after the diner, he'd recognized her
without even seeing her face. He stood for a minute examining her from

the rear before he approached: her slim hips, the outline of her spine visible through her white blouse.

She looked like Neil—the same height but slighter, her hip points poking through her drapey black pants. Even more than her body, it was the concentrated way she peered, neck crooked, at the tiny yogini inside the case that reminded him of Neil, who'd so vividly described the majesty and tragedy of the scarred Bamiyan Buddhas the night they'd met in a Kabul bar, Lance felt compelled to see them himself.

In a class at NYU, he'd read the Hemingway story about the girl in the Spanish train station who says the distant hills look like elephants and then pleads to the man who's impregnated her and now wants only to manipulate her, 'Would you please please please please please please please stop talking?' After reading the story, Lance had decided there are two kinds of people: people who can sense numinous undercurrents with their eddies of wonder, and people who cannot. Watching Ana that afternoon at the Rubin Museum, he saw that like Neil she was in the tribe alive to those currents. He remembered how at the diner she'd seemed to not know what to do when Alice hadn't shown up, and it occurred to him that while she was now in too much possession of herself for seven *pleases*, she'd once been that *please please* girl and there still existed in her the vestiges of someone who could be pushed around.

It disgusts him that as a teenager, he fashioned himself after men like the one in the story: the character's quiet slick-talking, as though all he cared about was what would be best for the pregnant woman. Lance had pulled that bullshit with the Joni Mitchell look-alike girl, leaving her alone in Kabul with her spider phobia after he'd met Neil and heard about the Bamiyan Buddhas looming like giants over a dusty village and he wanted to go there himself. Convincing her that what he wanted was best for them both. And when he came back from Kabul, she was whimpering in a chair in the hostel's kitchen with her hair in greasy clumps and red patches surrounding the scratches she'd made on her arms.

He'd been that man because he'd been raised by that man. As a boy, he idolized his father who, with his gaudy watch and pompadour and bookie racket, knew all the bartenders and union bosses and drug dealers and junkie prostitutes in Atlantic City. Idolized him until he grew to hate

him, a hate that cemented when he brought Gina, the only woman he'd
fallen in love with before Ana, and her five-year-old daughter to his parents' house for Christmas. His mother, her hands by then too misshapen
from arthritis to keep running a daycare from the sunporch, bought Gina's daughter a ballerina dress and a nurse Barbie and a child's book of
illustrated New Testament stories, all of which she wrapped in Santa paper and put under the tree. His father, star-struck by Gina, who'd been a
swimsuit model and cocaine addict before she moved from Rio to Kauai
to sing with a bossa nova cover band, felt her up in the kitchen.

Afraid Lance would cause a scene and ruin the holiday for her daughter, Gina waited until they were back in Hawaii to tell him. 'Hey,' she
said when Lance clenched his fists. 'Grow up. It's something old men
do when they've drunk too much.' She was right—his father did drink
too much, after which he got red in the face and said and did stupid
things—but Lance's revulsion at his father was like a pinhole in an air
mattress and the love for his old man slowly seeped out.

Sometimes he thinks he married Alice because his father would never
feel her up and she'd never been that *please please please please please please
please* girl. She, Alice, would have been the doctor counseling the girl to
do what was best for her.

AFTER HE'D RECOGNIZED ANA IN THE MUSEUM, HE CROSSED THE
empty gallery and stood behind her, looking over her shoulder at the
bejeweled statue. He counted to three before tapping her arm. It was the
first time he'd touched her.

She turned and he saw her look of surprise.

'Lance,' he said. 'The kindergarten guy.'

'Yes. I remember you.' A pink scrim rose from the open buttons of
her white blouse.

He pointed at the case. 'The Yogini Nairatmya. It's my favorite piece
here.'

She shifted so she was again facing the statue. 'I've been trying to figure out what's going on. She's sitting on a male figure. And then there's
that chain of tiny skulls . . .'

'Each time I see her, I think of the wife in that Hemingway story who scorns her husband after he runs from a lion.'

He immediately regretted mentioning Hemingway, on his mind because of the *please please* girl. The old man had fallen from his pedestal. Many women no longer liked him.

'"The Short Happy Life of Francis Macomber." That story shattered Hemingway for me. All his bluster fell away and I saw how terrified he was of women. How much he hated them.'

At the diner, she'd been drinking green tea with lemon. 'I'm headed to the café. I'm not a tea drinker except for here. They brew their own in Nepalese pots. Care to join me?'

She hesitated for a beat. She was taller than he'd realized, her shoulders nearly reaching his, but slighter too, her wrists the size of a child's. Before she could respond, he cupped her elbow and led her to the stairs and then to a table in the corner of the café.

When he returned with the pot of tea, he took off his bomber jacket. She blushed as he caught her glancing at the scar on his forearm.

She asked what brought him here. He explained that he was writing a book about the Bamiyan Buddhas, attacked by the Taliban with rockets and anti-aircraft guns and dynamite in March of 2001; he'd come to look at some artifacts from the same era.

He removed the tea ball from the ceramic pot and poured Ana a cup of the murky brew. He'd first seen the Buddhas, he told her, when he was nineteen and went to Bamiyan with a filmmaker he'd met in a bar. Eighteen years later, when Neil, the filmmaker, began work on a documentary about the lost Buddhist history of the Bamiyan region, he contacted Lance to ask if he'd come along as a production assistant.

'By then, the country was under the control of the Taliban. Neil knew from our traveling together that I got it. If we treated the Taliban men with respect—asking permission before we filmed, not trying to pull the wool over anyone's eyes—they'd be more likely to cooperate.'

He'd made a third visit to Bamiyan after the Buddhas had been blasted, this time as a journalist. It was the summer before 9/11. Two months later, and he'd never have been granted access. With the help of a fixer, he was able to interview several people in contact with Mullah

Mohammed Omar, who'd ordered the Buddhas' destruction. His goal in the book, whose proposal he was writing then, was to explicate all points of view, including that of the mullah, and to describe the internecine but also fundamentally philosophical arguments about what to do with the remains of the statues.

He paused to gauge Ana's reaction. She nodded slightly.

'There are concrete-minded people who think the act of understanding is an endorsement. When they hear that I interviewed associates of the man behind the dynamiting, they brand me as a supporter of terrorism.'

Instinctively, he glanced around the museum café, making sure that no one was in earshot. 'Even worse for me, as a journalist, is the accusation that I'm a rube believing Taliban lies. I know I've succeeded in depicting another person if I can imagine myself so fully in their shoes, I can feel their words coming out of my mouth. But that doesn't mean I lose my own point of view.'

'What was the reason for attacking the Buddhas?'

He downed the rest of his tea. As a surfer, he'd learned to recognize watershed moments, moments when you had to heed caution so as not to break your back and moments when you had to shove it aside to catch what might be the best ride of your life. 'Let me show you a section of my friend's documentary, from before the Buddhas were attacked. It will make a lot more sense to you if you see the village.'

The look he gave her was one he'd given his buddies as a teenager, when he had no doubt that *he* would swim into the roiling waves before a storm. Buddies whose fear he could smell. He wouldn't have put money on whether she would take the dare. If he'd had to bet, he would have said no. But she whispered okay, so softly he wasn't certain she'd said anything until he saw her putting on her coat.

Outside the museum, he fastened the extra helmet he kept strapped to the rear of his motorcycle under her chin. She climbed on behind him, and placed her hands lightly on his shoulders. He'd forgotten to instruct her to lean with him, but either she'd ridden bikes before or she intuited his movements. For a few seconds, as they rounded Columbus Circle, he felt her cheek rest on his back.

He parked the bike in front of his house. Ana followed him up the

stairs to his studio. It was nearly four. Marguerite would have dropped
Zena off at her math tutor's building and gone to fetch Wally from his
fencing class, the timing orchestrated by Alice, still at work. From the
stairwell, he could faintly hear the flutist who rented the other half of
the top floor.

Once inside, Ana sat motionless on the edge of the futon while he
loaded a cassette into the video recorder. She looked terrified. He wished
he could touch the hollow in her neck and tell her to breathe. Instead he
pressed start.

Neil's documentary opened with a panoramic shot of a lush green
valley. There were rushing streams and the snowcapped peaks of the surrounding Kush range that save for the oases of pomegranate trees could
have been Montana. Everyone he'd shown the film had been fascinated
and had lots of questions, but what he was looking for in Ana, who he
watched from his rolling desk chair, was something different: awe. And
he saw it on her face when her eyes opened wide with the first shot of the
two ancient Buddhas, each in its own grotto dug into the limestone cliff.

In a voice-over, Neil explained that the Buddhas are thought to
date from the sixth century. The smaller one, standing at 120 feet on
the eastern side, is presumed to be Buddha Shakyamuni, the historical
Buddha, while the other, on the western side and 175 feet in height,
depicts Buddha Vairochana, known as the transcendent Buddha. The
stone bodies were clad in the flowing robes of the Greek era when they'd
been carved, prior to Islam arriving in Afghanistan, the heads sculpted
such that a person, having climbed through the tunnels that lead to the
tops of the statues, could walk behind them.

Long before their dynamiting by the Taliban, Neil continued in the
voice-over, the visages of the two Buddhas had been defaced, first by
assailants during the reign of Genghis Khan and then by more recent
zealots, both cleaving to Islam's prohibition of human representation.
For many of the Hazara people who live in the village shadowed by the
statues, the figures are divorced from their Buddhist origins and are
viewed, instead, as the frozen forms of lovers tragically forbidden to
each other.

Lance wanted to roll his chair next to Ana so he could kiss her, but he knew it was too soon. Instead, when the film clip ended, he took a folder from his desk.

'You asked why the Taliban destroyed the Buddhas.' He rifled through the folder until he found the newspaper clipping he was looking for, then pointed at a highlighted passage. 'This is from a published interview by a Pakistani journalist with Mullah Omar.'

> I did not want to destroy the Bamiyan Buddha. In fact, some foreigners came to me and said they would like to conduct the repair work of the Bamiyan Buddha that had been slightly damaged due to rains. This shocked me. I thought, these callous people have no regard for thousands of living human beings—the Afghans who are dying of hunger, but they are so concerned about non-living objects like the Buddha. This was extremely deplorable. That is why I ordered its destruction. Had they come for humanitarian work, I would have never ordered the Buddha's destruction.

'Do you agree with him?' she asked.

'I understand how Mohammed Omar felt. Many Afghans felt the same way. They'd tolerated the Buddhas as a tourist attraction despite their being idolatrous. It felt to them like a slap in the face that western organizations seemed more concerned with these statues than the million starving children in their country.'

He hesitated. This woman would never call him Osama and threaten to bomb his house, as had a man who phoned into a radio show where Lance had been a guest, but that did not mean she understood.

'Do I think it was a tragedy that these Buddhas, some of the oldest and the largest that remain, were destroyed? Of course. It was a symbolic, not a practical act. It didn't put a grain of rice in anyone's mouth. There were museums that had offered to buy the Buddhas, which would have provided funds for food and medicine. But do I get it why the Taliban fighters I interviewed experienced the interest in restoring the statues rather than feeding the Afghani people as an obliteration of their humanity?'

Ana was studying his face.

'Yes, I get it.'

He props the wrapped photo against his desk. The photo is of the Buddha Vairochana, the transcendent Buddha. Had Neil arrived a day earlier, he would have been able to show it to him.

During the three weeks the documentary crew spent in Bamiyan, they stayed with local families in their cave homes. Their Afghan hosts spent many hours each day gathering wood for the open fires over which they prepared meals for the crew. Hospitality was an obligation under Islamic law, and although their Afghan hosts were paid, they treated the crew like guests.

The film crew had been working for ten days straight when Neil announced a day off. Wanting to explore the surrounding area, he and Lance borrowed two dilapidated motorcycles from some villagers. By late afternoon, they'd covered a hundred kilometers, passing farmers in turbans cutting alfalfa by hand and villages with one-room houses built of clay. Dust was baked into their arms and the backs of their necks.

Spotting a stream through a break in the curtain of trees, they stopped to swim. Alone and sheltered from the road, they stripped and waded into the cold mountain water. In the past, when Lance had seen men undressed, he'd responded with a clinical eye: this one had prominent pectorals, that one feline legs. Now, seeing Neil's white skin washed clean from the stream, his long hairless torso, the shock of black curls between his legs, Lance's breath caught. To his horror, he felt an erection, that hardened further when Neil turned toward him with bedroom eyes. As in a dream with a stranger, Lance approached the beautiful naked man. With Neil's hard cock pressing against his own, his heartbeat quickened and a warm sensation pulsed up from his groin. Never having done this before, never having even fantasized it, he sank to his knees and cupping his hands over Neil's firm buttocks sucked Neil off. And then he lay down on the scrub grass and looked up at the white cumulus clouds while Neil did the same to him.

'I'm not gay,' Lance said afterward.

Neil smoothed Lance's hair off his damp forehead. When Neil kissed him, he tasted of Lance's own cum. 'Got it, mate.'

They'd been physically intimate on three more occasions, spread across ten years. During that decade, Lance had never lusted for any other man. The sex had to do with Neil. Like certain paintings that don't fit a category, their connection defied definition. It was nothing new, Neil said. In ancient Greece, men studying in the schools of philosophy that gathered in the agoras of Athens or visiting the baths often pleasured one another, returning home then to wives with whom they did the same.

Neither felt jealous of the other's partners. As Neil put it, could Cindy Sherman be jealous of Dorothea Lange? Could Mark Twain be jealous of George Eliot? When Neil fell in love with a young sculptor, who he lived with for six years, Lance was happy for him. Later, when Lance fell for Gina, Neil welcomed her and her daughter. Not until Lance married Alice, by then five months pregnant with Zena, did he and Neil decide there would be no more sex: it was too important to both of them that their relationship be folded into Lance's new family, and that couldn't happen if they were carrying on behind Alice's back.

Neither has told anyone about the river, the salty taste of each other, the cumulus clouds. It's a landscape they alone share.

THE WINDOWS OF LANCE'S STUDIO LOOK OUT OVER THE GARDEN: the Japanese forest grass, the bluestars that attract butterflies in the spring, the slatted teak table shaded by a cantilevered umbrella. During the seven years of their affair, Ana has never set foot in the garden. She once joked that she'd give up a month of their lovemaking if they could sit together at the outdoor table, drinking tea.

The first time he kissed her, leaning in from his rolling desk chair, the newspaper clipping of the interview with Mullah Omar still in her hand, she wept. Wept as if she'd broken something precious, then listened as though to a fairy tale while Lance explained that nothing between them would change how he feels about Alice, and it could be the same for her with Henry.

'I believe in marriage. For me, that means Alice and I will work as a team to raise our kids and we'll stay together as long as we're both alive. But Al is not my erotic partner. I don't mean we don't have sex. We do. But it's not the way we connect.'

He put the newspaper clipping back in the folder, then moved next to her on the futon, inhaling her hair, the scent he'd first noticed when he sat across from her at the diner: the hint of wild berries and ginger. 'I no longer think it's simply a mismatch in our erotic imaginations. It's more basic. For Al, sex is fundamentally a physical sensation. It brings her pleasure like chocolate or a breeze on a hot day, but it's not part of a creative space for her.'

'A creative space?'

'Yes. Sex is part of my creative space.' He paused. 'Same as for you.'

She raised an eyebrow.

'It's written all over your body. The way you dress. The way you move.' He touched her mouth, ran a finger over her chin and down her neck. 'I've accepted that I need to go elsewhere for sexual satisfaction that's more—sorry to sound crude—than getting off. It doesn't seem that different from other things I do without Al. Surf, ski, travel to places unmarred by tourist amenities.'

His hand settled on her breast. 'Not yet,' she whispered. She needed to talk more first. She wanted to know about Alice, what she's like. 'Aside from thinking about sex as chocolate.'

'You want me to tell you about Alice now?'

She nodded.

He sighed. He hadn't learned much from his father that he felt proud of, but he had learned from him how to size up a situation. With Ana, he saw there could be no rushing. He crushed a pillow, wedged it beneath his neck, and rested against the wall.

'Alice is one-of-a-kind. There are people who put in what they deem an acceptable level of effort and there are people, like Alice, who always go to the max. She never gives up, whether it's finding the right shoes for Wally with his pronated gait or figuring out why a twelve-year-old patient is still wetting his bed. Put that together with a brain that operates better than almost anyone else's, and Alice is a superwoman.'

Ana had taken off her boots and was sitting now cross-legged on the futon. He loved Alice, he explained, but he'd never fallen in love with her. It wasn't physical. It was more fundamental: a limitation in his character. A need for mystery. 'There's no getting to the bottom of Alice because she's lacking in guile. What you see is who she is. Basically, I understood her fully the first day we met.'

'How did you meet?'

He touched Ana's ankle, traced the tiny bones. He could feel himself sinking into her, in a way that hadn't happened since Gina, when he feared he would kill any man who put a hand on her—and that included his father.

He'd met Alice five years ago, he said, though with his life now so different, it seemed longer. Then, he'd been living in Kauai, in a small house he owned in Poipu, splitting his time between writing and surfing. It was dusk and he'd just come out of the water. Near where he'd dumped his stuff was a woman in a beach chair, in baggy khaki pants and a canvas hat, reading what appeared to be an academic journal.

'She caught me checking out the title, *Pediatric Emergency Care*, and gave me a look that suggested she knew it was weird beach entertainment, but she didn't give a damn. We struck up a conversation about the article she was reading—the treatment of hypothermia in children, which I re-membered a bit about from my lifeguard training when I was sixteen.' He paused, hoping this was enough.

'Continue.'

He thought about joking that he could give her pen and paper to take notes, but he saw she was dead serious.

'When I told Alice I had to get something to eat, she asked if she could tag along. I was impressed that she asked outright. Usually, people just drop hints. I took her to my regular poke place. That's when I learned that if you ask Alice about herself, she'll tell you everything.'

'What did she tell you?'

'Mostly her family's Jewish story. Her grandfather had been the president of her family's synagogue. Her father was an orthodontist, her mother a guidance counselor in the next town. They celebrated the holi-days, but more in a cultural than religious way. In high school, she spent a summer on a kibbutz in Israel and freaked her parents out when she returned a Zionist zealot.'

The room was growing dim. He turned on a lamp. With the light on her face, he could see the lines around Ana's eyes, but they only made her appear more delicate. Like the patina on a porcelain vase.

'Alice's Zionism lasted through college, then crumbled during a medical school rotation in Gaza, when she saw firsthand the treatment of Palestinians. She ditched her plans for a pulmonology residency and instead did pediatrics, after which she went to work for Doctors Without Borders. That's Alice in a nutshell.'

'And what did you tell her?'

'What did I tell Alice about myself the night we met?'

'Yes.'

'Clever lady. Getting me to tell you my story through Alice.'

'Go on.'

'Mostly I told her about my time in Afghanistan, where I'd seen some of the same diseases she'd seen in Gaza, and how I traveled on to Kathmandu, where I met Elsa, a writer from *Rolling Stone*, who was chasing a failed romance with a photographer. How, after he split, she appointed me her rebound guy.'

Elsa. He hadn't thought about her in a long time. 'Even for Elsa, none too picky about her bed partners, we didn't last long. I was too young for her, but as her parting gift, she recommended me to her editor for a piece about the hippie kids flocking to Dharamshala.'

One assignment, he continued, tumbled into another. By the time he got back to the States, he had a reputation as a gonzo journalist for off-the-grid destinations. An agent approached him about doing a Hunter Thompson–style memoir about his travel adventures. 'I don't think more than a dozen people bought that book, but then, out of the blue, it was optioned for film and made into a movie in France. The money was nothing special, but it was enough for me to buy the house in Poipu, where I was living when I met Alice.'

'And?'

'And what?'

'What happened with Alice after your dinner?'

'It was not postcard pink sunset Hawaii or anything you could really call dinner. We're talking a picnic table next to a parking lot, plastic forks, beer in Styrofoam cups.'

Did he really have to say more? Ana was watching him intently. Yes, it seemed he did. 'As I was gathering up our trash, Alice asked me if I'd like to have sex with her. To be honest, it hadn't crossed my mind. I said yes mostly because I thought it would be hurtful to her if I said no.'

'That's terrible.'

'It wasn't terrible. It was like Sleeping Beauty without the beauty or the prince. Alice was thirty-nine and had only had sex with three other men. Really two—I'll spare you the details why the third didn't count. She'd never had an orgasm with any of them. I was forty-three and, I'm not proud to say this, I'd never been with a woman because of her mind.'

In another hour, Marguerite and his kids would return. He needed to get to the end. 'Three days later, Alice went back to New York. Neither of us expected we'd be in touch again, but then she discovered she was pregnant. She'd always hoped to have a child and couldn't believe her good luck at getting pregnant at her age. She gallantly offered to have the baby on her own and release me from any obligations.'

He inhaled deeply. 'It was Alice's giving me the choice that made me realize I wanted to have a family.'

He wondered what Ana would think of him if he told her he'd had what he thought of as an epiphany: It made sense to choose a partner based on who would be a good parent rather than sexual infatuation. 'We got married, and from there fell down the rabbit hole of having a baby and buying and renovating this house and then having another baby.'

He drew her toward him. 'End of story.'

ON THE YEAR ANNIVERSARY OF THEIR FIRST TIME TOGETHER, HE replaced the futon with a queen-sized mattress.

'Won't Alice wonder why you did this?' Ana asked.

They were lying atop the new mattress. He rolled her toward him so he could see her face. She knew that Alice never came to his writing studio. That she didn't even have a key. So what was Ana asking?

'If it weren't for Alice, I wouldn't know you.' He spread his hands across the wings of her shoulder blades and kissed the hollow between her breasts. 'It's all Alice's fault,' he whispered. 'Alice who leaves no stone unturned.'

Now, in honor of Ana's sixtieth birthday, he changes the sheets. Ana will notice. She always does.

The last time Ana was here, she told him that she's been thinking about a fairy tale she used to read to Simon. Lance had probably read his kids a version of it. There are three brothers. One by one, they each meet the same beggar on the road. The oldest self-absorbed brother tells the beggar not to bother him; he has his own problems. The mean middle one kicks the beggar in the shin. Only the youngest gives the beggar the food in his knapsack and fetches him clean water to drink from a stream. And for this, the youngest brother is rewarded by the beggar, who's really a king, with the hand of his daughter. 'I'm not looking for a reward,' Ana said. 'Only to do better.'

Hearing the fairy tale, he was flooded with misery, though he'd been unable to say why. Now it dawns on him. He's not the beggar, not one of the brothers, not the king, not the king's daughter.

He can't say who he is in Ana's story, only that nothing about him will help her do better.

7

ANA

I PUSH THE BUZZER FOR LANCE'S STUDIO. AT THE BEGINNING OF our affair, we talked so endlessly about how we're both committed to our spouses—both exceptionally good people, better, we agree, than either of us—I began to think the conversation was vulgar foreplay and insisted we stop. Now I look over my shoulder. The street is empty save for an elderly man walking his golden retriever and a UPS delivery person.

When I told Fiona that if I ever saw Alice, I'd have to turn and leave, she looked at me sadly, as though I were a child who'd just realized Santa Claus is not real. 'You're stuck, love, in a rigid way of thinking. Marriage is not a thing. It's a relationship within a context—for most of recorded history and still in most of the world, it's basically a business partnership. The idea that men were truly expected to be monogamous didn't become widespread until the Romantic Age.'

Lance buzzes me in, and I climb the carpeted stairs. Museum-framed photographs, all portraits, hang on the walls. I inquired about them the first time I came here to see the documentary about Bamiyan. Most of them had been taken by the photographers on his assignments, Lance told me, though he'd taken two himself. He likes portraits, he said, because if you look in the subjects' eyes, you can imagine a way into their minds. Studying the faces of some of the Taliban men had helped him understand that there's no such thing as a *senseless act*. 'We may be outraged by the rationale, but that doesn't mean it doesn't exist.' He considered me as though wondering if I was following his train of thought.

I nodded, unsure if I was agreeing *with* or *to* something. There was something respectful, maybe even compassionate, about the idea that people never do anything without a reason. Had it been Henry, with kindness encoded in his DNA, who'd said this, it would not have surprised me, but coming from this lanky boy-man with his disarming looks, it felt discordant, like rounding a bend on a dusty trail, as I'd once done hiking with Fiona, to discover a hundred feet of bushes laden with ripe blackberries.

It was intimidating, at first, to realize not only how much more of the world Lance has seen than I have, but how different his lens has been. Yes, as children George and I traveled to Europe and North Africa and South America to meet our father, but our destinations were the hotels where he was working. We were doted upon on account of our father's *starchitect* status, but I never felt I was anyone's guest. Before Henry's back injury, we'd visited the usual places where affluent travelers go: Iceland, Turkey, Costa Rica, the Galapagos, Japan. We never did the *If this is Tuesday, it must be Belgium* sort of trips, but we were still, at heart, tourists joining other tourists in ticket queues: looking at relics or artworks or vistas displayed as experiences to be checked off a bucket list. We never traveled the way Lance has: seeing what's not packaged for consumption; eating and sleeping with residents of a place, rather than being served by them. Travel as an act of imagination—a window into understanding others, past and present.

Not until my second visit to Lance's studio was I able to take in my surrounds: the watery blue of the walls bleached by the fading afternoon light to the shade of whale bones, the glass artist's table that serves as a desk, the Palladian windows overlooking the yard. Lance stood behind me, his fingers splayed across the plane between my navel and pubic bone, while I studied the brick pavers to a tree swing, the long grasses flanking a darkly stained fence. He nuzzled my neck as I asked who'd created the garden. 'Al is too good for beauty, too generous for orderliness. I'm the one who can't tolerate ugliness and disarray. It's one of my worst traits.'

Lance claims that with my long, narrow bones and pale lashes and hair, I'm the physical embodiment of the same aesthetic with which he'd designed the landscape: 'The perfection of no excess. The anti-Rubens.' 'You mean,' I said, 'I look like a fourteen-year-old boy.'

You, this is all you, I think now, as Lance appears at the studio door, barefoot, in jeans and a white T-shirt.

He pulls me inside, closes the door, and encircles me with his gym arms. 'Happy birthday, baby.'

'Baby, I am not.'

'You'll always be my baby.'

He covers my mouth with his and I feel my body taking dominion over my mind, as it's done since the first time I came here. Today, though, is my sixtieth birthday. I refuse to let a number define me, but still, it feels like a portal. A portal to? Well, isn't that the point? To something I don't yet know.

'I can't,' I whisper.

'Yes you can.'

I push against Lance's chest and slither away from the door.

'I'll make you a green tea and we'll talk it over. Okay?'

'Okay to the tea.'

My first afternoon here, when Lance told me how he'd met Alice and announced *end of story* and guided me back onto the pillows, I also said *I can't.* My breath was so shallow, I feared I might faint. He nodded after I said that since I'd met Henry, I'd never been with anyone else. I didn't need to ask how he knew. I knew how he knew—it was written all over me. And I knew, too, as my *I can't* dissolved and he kissed the mountainous ridge of my knuckles and I touched the hardened seam of his scar, that what would happen soon would not be the first time for him.

He lifted my hand from his arm and brushed it across his mouth. 'You've been eyeballing my scar since the day we met in the diner.'

'That obvious?'

'Is this what you do with your clients? Find an entry point into their stories?'

'Actually, it is.'

'Nothing original about this one. Protagonist: rube American. Setting: a club in Zagreb, where rube comes to the defense of a local girl.'

'How many others?'

'How many other knife scars do I have?'

I paused, taking in that the scar was from a knife. 'You know that's not what I'm asking.'

Lance raised an eyebrow. 'You want me to tell you how many other women?'

'My mother's an actuary. I grew up with statistics. It would help me to know.'

'Three. Three infidelities over five years of marriage. So, math lady, you figure out the rate per year.'

'No one-night stands? No flings?'

'I stopped those when I got married.'

The real numbers on my mind that first afternoon were our ages. I was fifty-three. Lance was forty-eight. He tipped my chin upward when I pointed out the five-year difference. 'You're ageless,' he said. 'Odds are I'm the one who's going to suffer here.'

Now I'm sixty, I think, as Lance hands me a mug and sits beside me. Sixty years old. Odds are we're both going to suffer.

Lance kisses my throat and slowly moves his mouth downward. 'My first sixty-year-old woman,' he says. 'I like it.'

'I really don't want to.'

He slides his hand under my T-shirt, and I'm sure he can feel my heart beating. 'Liar,' he whispers.

'I'm sweaty from yoga.'

'Love sweaty, babe.'

'I'm going to spill the tea.'

He takes my cup and puts it on the floor.

AFTERWARD, I THINK ABOUT WHAT SAGE GORDON IN HIS BIRKEN-stocks would say: You made the choice. Own it. Don't ruin it with regret.

I reach a hand out from under the sheet and trace the scar on Lance's inner arm. 'All these years, and you still never really told me how you got this.' With my finger on the craggy line, I feel as though I'm pointing at the boundary between us. The parts of him that are separate from me. 'All you ever told me was it had to do with your defending a girl in a Zagreb bar.'

'That is the story.'

'That's not a story.'

'You want, pun intended, the bloody details.'

'As my father was fond of saying, God is in the details.'

Lance turns onto his side so he's propped on an elbow, facing me. 'Really? You want me to tell you now? On your birthday?'

I nod.

With his free hand, Lance pushes my hair off my forehead. 'It happened a few months after I'd taken the *Let's Go* job. An editor assigned me what was then Yugoslavia—not a place on even low-budget travelers' radar. It seemed like a test. What could I come up with for Zagreb.'

He pauses, deciding, I think, how much to tell me.

'I got there by train, arriving at dusk at this surprisingly grand nineteenth-century station. I was studying the frieze on the façade and jotting some notes I hoped I could turn into something when a street kid started pulling on my shirt. He looked like he was eight or nine, but once he started talking, a mile a minute in decent English, I could tell he was older. Before I could say anything, he snatched my backpack and insisted on escorting me to a hotel.'

I picture the child: large dark eyes, beat-up sneakers, an American T-shirt.

'At the hotel, the kid gestured for me to lean down and whispered in my ear that I should ask for a different room. The one the clerk was giving me had a broken toilet. I thanked him, handed him a few dollars and the remains of a pack of gum, and assumed he'd be off, but when I came downstairs an hour later, there he was, crouched outside the hotel door. I knew I shouldn't encourage him, but he looked so ravenous, I bought him a meal and then, after we'd eaten, asked him to take me somewhere with live music.'

From the way Lance is watching me, I know that he's getting now to the heart of the story. I tighten the sheet around my naked body.

'He walked me to this divey club. I handed him a few more bucks and figured he'd finally be off.'

Lance looks at me, and I nod. I have no idea where this story is going, only that it's not going anywhere good.

'I was sitting at a table, having a few beers and listening to a local crooner, when I heard a scream. I looked over, and a guy with tattoos on his arms and neck was hitting the young woman beside him at the bar. I grabbed the guy, to pull him away from her. Next thing I knew, he slashed my arm with a knife.'

'Oh my God. Did they call the police? Take you to a hospital?'

'I wish. Instead, I saw the blood streaming onto the floor and something snapped in me. I landed a throat punch and the guy crashed to the ground. The kid jumped out—he must have been hiding in a corner. He grabbed my hand and led me through back alleys until we got to the edge of town, where he lived in a little apartment with his grandmother. She butterfly-bandaged my arm.'

'You never saw a doctor?'

'The kid wouldn't let me leave. He claimed I'd killed the guy with the knife and the family was dangerous: they'd been Ustaše during the war and if they found me, I'd never be seen again.'

I'd imagined various stories about how Lance got his scar, but not this. 'Did you believe him?'

'I knew the Ustaše had been even more brutal than the Nazis. Alice's grandparents left Zagreb after they came into power. But I didn't think I'd actually killed the guy. I would have had to crush his windpipe with the punch. And if I'd killed him, someone would have made it their business to find me.'

'Did you ever learn why the guy was hitting the woman?'

Lance shifts to his side. He touches my cheek. 'Do you really want me to tell you?'

I nod.

'He was coming on to her and he put a hand up her skirt and discovered she was trans.'

My stomach clenches. For a moment, I think I might be sick.

'It was Yugoslavia in the 1970s. The country doesn't even exist now.'

I imagine a map with lines dissolving. 'Does Alice know?' I ask.

'Know what?'

'How you got the scar.'

'Not beyond what I told you when you first asked.' He smiles. 'She's not a meddler like you.'

'You should tell her.'

'You don't think it would be upsetting for Alice that relatives of the guy who knifed me might have been the murderers her grandparents escaped?'

No more, I think, than my hearing about a trans woman being hit in a bar.

I want to ask more—Did Lance hear what happened to the trans woman? —but it's getting late. 'I have to go. I have a client soon.'

'Not until I give you your birthday present.'

Lance gets up from the bed. I'm not blind to the changes in his body since we met—a slackening of his belly, some gray pubic hairs—but it's still easy to imagine him as the sixteen-year-old lifeguard who saved a brother and sister from a riptide or the twentysomething coming to the rescue of a woman in a Zagreb club.

Propped against the side of his desk is a package covered in green and gold paper. Lance hands it to me. Sitting up, I unwrap a framed photograph.

'It's the Buddha Vairochana—the larger of the two.'

A stone face stares out, impassive to those who for over a millennium made pilgrimages to stand at its feet.

'I bought it for you the last time I was in Kabul. An Afghan photographer took it three days before the statues were dynamited.'

'You were thinking then about my birthday?'

'Of course, babe. I think about you every day. Every hour.'

I study the Buddha's face, scarred by acts of earlier hatred. Chastising is the word that comes to mind, but also beautiful in its cold imperfection.

'Thank you. It's a magnificent gift.'

Lance rewraps the photo and sets it on his desk. He pulls on his jeans and sits in his desk chair. 'Since I was last in Bamiyan, a German group reconstructed the feet of the smaller Buddha, and a Chinese couple funded a laser show that creates the illusion that you're seeing the statues as they were before 2001.'

He looks at me intently. 'I'm going again in September. You should come with me.'

Lance has gone to Bamiyan twice since we met. Both times he asked me to accompany him, and both times I was tempted. Tempted not because of the Buddhas, but because it would be amazing to experience traveling with him: how his antennae go up for people who hold the keys to the hidden story.

'It's the best season to go there, without excessive heat or rain or snow. We've never been away together. It's time.'

'We were in Poipu.'

'That was not going away together. You tacked me on to the end of your hiking trip with Fiona.'

It's true. Two years ago I accompanied Fiona on a trip to the Napali coast of Kauai, where she'd wanted to go since she was ten and saw photos in her parents' *National Geographic* of the cliffs sharp as incisors and the bays the blue of Navajo turquoise. It was the beginning of March, our time in Kauai overlapping with the two weeks Lance spends alone each year at his house in Poipu before his family joins him for his children's spring break. I stayed after Fiona returned, taking a hotel room close to Lance's house, which I hoped would make the five extra days feel less deceitful. There was no difference, I told myself, having sex with Lance in his Hawaii house than being with him in his studio in New York. But it was different. We'd never before actually slept together, made love at dawn. We were seven thousand miles from our spouses and children.

Our last morning in Poipu, Lance told me his fantasy that Alice and Henry would die young enough for us to live together. 'We'll get married, then.' I was dismayed at his wishing—and in that moment my joining him in wishing—that our spouses would die before us. As for getting married, I'd witnessed enough women, wives and girlfriends, cycle through my father's life to understand that marriages and affairs are different animals.

I kick my feet out from under the sheets. 'Now I really have to go. Not a word more.'

USUALLY, THERE ARE FEW CABS IN LANCE'S NEIGHBORHOOD, BUT today I'm lucky. There's one approaching as I reach the corner. I place the photo, wrapped in the green and gold paper, on the seat beside me. When the driver catches my eye in the rearview mirror, I have the awful thought that he can smell the residue of Lance between my legs. If there's no traffic, I'll be home in ten minutes: time to take a washcloth to my crotch and change my clothes before Bettina arrives.

I turn off the taxi TV and crack the window, my mind still on the trans woman who was hit in the Zagreb bar. *Do not go there,* I tell myself. It's not good for Simon for you to go there. Think about the trip to Kauai: the intense pleasure of the hiking with Fiona to torrential waterfalls with mists that slowed my heart rate and muted my thoughts.

From the mists, my thoughts shift to Lance's frangipani-scented house. Waking together, reading on the beach while Lance surfed, chopping the dinner vegetables as he cleaned the fish—it all felt more intimate than sex. Learning that we really could live happily together was painful. Could live happily together were we not each married to spouses we would never leave. And then, all of this, buried by the terror of the plane ride home.

'YOU CAN SAY I'M YOUR VAN DRIVER,' LANCE TEASED WHEN I OBjected to his driving me to the airport, afraid we might bump into someone who knew Henry or Alice. 'I'll wear a baseball cap and you can sit in the back of the jeep.'

'Only if we say goodbye in the parking lot.'

'Yes, Ma'am.'

At check-in, I learned that I'd been upgraded for my second flight, the LA to New York leg of the trip. Having always flown economy, it felt pointed that my seatmate was a child, escorted onto the plane by a flight attendant and oblivious to being in first-class. I had the aisle seat and the child—Dory, with a *y*, not an *i*, she announced—had the window seat. She was eight and a quarter years old, going home to her mom in New York after visiting her dad in Santa Monica.

Across the aisle, with no one beside him, was a heavyset man, breathing loudly and blotting his forehead with a paper towel. He ordered a double vodka and orange juice, never unwrapping the complimentary cheese platter.

After the flight attendant brought Dory crayons and two juice boxes and a handful of mini snack bags, Dory asked if I'd like to play hangman. I smiled. I'd not played hangman since Simon was Dory's age.

We played hangman and tic-tac-toe and connect-the-dots, which I taught the child. When she yawned for a second time, I suggested she might like to rest. I lowered her seatback and helped her settle in with a pillow and blanket.

Once Dory was asleep, I leaned down and rifled through the tote bag at my feet for my book. I was rereading *To the Lighthouse*, and the time amusing the child had left me feeling like Mrs. Ramsay. As I sat back in my seat with the book now in my lap, I saw from the corner of my eye the man across the aisle unzipping his laptop case. In the strange way the body recognizes something before the mind, my heart pounded as he opened the laptop's battery compartment and removed what looked like the blade of a surgical knife Henry had once shown me.

I must have emitted a sound because the man looked over at me as he slipped the blade into his seat pocket behind the safety instructions. Everything had taken place so fast, for a moment I thought I'd imagined it all. How could there be a blade in the battery compartment? Hadn't the man gone through the same security scanners I had? But when he made a menacing face and pointed at Dory and drew his forefinger across his throat, I knew I'd not imagined anything.

There are moments when our lives hang in the balance, and if we are to prevail we must access our greatest wisdom and strength and self-control. I instantly recognized that this was one of those moments. It was as if I was speaking to myself in the voice I use with my clients when I say, with their pages stacked on the table before me, that they have to distinguish between what they intend to say and what they've actually written. I heard that voice, talking now to myself, which is a peculiar conceit: the idea that we have different parts with different weights such that a more ethereal orator can address a more corporeal self. *Listen up, Ana. Do not waste a moment puzzling how the blade got on the plane. What matters now is what you do.*

Sweat beaded on the man's hairline. I held up the juice box Dory had not opened and waved it slightly, the way one might a flag at a parade. The man followed my hand with his eyes. I pushed the straw out of its sleeve and into the box and gave it to him. He drank the juice, in three gulps, while I ripped open a packet of Goldfish crackers. Passing the little bag to him, I tried not to stare at the tip of the blade peeking over the top of the safety instructions.

The man stuffed the crackers into his mouth, five or six at a time. He pointed at the book in Dory's seat pocket: a Disney version of *Peter Pan*. 'I know that,' he said. His voice was gravelly, as though there were clots of phlegm on his vocal cords. 'I know that story.'

I pulled the book out of the seat pocket and gave it to him. He flipped through the pages, studying the pictures, but not reading any of the text. It occurred to me that perhaps he couldn't read.

'Should I read it to you?' I asked.

He looked as though he might cry.

I took *Peter Pan* from him and, holding it aloft in the aisle, began:

All children, except one, grow up. They soon know that they will grow up, and the way Wendy knew was this. One day when she was two years old she was playing in a garden, and she plucked another flower and ran with it to her mother. I suppose she must have looked rather delightful, for Mrs. Darling put her hand to her heart and cried, 'Oh, why can't you remain like this for ever!' This was all that passed between them on the subject, but henceforth Wendy knew that she must grow up. You always know after you are two. Two is the beginning of the end.

'Why don't you lower your seatback'—I pointed at Dory— 'and you can relax while you listen.'

The man stared at me. He seemed to be in a trance, and I wondered if he might be hallucinating. I stood so I could reach the button on his chair and, as I'd done with Dory, helped him adjust the seat. I could smell the dried sweat on his forehead: acrid like the remains of cleaning fluids in a public restroom. Removing the thin blue blanket from its plastic envelope, I covered him with it the way I had the child.

After I sat back down, I continued reading aloud from *Peter Pan* until I could tell from the man's light snoring that he'd fallen asleep. I reached into my tote for a pen and paper, wrote a note, and pushed the call button for the flight attendant.

When the attendant arrived, I touched a finger to my lips, pointed at the man across the aisle, and gave her the paper. Reading the note, the attendant clapped her hand to her mouth, and turned on her heels.

A minute later, she was back with a male attendant, who situated himself in the aisle next to the sleeping man while she moved through the first-class cabin, gently shaking the passengers who'd fallen asleep and holding up a piece of cardboard on which was printed EMERGENCY: EXIT IN TOTAL SILENCE. Pantomiming by tapping her mouth the urgency of quiet, she escorted the first-class passengers row by row into the economy section of the plane.

Once the cabin was cleared save for the sleeping child, the sleeping man with the blade, and me, the male attendant signaled for me to stand so the female attendant, who'd returned, could lift Dory from her seat and carry her out. With Dory gone, the copilot emerged from the cockpit, relocking the door behind him. He stood guard, with a pistol in a belt-holster and a hypodermic needle in his hand, watching as the male attendant cuffed the man's wrists to his seat arms.

The man bolted awake. He flailed and screamed while the attendant held him down and the copilot sunk the needle into his thigh.

I DIDN'T CALL HENRY UNTIL I WAS IN THE CAB HEADED HOME. 'I'm fine, I'm fine,' I said over and over, trying to convince myself as much as Henry, before telling him the outlines of what had happened on the plane and after we'd landed—the TSA officials storming the cabin, the questioning they'd put me through.

'Ana,' Henry said. I could hear the alarm in his voice. 'Are you sure you're alright?'

'I am. I'll tell you the rest when I get home.'

I hung up and put on the taxi TV. The story was scrolling across the bottom: Possible hijack deterred on flight from LA to NYC. I'd declined permission for the airline to release my name, so I was identified only as a fifty-eight-year-old woman en route from Hawaii whose cool thinking had prevented what might have been a disaster.

When my cell phone rang with my mother's number, I knew from this breach of her usual email-only policy that the story must have been on the five o'clock news, which she watched religiously. 'It was you, right?' my mother said triumphantly, as though what mattered most was that she'd figured out that I was the woman. I hesitated but then, not wanting to lie, said, 'It was, Mom, but please be discreet about it.' I waited, hoping to hear from my mother some sort of commendation about how I'd handled the situation or at least relief that I was safe, but my mother changed the subject to George. He and Catherine also had a terrible time getting home from their fire and ice vacation. The plane from Anguilla was delayed and they missed their connection. The only seats left on the new flight were economy.

Still, my story must have impacted my mother, or maybe she simply wanted to gloat about having correctly guessed that I was the woman in the news, since she phoned George, who then phoned me just minutes later. George mumbled that he and Catherine were glad I was okay, before beginning a what-the-fuck rant. 'Why didn't you give your name? You were handed a monetize moment: this is *Good Morning America* and *Today* show stuff. A book. A movie with Tilda Swinton playing you.'

PULLING UP TO MY BUILDING NOW, I REMEMBER HENRY WAITING for me on the curb that evening. From his stiff movements, I could tell he'd not used his vaporizer. He held the cab door, then hugged me tightly while the driver gave my bags to Carlos, our evening doorman. 'I could have lost you,' Henry murmured.

Henry made tea while I described the flight, from playing hangman with Dory to the man's scream when he was restrained, and then my decision to not permit airport security to reveal my name to the press.

'To use my brother's word, I don't want to *monetize* the experience.'

Henry nodded.

I was glad not to have to say aloud what I'd been thinking since I'd watched the sedated man carried off the plane on a stretcher: I'd drawn on everything I understood about people—from social work school, from taking care of children, from the work with my clients, from the thousand novels I'd read over half a century by writers who'd depicted the interior lives of the most depraved to the saintliest. Still, there was so much that could have gone wrong. I'd be thumbing my nose at Lady Luck to make myself the heroine of the day. To not see that there'd been white magic at play. The man had fallen under the spell of Peter Pan. Dory had remained asleep.

Henry took my hands in his. 'No truly good deed is advertised.'

I've never told Lance what happened on that plane. Once I realized he hadn't heard, the story apparently not having spread beyond New York local news, I felt an aversion to sharing it with him, though I couldn't say why.

With Carlos standing outside as he'd been that evening when I returned from Kauai, it seems obvious now: Henry's response so elevated my experience, I'd felt it belonged to him as much as me. I'd kept it between us. Between Henry and me.

LANCE CALLS WHILE I'M WAITING FOR THE ELEVATOR. THE LOBBY is empty, Carlos still outside, chatting with a neighbor. I rest the wrapped photo against the wall before I answer.

'You ran out so fast, I didn't get a chance to tell you my real gift.'

'The photograph isn't a real gift?'

'I got a grant to work on the book, so I can pay your way to come with me to Bamiyan.'

I'm not sure if I'm going to laugh or cry. 'And what do you propose I tell Henry?'

'Oh, dear lady, I am a step ahead of thou . . . The truth. Brilliant, yes? You'll tell him I want to hire you to help with my book. And I'll tell Alice the same. We'll be covered by the beautiful truth.'

It's too frivolous an idea to merit Fiona's truth and lies adage. Still, there's a sweetness to it. I study the green and gold wrapping paper and imagine the photo underneath: the expressionless face, the eyes half closed. Imagine sitting with Lance in interviews with the men who carried out the explosions sixteen years ago, with the German restoration experts soldiering on now. Sleeping in the cave home of one of the Hazara families who live in the village at the feet of the destroyed Buddhas: moderate Muslims, Lance has told me, the women wearing hijabs but not long robes, letting their children play cricket and basketball as long as it's not during the call for prayer. Our hosts presuming Lance and I are married.

'We'll fly to Paris, stay at my favorite hotel, tucked behind Saint-Sulpice, and then drive to Marseilles. We can visit my friend Maurice, who'll make us his special bouillabaisse. From there, we'll take a boat to Haifa and buy a used motorcycle to go on to Kabul.'

The night at the Merzouga Dunes is my only experience that comes close to how I picture Bamiyan. With my father and the camel tenders gone to search for Mathilde, the ominous snorting of the tethered animals, my brother calling Mathilde a *cunt*, a word I couldn't define but knew was horrid, I'd been terrified.

'I turned sixty today.'

'Long overdue to make love in a cave.'

'Lance . . .'

'From Kabul, we'll take a four-wheel drive van and then camels on to Bamiyan.'

'Lance . . .'

The elevator arrives and I step inside. I see Lance's jagged scar, the watery blue of his studio walls, the long grasses in his garden. I smell the frangipani outside his window in Kauai.

'Ana,' Lance whispers. When the door closes, we'll lose our connection.

'Ana . . .'

8

GEORGE

AT FOUR O'CLOCK ON THE AFTERNOON OF HIS SISTER'S SIXTIETH birthday, George Koehl is in the wine cellar he installed in a former elevator machinery room in the basement of his building, selecting the bottles to be delivered for her party. He pays the co-op three hundred dollars a month for use of the space, which he spent eighty thousand dollars to convert. When he's done, he'll go upstairs to work out on the elliptical Catherine set up in what was once Ella's bedroom, shower in their newly renovated bathroom, and then stretch out on the family room couch to watch the basketball game he recorded last night. Catherine will fetch him when it's time to get dressed for the party. Because they'll spend the weekend at their beach house, she will have already packed his suitcase for the overnight trip he'll leave for Monday morning: a visit to a Chattanooga refrigeration parts company whose value he'll assess.

George can no longer recall when Catherine took over packing for him. Before they had children (when her work as a financial analyst at a competing firm had, in truth, led to her advancing at a faster pace than him), she would hover while he stuffed briefs and socks and gym clothes into his hanging bag and then, after he left their bedroom, refold and reorder everything. Now, he simply tells her his itinerary and she tucks a list of what to wear each day in the outside pocket of the bag. Having Catherine match his shirts and ties feels a bit infantilizing—not that he remembers his mother ever concerning herself with his or Ana's clothes aside from insisting that a pair of shoes could last another season—but who wouldn't prefer to watch a basketball game on an eighty-five-inch screen than pack a suitcase?

He looks at the make of his six wine refrigerators and wonders if the Chattanooga factory he may well recommend be shuttered fabricated any of the parts.

THE CARPENTER WHO CONVERTED THE ELEVATOR MACHINERY room into George's wine cellar was a muscular Lebanese man named Aziz with a gray beard as closely cropped as the hair on his head and a messenger bag from which he took at their first meeting two very sharpened pencils, his calendar, and a quadrangle notebook where he sketched the room. The man had a quiet but powerful aura to him. Catherine had found him—there was some connection to Henry—as she did everyone who worked on their apartment or country house. It disturbed George that during the weeks Aziz built the wine cellar, he thought about Aziz more than he liked: What did his wife look like? Did she wear a head scarf? How often did they have sex? Did Aziz have male friends? Did they bike or camp together?

On one occasion, Aziz brought his son, a boy of three or four, who sat silently on the floor playing with an action figure while George and Aziz talked. Afterward, Aziz knelt to button his son's coat, starting at the hem and advancing up to the collar, and then reached into his own pocket for the wool cap he put on the child's head. Watching the two of them exit hand in hand, George felt a sharp sadness.

As a gift, Aziz added a small built-in desk. Seated now at the desk, George surveys the floor-to-ceiling racks, with his bottles sorted by varietals. He'd learned about varietals at a wine course in Burgundy: a fiftieth birthday present organized by Catherine to not overlap with Ella's bread-baking class or Gemma's internship at a cancer research lab. He never told Catherine that by the fourth day of the course, he'd tired of it: the morning lectures by enologists on *terroir* and the French system of *L'Appellation d'origine contrôlée*; the tastings paired with a too-leisurely luncheon on a terrace giving onto the vineyards; the afternoon trips to wineries, nearly everyone dozing in the van. With Catherine and the girls gone until early evening on a program she'd mapped out of visits to nearby cultural sites, he began slipping off following the luncheon so he could return to the villa Catherine had rented for them. Tipsy from the wine and pushing aside his guilt at spoiling the experience Catherine had so meticulously planned for him, he would collapse on a chaise lounge by the saltwater pool.

George and Catherine's friends marvel at Catherine's ingenuity. When the girls were young, she was known for her skill at finding the perfect enrichment programs and then, when Ella at fourteen declared she just wanted to come home after school and bake with their house-keeper, Lourdes, accepting that too. I'm an excellent shopper, Catherine says, and although their friends pooh-pooh this as minimizing her skill, George thinks Catherine is right. Shopping—be it for furnishings or contractors or hotels off, but not too-off, the beaten path—is her passion, to which she applies the same scrutiny of variables she had as an analyst. Mostly, he is grateful, but it's also exhausting. There are times when he wishes Catherine would, for even a day, slack off. Let the dinner hour roll round without the line-caught fish in a marinade from a Turkish cookbook so he could fry some baloney to eat with saltines and pickles the way he had as a kid on the nights when his grandmother was too tired to make even sandwiches.

The greatest testament to Catherine is that both girls remain close to her: to this day, she and Ana are the first people they go to for advice and comfort. While George never doubted that his own mother worked hard to provide for his sister and him, he understood from a young age that she viewed suffering as weakness. When he was so repulsed by his acne that he couldn't stand seeing himself in a mirror, when he was cut from the freshman football team and the rejection felt like *Loser* branded on his chest, it never occurred to him to talk to his mother. She was in bed two hours after she arrived home from work; if he'd approached her during the interim window, she would have looked at him as though challenging him to explain what she should do.

He opens his ledger, a notebook he was given at the wine course, and enters today's date—his sister's birthday—and the bottles he has selected for tonight. Seated next to him at the table by the villa's pool, fifteen-year-old Gemma insisted on setting up the ledger for him the way she did her lab notebooks. He sees her as she was then, a serious girl wielding a wooden ruler and red pencil as she bent over the first page and drew the columns, and then as she is now—pregnant, a scientist, still serious.

WHEN GEORGE WAS FIFTEEN, HE'D SPENT WHAT WOULD BE HIS last summer with his own father. The trip began strangely, with his grandfather, who they lived with then, having died a week before but no one questioning that he and Ana should still fly to Marrakesh. George had hated his grandfather for being so mean to their grandmother, but loved him, too, for the evenings they'd spent together watching sports on his grandparents' black-and-white television, sharing bowls of potato chips and Oreo cookies.

Arriving in Marrakesh, George at first paid little attention to his father's latest girlfriend, Mathilde, a recent graduate from a French architectural school, aside from noting that she disregarded the gestures toward modesty made by other female Westerners: long skirts and never pants or bared arms. He was surprised when Mathilde succeeded in convincing his father, who'd always worked through their summer visits, that they should make a trip to the Sahara so they could spend a night in a caravan camp. A classmate of Mathilde's had done this when she was in Morocco. They'd be served an authentic Berber meal, Mathilde promised, sleep in tents pitched near the dunes, and then at four in the morning mount camels so they could ride to the highest summit to watch the sun rising from the seam of sand and sky. It would be *magnifique*.

Mathilde arranged a driver, who after an eight-hour car ride deposited them at a bleak café at the end of a road, where they waited in the 105-degree heat for the sun to set before climbing into dune buggies for the final thirty kilometers to the camp. Hot and tired as he was, George had a frisson of triumph—his father and Mathilde were idiots—when on reaching their destination, the camp owner explained that the heat would make sleeping inside the tents unbearable. The camel tenders had dragged the moldy carpets onto the sand. The camp owner showed them the bathroom: a concrete structure with a wash sink and a toilet without a seat. George looked at his acne-marred face in the small mirror. He'd brought his tube of Clearasil, but would feel too self-conscious about the pink spots it would make to use it now that they would all be sleeping side by side on the carpets outdoors.

During the long wait for dinner, Ana sat cross-legged on one of the carpets, shining a flashlight on an English translation of a French novel Mathilde had insisted Ana would *adore absolument*. The third time Ana asked George the meaning of a word, he grabbed the book. This looks like filth, he announced after glancing at the title, *Gigi*, and the come-hither look of the cover illustration. His sister furrowed her brow. She was tall for her age, but because she was skinny, she looked younger than her twelve years. Too young to even understand what he meant, he thought. Without protesting, she took another book from her backpack and opened it. Usually, he mocked her constant reading, but now he envied her: she could escape the disappointing camp for the world on her pages.

Mathilde emerged from the washroom in a sleeveless top that tied behind her neck and what the girls from the sister Catholic school to the all-boys one George attended called hot pants. She looked nothing like those girls, with their sheaths of blonde or chestnut hair and soft thighs and plentiful busts. Everything about Mathilde was small and tight, from her cap of dark hair to her apple breasts to her tiny butt. Seeing the barely covered vee between her legs, he feared he might have an erection.

'For Christ's sake, put on some decent clothes,' his father hissed.

'Fuck off, Rolf.' Mathilde's English was only passable, but she cursed as proficiently as George's grandfather had. She picked up one of the bottles of wine set out for their dinner, cooking now over an open fire, swigged from it, and then flashed the camel tenders a smile with her little teeth, browned from her incessant smoking.

Since they'd arrived in Morocco, George had tormented Ana by telling her that what was on her plate was goat or pigeon, after which she would politely poke at her food, eating around the meat. Tonight, though, she was looking so nervously at the camels and chewing the tip of her finger, when their dinner was finally served, he couldn't bring himself to upset her further.

Following the meal, the camel tenders brought out drums and stringed instruments shaped like elongated banjos. George watched from the outskirts of the group, his face set in a smirk that hid his envy while one of the musicians showed Ana how to strum the largest of the instruments. Mathilde danced, at first standing next to George's father, but as the night progressed and she finished the bottle of wine she'd kept for herself, only arm's length from the drummers. She arched her neck so her apple breasts faced the stars and gyrated her hips. She yelped and shimmied. Not until she stumbled and his father walked her to the washroom, where he must have pushed her head under the faucet because when she emerged, screaming, she was dripping water, did George realize how wasted she was.

'Asshole. Son of a *beetch*,' Mathilde bellowed as she darted behind one of the tents.

His father waited ten minutes before going to get her. When he returned, there was a look of alarm on his face. He couldn't find Mathilde: not inside any of the tents or the washroom or anywhere.

The camp owner gathered flashlights and lanterns so they could break into teams to look for Mathilde. 'Go to sleep,' their father instructed before he left. He said it calmly, but George could tell he was agitated. They'd been warned not to wander far from the camp due to poisonous snakes that came out at night.

George remained standing with his arms crossed over his chest, but Ana obediently lay on one of the carpets spread out on the sand. She turned on her flashlight and opened her book. George could tell she wasn't reading because she never flipped the page. A few minutes passed before she asked, 'What if they can't find her?'

'Don't be a dope. They'll find her. She can't have gone far.'

After a while, George stretched out next to his sister. The carpet smelled like it hadn't been washed in a hundred years. Ana put down her book and turned off her flashlight. He stared up at the sky. Never had he seen so many stars. He wished he knew how to identify some of the constellations. No one in his family had ever talked about the stars. When his mother went outside after dinner, it was to sit on the stoop with her iced tea, listening to a transistor radio. His grandfather's nighttime forays had been limited to the cement yard behind their house; smelling of whiskey and often a bit unsteady on his feet, he'd smoke a cigar. Had he ever looked up, he would have seen little, the city lights leaving the sky opaque.

Ana touched George's arm. Usually, he would tell her to get her grubby hands off him, but it was reassuring to know someone else was here, even if it was only his stupid twelve-year-old sister. She gripped his elbow, holding on to it like a buoy in a sea turned rough. That his father hadn't thought to have one of the camel tenders stay back with them irked him. What if thieves came to rob the camp? Or, with the camp now so quiet, a snake slithered onto the carpet where he and Ana lay?

ONCE HE WAS CERTAIN ANA WAS ASLEEP, GEORGE GOT UP TO PISS. Shining his sister's flashlight in front of him, he made his way to the concrete washroom. He was almost there when he heard whimpering. With his heart pounding, he pointed the light through the open flap of the nearest tent. The carpet had not been removed. Mathilde was curled atop.

'Mathilde?'

George ducked under the flap. Closer now, he saw that Mathilde's face was tear-streaked. Not knowing what else to do, he plopped down next to her.

For a good while, she remained curled in a ball and continued to cry. Then she sat up. 'I hate your father,' she said, seizing George's arm. 'He is—what is the word? A bull.'

'Bully.'

It was true that his father could be domineering, but George would not have described him as a bully. Besides, he had to admit that he agreed with his father. Mathilde should not have been shaking her butt in front of the camel tenders.

He was still thinking about this when Mathilde leaned her face toward his.

Instinctively, he touched his acne-covered chin. The boys in his class called him chicken-pox. But Mathilde seemed unaware of his blighted skin as she kissed him, her mouth tasting of wine and cigarettes.

It was so hot inside the tent, George could feel beads of sweat dripping from the back of his head onto his neck. Taking his hand with her tiny soft one, Mathilde slipped it under her halter top. Her skin was slick, as though he'd licked it with his tongue. His stiffening penis pressed uncomfortably against the elastic of his gym shorts. His chest tightened and he felt the way he did before he would have to lock himself in the bathroom to jerk off. Should he squeeze Mathilde's breast? Could he put it in his mouth?

Mathilde slid her fingers below the waistband of his gym shorts. She grasped his now hard penis.

He groaned. What if he came in her palm? She laughed, then removed her hand so she could unsnap her hot pants. Lifting her hips, she pulled them and her underwear off.

He'd never seen a woman's pubic hair before. Mathilde's was black and curly, thicker than the hair on her head. She lay back, planting her feet wide on the carpet so her knees pointed up. Mesmerized, he watched her wet her forefinger and then make circular motions near the bottom of the triangle.

'Now, boy,' she said. She arched her pelvis. 'Now.'

He was in the washroom, cleaning himself up, when he heard his father's low steady voice and Mathilde's high-pitched yelling. By the time he came out, Mathilde and his father were sitting together on the furthest carpet from the place where Ana was sleeping. Mathilde had put her hot pants and he presumed her underwear back on. Her face was pressed against his father's chest, and George could hear her sobbing.

'Go to sleep,' his father said when he saw George. It seemed strange that his father repeated the same words he'd used before he left to look for Mathilde. As though Mathilde hadn't, just moments ago, guided George's cock to the damp place beneath the black vee. As though, after he came in two thrusts, she hadn't propped herself on an elbow so her head dangled back and then rubbed his finger on a hard little bump. As though she hadn't groaned 'Keep going, boy' while he moved his finger faster and faster until she sank back on the carpet and clasped him to her and he felt her shake.

'We have to get up at four,' his father said.

George lay down next to his sister. Ana turned toward him and rested her hand again on his elbow. A few minutes later, he saw his father helping Mathilde to her feet. She raced to the edge of the encampment and vomited onto the sand.

It was still dark when they mounted the camels and began ascending the dunes: one camel tender in front, then his father, then Ana, then him, then two other tenders. The camp owner had stayed back with Mathilde, who his father had been unable to rouse. She would be furious at missing the sunrise over the mountains of sand—why they'd made this ridiculous trip—but even if they'd managed to get her onto a camel, she probably would have been sick again.

Over the top of his sister's head, George could see his father's wide-brimmed hat and the back of his neck. After he'd watched Mathilde puking, George had remained awake for a long time, torn between a queasy feeling and a sense of victory: he'd lost his virginity, his pimply chin and the welts on the sides of his nose had not mattered to Mathilde. In ninth grade, they'd read *Oedipus Rex* and learned from the lay teacher who taught English about the oedipal complex—the wish to sleep with your mother and be rid of your father. All the boys had tittered. 'Okay, lads,' Joey, the class clown, stage whispered. 'Keep away from your mums.' The idea revolted George: his mother's back was padded with a layer of fat, like a seal, and her cheeks looked like they'd been scrubbed with steel wool. Not a one of the boys in his class would have turned down Mathilde with her tight butt and her apple breasts. But wasn't fucking his father's girlfriend just a step away from fucking his mother?

The camels grunted as they climbed the dunes. George had always thought he hated his father, but now it seemed more complicated. Yes, he hated his father for never asking how he was or spending any time alone with him, but he also felt sorry for his father that he had a girlfriend who would have sex with his fifteen-year-old son.

His father broke it off with Mathilde when they finished the Marrakesh project. By Christmas, he was with Isadora, an interior decorator for the hotel he was renovating in Rome. In the spring, his father and Isadora married and moved back to New York. A few weeks later, they took the train to Baltimore so Isadora could meet George and Ana. Unlike slutty Mathilde, Isadora was quiet and elegant. She'd never had children, but she was close to her brother's three sons. Immediately, she recognized how miserable George—by then, smoking pot daily and drinking heavily on weekends—felt about his acne. Without asking her new husband, she made an appointment for George with a dermatologist at Johns Hopkins, with instructions that the bill be sent to her. It amazed George how quickly the medications the dermatologist prescribed cleared up his skin, but it also angered him. Had his mother not known he could be helped—or did she not think it worth the expense?

WHEN GEORGE FINISHES HIS ENTRIES FOR THE DEPARTING BOTTLES of wine, he returns the ledger to a cubbyhole in the desk. The room has a musky smell from the racks of corked bottles that reminds him of Mathilde inside the tent: her mouth tasting of wine, the moldy carpets, the scent on his fingers after he rubbed what he'd not known then was a clitoris.

He locks the wine cellar door and takes the elevator upstairs to his apartment. The hanging bag Catherine has packed for his Monday trip is propped next to the front hall table, where there's a note that she'll be back by five thirty. There's no mention of where Catherine has gone, and perversely, it flits through his mind that he'd like it if she were off doing something out of character, something that would let him feel morally superior—fucking a greasy thirty-two-year-old guitar player or, better yet, shooting heroin with him—rather than to her spin class or to have her hair blown dry.

After his elliptical workout, he kicks off his sneakers and heads into the new master bathroom: a marble mausoleum with double sinks and heated towel bars. When he'd once described to Catherine the ancient plumbing of the sole bathroom in his grandparents' house—a sink with separate faucets for hot and cold water, a tub with no shower—she looked horrified. Her parents' Greenwich house had five bathrooms, including a gleaming pink-tiled one between her sister's and her Jack and Jill bedrooms. He was unable to bring himself to mention that he could hear his grandfather's toileting grunts through the door or that he'd always let Ana take her bath before him because by then the room would be cleansed of old people smells and she always scrubbed the tub afterward and no one would be waiting for him to finish popping his pimples.

Using the shaving mirror installed by his sink, he trims his nose hairs with the grooming scissors Catherine bought him years ago. Early in their marriage, she teased him for being a peacock—more concerned about his appearance than she is about hers. He would counter that with her heart-shaped face and size-two figure, she'd look good in a burlap sack whereas he has to make an effort, but didn't tell her the real reason: he's never fully recovered from the awful years, before Isadora sent him to a dermatologist, when he felt so hideous. His mother was largely oblivious, but Ana knew. Once, when his nose was bleeding after he'd squeezed too hard, she brought him a hot washcloth, not saying a word, only pointing to the spot. Another time, when she found his tube of Clearasil behind the sink, she cleaned it off and knocked on his door to give it to him.

He's aware that his obsession with other men's appearances comes from those years. Last Memorial Day, Ella's live-in boyfriend showed up with a day's beard in a flannel lumberjack shirt and mud-caked construction boots for the annual party George throws at his beach house for the group he heads. 'Does being a pickle maker mean you don't have to shave or clean your shoes?' he asked Ella, who then snapped at him: 'Dad, it's so disturbing that the only thing you care about is what Austen is wearing and how he's groomed. Is there anyone else here who runs a rooftop organic farm that provides free greens to people in the neighborhood?' She glanced over at three associates from his office, all with ice-pop-colored Bermuda shorts and gelled hair and expensive watches, sipping his Puligny-Montrachet by the pool while they placed bets on who would win the presidential election. 'Anyone else who goes door-to-door campaigning for Bernie Sanders?'

George had to control himself to keep from snickering. He was certain that none of these young men knocked on doors for Bernie Sanders or, for that matter, would ever vote for him. They might not even vote for Hillary. In November—he'd not dared tell Catherine or his daughters—he was unable to himself. He just couldn't do it. He knows it's dangerous to have a president who gets his information from crap sources and fires anyone who doesn't pander to him and gets off inciting crowds to violence. But if George is honest, it's easier for him to stomach than a woman in charge. Were he to consult with a psychoanalyst, he—and it would be a he because George would never see a she—would probably say it has something to do with George's feelings about his mother or perhaps his sister or wife, but it's a moot point because there's no way he's going to see a psychoanalyst.

Having finished trimming his nose hairs, George feels the creeping edges of the dark mood that regularly enveloped him during his younger years but, since he's been married to always encouraging and doting Catherine, rarely visits him now. The dark mood is not as bad as it once was, but it's smothered his desire to watch the basketball game. Instead, he lies down on the bed.

It's hard to believe his sister is sixty. In his mind's eye, she's still the twelve-year-old he felt compelled to taunt, as though something endangered in himself depended on her eyes welling with tears. Then, she was so skinny, he called her *Pick*, short for toothpick. She tried to ignore his teasing, but he knew it wounded her. Her best friend, LuAnn—What was her last name? Something Polish. *Wa* something or other—was her opposite, with what the boys at George's school called a set of knockers and a nice-sized ass too. Once, when LuAnn spent the night at their house and he heard her get up to use the bathroom, he crept into the hallway and peered through the keyhole. For weeks, he jerked off thinking about her thighs splayed over the toilet seat.

After he saw the dermatologist and his skin got so much better (he was lucky, the doctor told him, to have the kind of acne that doesn't leave scars), he was astonished to discover that there were girls interested in him. He was still far outside the Brahmin caste of the most popular boys—the football players who got the blonde cheerleaders or the

James Dean guys who landed the artsy, exotic-looking girls—but he fell squarely in the next caste for whom pretty, quiet girls or flawed, bolder girls were in reach. Years of diligent and often tedious hard work and the good luck of a boss who'd gone to bat for him led to his acceptance to the Wharton business school and then to a job at a top-tier consulting firm, which leapfrogged him to having access to beautiful, classy girls, who'd gone to elite colleges and came from wealthy families. Having by then had more sexual partners than he could recall, his thoughts about Mathilde shifted from something akin to spitting in his father's soup to gratitude that she'd seen beyond his acne and admiration at her insistence on her own pleasure. He was relieved to settle into a monogamous relationship with Catherine, a girl who men in his newly acquired set would call *marriageable*. A girl who, although not a virgin (Catherine had slept with her college boyfriend and had a few hookups), still seemed pure and clean.

Only once since he's been married was he at risk of straying. It was nearly twenty years ago, in Cartagena, at a retreat for his firm. Following a dinner where everyone was drinking heavily, a young associate from the Chicago office convinced him to take a horse-drawn carriage with her through the old city. It was the setting, she told him, for some of the scenes in Gabriel Garcia Márquez's *Love in the Time of Cholera*. He'd never read anything by Gabriel Garcia Márquez, but Catherine had spent a semester abroad in Barcelona, where the writer was living at the time, and had read his novels in Spanish. It would amuse her, he thought, to hear that he saw these places.

The night was balmy, the air fragrant with jacaranda. He sat side by side with the young associate on the cracked leather seat, listening to the steady *clop* of the horses' hooves as they moved through dark cobblestoned streets and across colonial squares. A breeze from the nearby sea blew strands of her long red hair onto his face as she pointed out the plaza where Florentino waits to see his beloved Fermina. The girl—she really was more girl than woman—laughed as she peeled her hair off his neck and cheeks, sidling closer to him, until she was leaning on his shoulder. She looked up at him, smiled, and then slid her hand inside his pants and slowly began to caress him.

When he felt on the verge of coming, he saw Mathilde's face—not as it had been that night inside the tent but tight with rage as it was when they returned from the dawn camel ride without her. He pulled the girl's hand out from his briefs.

'What the hell?' she said.

In the distance, George could hear the waves pounding the ramparts. His cell phone vibrated in his pocket, and he was certain it was Catherine calling from the couch in their family room, sipping chamomile tea with her knees tucked under her, the girls asleep in their beds.

'I'm married.'

'You don't think I know that?' She fished through her purse, retrieving a small bottle of sanitizer with which she meticulously cleaned her hands. '*Terminado,*' she hollered to the coachman. '*Queremos volver.*'

For the rest of the ride, she kept her back to him. Feeling her fury, George thought about the look his father had given him while Mathilde ranted about Rolf having purposefully deprived her of the sunrise over the dunes. At the time, George had thought his father's expression was exasperation with Mathilde. Now, with the hypnotic beat of the horses' hooves as they passed balconies where virgins in colorful mantillas had once gazed down at their black-suited male callers, he realized that in his father's look, there'd also been begrudging respect—respect of him, George. Mathilde must have told his father that she'd fucked him. Not one of the camel tenders. His son.

Back at the hotel, he asked the red-headed associate if she'd like to have a drink. She gathered her hair with her very white hands into a high ponytail atop her head, and then released it in a cascade over her shoulders. It took all of his self-control not to pull her toward him. Smirking, she turned and entered the bar, slipping into a booth with two men from his office—one married, one recently divorced.

In the morning, when he came down for breakfast in the hotel dining room, she was talking animatedly with the divorced one. She'd kicked off one of her sandals and her bare foot was nestled against his ankle. George could tell she knew he was there, but she ignored him. Instead, she plucked a slice of papaya from her companion's plate and, opening her mouth, dangled it between them.

He buries his face in one of the dozen pillows atop the bed. It smells of lavender and something that tickles his nose. Laundry detergent? Catherine's astronomically expensive eye cream?

When his father died, there was an obituary in the *New York Times*. It mentioned the many prizes his father had won and the storied hotels he'd worked on. George and Ana were named, along with Ella and Gemma and Simon. At the funeral, George gave a eulogy. It was the first time he'd been able to express pride in his father.

Last September, on what would have been their father's ninetieth birthday, Ana left him a voice mail acknowledging the day. She didn't explicitly ask that he return her call; rather, she said that she would be home for the rest of the afternoon and evening. It was sufficiently vague that he could play dumb—as though he didn't know she would be hurt if he didn't call back. Instead, he tweeted their father's obituary and photographs of two of the hotels their father had renovated. Ana wouldn't have seen the tweets—she doesn't use social media—but he told himself that his posts sufficed as his own acknowledgment of the day.

He turns onto his back and tosses half the pillows off the bed. He wishes he'd opened one of the bottles he chose for Ana's party. That he had a glass of Châteauneuf-du-Pape here on the bedside table next to the latest volume of the Lyndon Johnson biography Catherine had bought him.

Staring at the ceiling, he sees the stars as they looked that night over the Merzouga Dunes: the sheer magnitude of the pinpricks of light. He recalls Ana's face after he returned from the washroom. Her lips parted in the way of a child sleeping deeply. His relief that she didn't awaken as he lay down beside her.

He wonders if tonight at Ana's birthday party he could ask her if she remembers the musty smell of the carpets or Mathilde shaking her butt in front of the camel tenders or Mathilde's shrieks when she realized she'd missed the sunrise. If he could bring himself to ask Ana if she ever thinks about holding his elbow under the Sahara sky.

9

ANA

I BRING A CARAFE OF WATER AND TWO GLASSES INTO MY STUDY, take out the last draft of Bettina's manuscript, and replay her voice mail from this morning. Bettina sounds shaky, but she's using what I think of as her real voice, so different from the chipper one she kept up the first time we met, now two years ago. Had I not known that day from Bettina's preliminary email the subject of her book project—an account of her experiences as the manager of a recovery house outside Boston for girls who'd been brought to this country as sex workers—I would have assumed she was one of those temperamentally cheerful persons with a blind eye to the dark side of their fellow brethren and a Teflon skin that protected her from daily frustrations. Knowing, however, her chipper tone seemed bizarre, like wearing a yellow dress to a funeral.

In that first email, Bettina wrote that she was reaching out because she was blocked with her manuscript. She'd heard about me from her partner's friend, who'd worked on a book with me. Bettina would be coming to New York later in the month. She'd be staying with her aunt and was hoping we could meet. Aside from a visit with her mother and sister, who'd be driving in from New Jersey, she could come any time. What most strongly stuck with me from that first email was that Bettina would not be staying with her mother.

I wrote back, explaining that I offer potential clients an hour free consultation, suggesting a time, and asking that Bettina send in advance a synopsis and a sample ten pages. A week later, an envelope arrived with both. The pages left me with the disquieting feeling I'd had so many years ago reading what Nan, my first client, had sent me. Like walking into a silent house and suspecting someone is hiding, I sensed a shadow story to the one Bettina was telling. Usually, I could picture the writer from a manuscript sample, but with Bettina's pages, all I could imagine was a caricature of a lesbian: a wide back, crew-cut hair, construction boots.

Arriving my usual ten minutes early, I noticed at the corner booth a pretty woman, a decade younger-looking than the forty-four years Bettina had written she was. Dressed in a navy jumper over a white blouse with a Peter Pan collar and Oxford tie shoes, she could have been a nun in lay clothing.

The woman half stood. 'Ana?' She extended a hand with nail-bitten fingers and smiled, revealing a mouthful of perfect teeth that suggested a childhood of regular dentistry and braces.

I slid into the banquette across from Bettina. A small gold barrette above each ear held her hair back from her face. She hoped the booth was okay; she'd come a bit early to have something to eat. Pushed to the side were the crusts of a grilled cheese sandwich and a chocolate milk, foods I hadn't seen anyone order since I used to take Simon out to lunch after a Saturday morning at the Museum of Natural History.

Without preamble, Bettina launched an account of how her proposal had interested an agent, but given that it was a first book, the agent told her she'd need a completed manuscript before they could go further. In the year since, she'd only been able to produce thirty-some pages, ten of which were what she'd sent.

We talked briefly about the structure of the book—how Bettina might reorganize it to open with a story about one of the girls rather than a history of the house—and then Bettina described how hard it had been for her to settle into a writing routine. She was responsible for all practical arrangements for the house: staff schedules, ordering supplies, the food shopping (which she did each week with a team of the girls), managing the logs of the residents' appointments with case workers and doctors and training programs. For a while, she'd tried dedicating Saturdays and a half day on Sundays to working on the book, but she found it difficult to pick up after the five-day break so that her weekend writing sessions were frustrating and unproductive and she would make excuses for skipping them. She'd tried other strategies—dedicating vacation time to the book, working for an hour at lunch—but none of them were successful, in part, because with the demands of running the house, it was impossible to take off time regularly for lunch, much less vacation.

Listening to Bettina, I noted that she seemed to have only two expressions: the wide smile of her greeting, and a look of terror that briefly surfaced when I suggested that the manuscript would benefit from including more about herself, a look that was so quickly replaced by the default chipper façade, I wondered if I'd imagined it. When we parted on the sidewalk in front of the diner, I thought, I'm not going to hear from this woman again.

Eleven months later, an email from Bettina arrived. She apologized for not having followed up after the first meeting. Would I give her another chance? She understood that this would be a paid consultation, but she was ready now to commence working together.

The second meeting took place in my home office. It was a November late afternoon with the trees in the park rendered a brilliant yellow and orange by the setting western sun. We sat side by side in rolling desk chairs at the library table under the window, the pages and synopsis Bettina had sent the year before (she'd produced no new pages) between us.

Again, Bettina detailed the demands of managing the house: how much food eighteen girls, some of whom had spent years fed amphetamines and little more than soda and chips, could eat in a week. Fifteen dozen eggs, twenty gallons of orange juice, twenty-five pounds of chicken and ground beef, thirty loaves of bread . . .

Although I mean what I always tells clients—I'm not a psychotherapist and if they need psychiatric help they must seek that elsewhere—over the years, I've found myself using what I learned from my classes in social work school, most particularly the idea of evenly-suspended attention. The Argentinian analyst charged with providing the three-lecture introduction to psychodynamic treatment claimed no one explained the concept better than Freud himself: the analyst aims to 'catch the drift of the patient's unconscious with his own unconscious.' Hearing this, I was reminded of *The Catcher in the Rye* and certain exhilarating experiences I'd had as a reader when I felt time and space liquefy so I entered a writer's mind and he or she, it seemed, entered mine.

While Bettina expanded her description of her job responsibilities, I observed my thoughts as they floated to another late afternoon, weeks before, when I'd been at the same table, looking out the same window, as the sky turned slate and opened like a faucet on full force. Rain bounced off the street and the wind battened the front windows with such force, the glass seemed to ripple. I'd raced through the house, locking the windows and wiping up the water that had already pooled on the sills. Moments later, there was a terrible crash, something hitting the pavement seven stories below, and I heard screaming and soon after ambulance sirens. When I went downstairs, presumably for the mail but really to inquire, Carlos told me that a piece of the cornice from the adjacent building had fallen. It killed a young woman running from the rain toward the awning of my building.

I gasped. Imagining a bloodied body splayed on the wet concrete, I gripped the lip of the doorman's station. Did anyone know who the woman was? Carlos shook his head no. 'Young, that's all I heard.'

By the time Henry arrived home, the sidewalk fronting the adjacent building was cordoned off with yellow police tape. A neighbor had told him that the victim was the Romanian housekeeper for a family with a brownstone around the corner. The newspaper report the next day included little additional information other than that the woman had been in this country for three years. Within days, she disappeared from the story, which morphed into a scandal about the neighboring building having failed to inspect the cornice on the required schedule.

I studied Bettina's nail-bitten hands. Bettina, too, had disappeared. Disappeared from the story she was telling so blandly.

I angled my chair so I could better see Bettina's face. 'Let's step back.' The words sounded canned even to me, but it was a start. Or rather a stop. I had to stop Bettina's droning so we could start. 'Why are you doing this work? What drew you to it?'

Bettina looked at me as though I'd asked her to smash the window in front of us and leap out. She clenched her jaw so tightly, I could hear her teeth grinding.

'You have an important story to tell about these girls you've been working with now for a decade. But you're trying to tell it while excising yourself. And you're who the reader needs to connect with. If they don't care about you and trust you, they're not going to care about your girls.'

Bettina covered her face. The flesh around her bitten nails was even more inflamed than I'd seen with Gemma. When she lowered her hands, her eyes were dry. Dry but filled with an anguish that seemed too powerful for tears. 'I'm sorry,' she said. 'I have to go.' She stood, mumbling something about meeting her aunt. I raised my eyebrows, but did not point out that Bettina was leaving only fifteen minutes after she'd arrived or ask if she'd like to schedule another appointment.

Ten days later, an envelope arrived from Bettina: a clump of handwritten pages with a note clipped on top. She felt terrible about the last meeting, she'd written in her schoolgirl's hand. It was childish and rude to run away like that. She knew it was asking a lot, but would it be possible to see me again? She would insist with her boss that she had to take a day off and she would come any time I offered. She gave her word she wouldn't bolt.

The only way, Bettina continued in her note, she'd been able to include herself was to tell what had happened as though it was a story, written from her mother's point of view. She knew it was weird, but writing this way came easier. She'd shown the pages to her girlfriend, Rea. Rea was a parole officer and used to hearing people tell their stories. Rea said Bettina had written through her mother's eyes because she didn't want to blame her mother even though her mother should be blamed. Everything she'd written, Bettina added, was, to the best of her knowledge, true—told to her by either her mother or her aunt Niss.

Reminding myself that the *I* refers to Teresa, Bettina's mother, I re-read the first of the handwritten pages:

At times, I think the only thing I know for sure is I got pregnant with Bettina on the purple rug in the back of Michael's van. It was the first time I had sex. Michael said I smelled like the frying oil and

*powdered sugar at the boardwalk funnel stand where I worked. He
smelled of the ocean where he'd gone to wash after his job.*

*I was shocked when Niss said she could help me figure out how to
get an abortion. What made her think I wanted that? I loved Michael. He'd been on his high school's basketball team, but he also
played guitar and sang sweetly like Paul Simon. I loved the peanut
growing inside me.*

I skim the next page about Bettina's father's death when she was six
and he crashed to the ground from a hastily mounted scaffold. With the
owner of the construction company nowhere to be found and no insurance payments coming, Teresa moved with Bettina into the basement of
her parents' house so they could watch Bettina while she cleaned offices
at night and took a secretarial course during the day. She and Bettina
slept on a pull-out couch next to a wall Teresa scrubbed with Clorox
to fight the creeping black mold, which she thought was the cause of
Bettina's sinus infections. When Teresa asked her mother not to smoke
in front of Bettina, her mother rolled her eyes.

With the secretarial course completed, Teresa got a job at the Midgman & Midgman law firm. At the year-end holiday party, there was a
Secret Santa gift exchange. Her gift came in a black velvet box with a
red bow on top.

*Inside was something shiny hanging from a gold chain. I thought it
was from the costume jewelry place at the mall, but I looked up and
saw Mr. Midgman (that's what I called Jack then) smiling at me. I
nearly fainted as I realized I was holding a diamond necklace.*

Bettina, still writing in her mother's voice, described how at the end
of the day, her mother knocked on her employer's door. From the doorway, he looked like a dwarf behind his enormous desk. She held out the
velvet box.

*I told him the necklace was beautiful, but I couldn't possibly accept
it. It wasn't right. "Who said I gave it to you?" he asked. I turned beet*

red. "Just joshing you, Teresa. Yes. I gave it to you." He puffed out his
chest. It scared me. "This is my firm. I decide what's right."

It wasn't as though I didn't know before I married Jack that he
drank—basically every night and on holidays too. Even Niss noticed
when she came to his Fourth of July barbeque. "He does like his booze,
doesn't he?" Niss said. But I told myself I'd be busy with Bettina, help-
ing with her homework and bath, and it wouldn't really bother me.

The pre-nup Jack handed me just three weeks before the wedding
as we were having our morning coffee by the pool—that was a sur-
prise. When I asked Jack why, he swept his hand from the pool, past
the summer kitchen, to the house. "Come on, Teresa," he said.

In a way, I guess, he was right. Not that I was marrying him for the
pool or the house, but that I was marrying him so my daughter wouldn't
have to sleep in a basement with black mold on the walls or eat her
breakfast in a room filled with cigarette smoke. Was that wrong?

Only now do I see that here Bettina switched into her own voice:

Wasn't that the case for most women through most of history and
isn't it still the case for most women in most of the world? They marry
to get away from something worse.

Arriving at our next meeting, a week after I'd read the pages Bettina
had written from her mother's point of view, Bettina began speaking
before she'd even taken off her coat. 'I talked it over with Rea. She said
now that I've told you about Teresa and Jack, I need to tell you everything.'

Bettina unclasped the barrette above her right ear and then refas-
tened it. She looked me in the eyes as though asking whether she should
go on. I nodded.

'It's such a common story, I'm afraid it will sound trite. Or fabricated,
as I sometimes think it did to my mother when I was eleven and finally
told her.'

What Bettina had told her mother was that Jack had been coming
into her room at night ever since they'd moved into his house, three
years before. It started with Jack lying on her bed. Let's have a nice cozy

chat, he'd say. Soon, the cozy chats were accompanied by his locking her bedroom door and unbuttoning her pajama top and massaging her chest, then putting his hands inside her pajama bottoms and feeling between her legs to make sure everything was okay down there. At eleven, she didn't have the words to tell her mother what would happen next. Instead, she cried and looked at the floor and said Jack had told her if she said anything to anyone, the police would put him in jail and she and her mother would have nowhere to live.

It would have been easier, Bettina said, if her mother had slapped her and said she was a filthy girl with dirty lies rather than telling Bettina to go to her room and not leave until her mother came to get her, which she did not do until the next morning, when she made Bettina her favorite blueberry pancakes and drove her to school. They never spoke about what Bettina had said, but Bettina was certain her mother told her stepfather because he never again came into her room and he started going to A.A. meetings. Not long after, Bettina's mother got pregnant with Bettina's half-sister. As far as Bettina knew, her stepfather had not had a drink in the thirty-some years since.

Bettina didn't tell anyone else until her first semester of college, when a roommate discovered her cutting herself and informed the dorm resident advisor, who escorted her to the college's mental health services. For a month, Bettina sat silently with the psychologist she'd been assigned, not saying a word. Then, one day, the details poured out of her like a flash flood, after which the psychologist advised Bettina to sever for the immediate future all contact with her family. Bettina adored her baby sister, Carol, then six, and for that reason could not bring herself to do what the psychologist advised, but she stopped going home. That's why, she said, she stays at her aunt's apartment. Her sister and mother come in from New Jersey to visit her there.

CARLOS CALLS UP FROM THE LOBBY TO ANNOUNCE THAT BETTINA is here with her aunt.

'I'm sorry I'm so late,' Bettina says when I open the door. Her forehead is furrowed but she's trying to smile, the two together more like a grimace. She touches the arm of a woman with shoe-polish black hair and penciled brows, and I assume that she doesn't want to say it took longer because of her. 'This is my aunt Niss. She rode the subway uptown with me and wanted to meet you.'

The woman looks at me warmly. 'It's Janice, but everyone calls me Niss. Bettina has said such lovely things about you. How much you've helped her. I just wanted to see your face and say thank you.' She turns to Bettina. 'I'll leave you, dear.'

'You're welcome to wait here,' I offer.

'I don't want to be a bother. I can take a little walk—get in my steps. An hour, is that about right?'

'It's no bother at all.' Hearing the solicitousness in my voice of a younger person to an older one, it occurs to me that Bettina's aunt is probably only ten years my senior.

I escort Niss to the TV room. Grateful that Henry is so discreet—always returning the vaporizer to the closet, running the air purifier—I show Niss the remote and then excuse myself for a minute. I text Henry that my client's aunt is waiting for her in the TV room. They'll be gone by 5:30, I add, knowing Henry will want to vape before my birthday dinner.

Returning, I find Bettina and her aunt staring at the TV. There's a photograph of the same young woman I saw last night when I woke Henry. The newscaster explains that after Kayla Greenwood learned that Williams, the man who'd killed her father, had a daughter Kayla's age who was trying to raise money so she could see him for a last time, Kayla and her mother and stepfather paid for a plane ticket for Williams's daughter and then drove her from the airport to the prison. A photograph of Williams appears. Kayla had forgiven him, the newscaster continues. She sent a letter to the Arkansas governor, pleading that he show mercy and overturn the order of execution for Williams, who she believed was a changed man. The governor, the newscaster reports, was unmoved.

'What a story,' Niss says. 'That girl—she has a heart bigger than the Grand Canyon. Now you go,' she tells Bettina. 'No more fussing over me.'

BETTINA TAKES HER USUAL CHAIR AT THE TABLE IN MY OFFICE. Within seconds, she is crying.

I hand her a box of tissues and wait.

'I'm sorry. I've been trying to keep it together all day. I didn't want to be a basket case with my aunt. She knows, of course, what happened when I was a child. But I didn't tell her about yesterday.'

Bettina blows her nose. She takes a few sips of water and looks sadly at me. 'I suppose I should tell you what happened.'

'That would be helpful.'

Her mother, Bettina says, called last Sunday. Jack, who'd been diagnosed with congestive heart failure over the winter, had taken a turn for the worse. He was on oxygen now twenty-four seven, and was suffering from severe edema. Her mother had hired a night nurse. He'd been asking to see Bettina.

Rea tried to discourage Bettina from going. Bettina didn't owe the son of a bitch a damn thing. 'I agreed with Rea. But I thought maybe he wanted to apologize, and if I didn't go, he'd somehow unload his guilt onto me.'

Bettina sighs. 'How could he hurt me now, I stupidly thought. He's old and sick and bedridden.'

I glance out at the treetops. I see my father's face during his last few weeks, drained of color, his tongue coated white.

'I took the train to the city yesterday morning, and then a bus and cab to their house. I hadn't been there since I was eighteen. The shutters were now black and the trees so much taller. The sun room—with all its windows, it used to be the one place in that house where I felt safe—was set up like a hospital. My mother gave me a hurt look when I didn't kiss Jack or say anything to him. I just sat there, ten feet or so from the bed, listening to the whirring sound from the oxygen tank while he coughed and talked about the Red Sox. Trying to put together this shrunken, wheezing man with the monster I remembered . . .'

Bettina takes her barrette off and then puts it back on. The bad part must be coming now.

'After about ten minutes, he asked my mother for juice. She looked at me, like she wanted my permission to leave. I was so thrown by the tone he used—requesting, not ordering, the way he did when I was a kid—I thought it's okay.'

Bettina averts her eyes, ashamed, it seems, at herself.

'Once we were alone, Jack smiled. His teeth were so yellow, they creeped me out. Betty, he said, calling me by the name he used when I was a child, could I pull my chair closer so he could hear me over the noise of the oxygen tank? I thought about Little Red Riding Hood and the wolf, but it was like when I was little and I felt I had to do what he said. As soon as I was in reach, his hand darted out from under the covers and clamped onto my crotch.'

Bettina shudders. I picture her sitting next to a hospital bed in her blouse with its Peter Pan collar and her Oxford shoes and an old man's veined hand between her legs.

'I ran out of the house, didn't even say goodbye to my mother. My sister was on her way over to see me. I texted her that I had an emergency and I'd meet her on the corner so she could drive me to the bus.'

'I had my laptop with me. All I wanted to do was erase everything I've written. When I called Rea, she said I should try to see you.'

The opening lines of a poem by Robert Lowell that Fiona loves float behind my lids, wobbly, like a banner pulled across the sky:

Tamed by Miltown, we lie on Mother's bed;
the rising sun in war paint dyes us red;

Bettina is crying again. 'I feel like a pathetic weakling. I run a house for girls who make what my stepfather did seem like a mosquito bite, and I can't even protect myself from him now that he's on his deathbed.' She shakes her head. 'I should have screamed and yanked the oxygen probes from his nose. My mother would have raced in and I could have told her right to his evil face that he's going to rot in the hell she still believes in.'

Is this why I thought of Lowell? A pathetic sick man in the wrong generation's bed? But Bettina is describing herself, as pathetic. She wipes her eyes on her sleeve. 'Will it ever change? Ever?' she whispers.

I don't answer. Anything I say will sound either saccharine or condescending.

'If I hadn't reached Rea, I really do think I would have deleted the manuscript.'

I point to the table: the neat pile with the typed pages Bettina has sent me and the handwritten ones from Bettina's mother's point of view. 'Well thank God, I have a copy. But why did what happened yesterday make you want to destroy your manuscript?'

'I wish I knew. Why one more disgusting act by this disgusting man made me worry even more about what it will do to my mother and sister if I publish what he did to me. Rea says, fuck your mother, she deserves it. I wish I could think that way. But, for me, it's more complicated. I've reached a place where I feel both angry at her and sorry for her. She was so young when my father died . . .'

Bettina is watching me, afraid, it seems, that I'll pounce on her for what she's saying. Pounce on her the way Lance has experienced when he's attempted to explain why the Taliban dynamited the Buddhas. The way, I worry, would happen were I to express to anyone other than Fiona and Henry my fears about Simon transitioning. 'My mother cleaned office bathrooms at night,' Bettina says quietly. 'She thought my grandparents' basement was making me sick. If she'd let herself be aware of what was going on in my room, after my stepfather had his martinis and bottle of wine, we would have had to move back into that basement.'

I nod. I'm certain Bettina knows I'm not condoning what her mother did—that I'm only acknowledging that I understand how Bettina sees her mother.

'It's Carol who I worry the most about. Not that I'm violating her privacy. We had different last names as kids, and then she changed her name when she got married.'

'So what are you worried about?'

Bettina touches her manuscript pages. 'How she'll respond to reading what I've written.'

I'm confused. I've always assumed that Bettina told her sister what happened with Jack. All through high school, Bettina has said, she watched Carol like a hawk. She'd sneak into her sister's room, after her mother kissed Carol goodnight, and sleep on the floor next to Carol's bed.

'Carol doesn't know?'

Almost imperceptibly, Bettina shakes her head no.

'She never asked why you slept on her floor or stopped coming home?'

'She was six when I left for college. By the time she would have been old enough to wonder, my never coming home was just the way things were.'

Bettina looks off. 'The truth is, we grew up in different households: me, with a drunken abusive stepfather, her with a father who was A.A. royalty. Carol loved everything A.A.—all the sayings, the *Big Book*—while I used to break into hives hearing Jack preach about making amends or talk about his work as a sponsor.'

I think about Bettina saying it would have been easier if Teresa had slapped her, easier than what had felt like unspoken accusations, and then about the time my own mother slapped me because I said if I married Dean, my life would turn out like hers.

'When the psychologist told me not to go home, the hardest part was that I couldn't stop worrying that ending my weekend trips would put Carol in danger. It took me a long time to accept what the psychologist said: that I'd never seen anything to set off alarm bells, and besides, the fact that nothing happened while I was home was not a safeguard that nothing would happen when I wasn't there. That thought so freaked me out, I almost dropped out of school so I could move back and stand watch.'

I pour more water for Bettina and wait for her to continue.

'Jack did stay sober, and I am grateful for that. And it's a comfort to me that my aunt knows. But even she asked if I could write my book without mentioning my stepfather. I explained to her what you've helped me understand: that it's my experience with sexual abuse that led me to my work and gave me insight into what the girls in the house have been through.'

Bettina throws a wad of crumpled tissues into the wastepaper can. 'My aunt said I shouldn't worry about my mother. She hasn't read a book since she graduated from high school, and she won't read mine either.

Carol, though, will definitely read it. She's already asked me if she could read what I've written so far.'

I've been here before with my clients. There's almost always something—not usually such raw material as Bettina's, but still something—they worry will harm someone. It's easier for my novelist clients. They can change the biographical and physical details, even the sex of their characters (how strange that I never thought of that: the gender reassignments fiction writers make all the time), while keeping the emotional heart—the original persons so disguised, they may not even recognize themselves.

'But you're not writing about your sister,' I say. 'You're writing about yourself. Your own experience. It's up to your sister to decide if she wants to know about your life if it means learning things that she'll find distressing.'

As I say this, a thought takes shape: Bettina's concern is the expression of someone whose body has been violated. A confusion about what belongs to her.

Bettina leans back in her chair. 'You mean,' she says very slowly, very softly, 'what I decide to write is separate from what my sister decides to read. I could warn Carol that what I've written might be painful for her.'

I nod.

'It would be her choice—not mine.'

AFTER BETTINA LEAVES, I SIT AT MY DESK, ATTEMPTING TO digest what she's told me. I let my eyes rest on the reservoir, the blue oval a balm. Most people, I know, would confront Bettina—certainly, her girlfriend, Rea—for making excuses for her mother. What I heard was Bettina viewing the past both through her mother's eyes as well as her own.

Fiona is fond of quoting F. Scott Fitzgerald that the sign of a first-rate mind is the capacity to hold two opposing ideas at the same time. Bettina's response strikes me as even more extraordinary: Bettina has both her own feelings about her mother having failed to protect her, and empathy for her mother not challenging what she'd worked so hard to gain. Are there people—I think about Kayla Greenwood and her compassion for the daughter of the man who killed Kayla's own father—who are born with a greater capacity for seeing the humanity in all? For forgiveness? Others—I think of my mother, who will go to her grave with her charges against her ex-husband still burning—who lack this gene?

Since Bettina first told me her story, I've been aware of the similarities between our mothers: both single parents who swallowed the humiliations of living with their own elderly parents so they could keep a roof over their children's heads. My mother, however, never placed George or me at risk with any man. In fact, as far as I know, my mother was never intimate with anyone aside from my father. I've always thought my father's explanation for why my mother never had another partner after the end of their marriage—she lost her looks, her model's figure reverting to that of her Swedish farm women forebears—was insulting, as though her only positive attribute was her appearance. Even worse, it cast my mother's trajectory as fated—akin to her sister's brain aneurysm that lay dormant until, like a bomb on a timer, it suddenly burst—rather than as a path my mother chose.

'What kills me,' I told Fiona a few days after my mother and I had agreed that I would have to live with her believing that George did nothing wrong with our father's estate, 'is that since she doesn't know why I'm anxious about Simon receiving his inheritance now, I can see why she thinks my objections are petty.'

As usual, Fiona and I were circling the reservoir. A lone duck, a straggler who'd remained after the others departed for the winter, hugged the shore. 'What my brother did *is* good for his girls. Ella will buy a house upstate where she and Austen and their dog can go on weekends. Gemma will be able to afford a nanny.'

I didn't tell Fiona that giving up on being understood by my mother was as hard to digest as George's betrayal, but Fiona must have sensed it.

'It's our phase of life,' Fiona said. 'Parents get old and dotty and that forces us, if we haven't already, to let go of wanting from them anything more.'

HENRY IS LYING ON OUR BEDROOM FLOOR WITH HIS EYES CLOSED.
I touch his arm. 'Wake up, Sleeping Beauty. My client and her aunt are
gone.'

He squints to bring me into focus, then smiles. 'Are you my prince?'

I refrain from making a not-funny quip that we all seem to be
gender-fluid now.

'Did you have a good day, darling?' he asks.

I feel a stab of the remorse that has never abated in the seven years of
my affair with Lance.

I nod. 'You have time,' I say, leaving the sentence unfinished so I
don't have to use the ugly word *vape*. 'If we take a cab, we won't need
more than twenty minutes to get to the restaurant.'

'I thought you'd like to walk.'

With Henry's back injury, it's been a long time since we've walked
together. My face, I'm sure, shows my surprise.

'It's your birthday. We're going to walk. And I'm not going to vape
before your party. I'll manage with an extra Aleve.'

I offer Henry my arm as he slowly stands and heads for the kitchen.
Alone in our bedroom, I look through the west-facing windows at the
sky streaked with plum and persimmon. As a girl, I'd dreaded this time
of day: the witching hour, when light turns inexorably to dark. The impending gloom that would blanket my grandparents' house with the
approaching return of my mother, irritable from her drive home from
work. Trying to think of the flesh as factory-produced rather than carved
from an animal, I would remove whatever protein my mother had left
to defrost from its Styrofoam package and use a paring knife to trim the
excess fat as my mother insisted. Afterward, I'd sterilize the sink the way
my grandmother had taught me: scrub with Clorox, rinse with the white
vinegar in the gallon jug.

In the shower, I remember the first time I told Henry about my ado-
lescent afternoons and how I hadn't cooked since. Henry looked stricken.
He'd not said it, but I later realized he must have been thinking about
his own childhood afternoons, the house filled with the noise of three
boisterous boys and the smells of his mother's roast chickens stuffed with

lemons and herbs, brownies with walnuts cut into squares, apple kugel dotted with bits of apricot.

I PUT ON A CORAL SILK SHELL I PURCHASED WITH THE BIRTHDAY gift certificate Catherine sent me from a Madison Avenue boutique, with instructions to see her personal shopper. Most of the clothes were too fussy—too structured or asymmetrical—and I prefer neutral colors, but I bought the coral shell after Catherine's lady insisted I try it on and then raved extravagantly: 'It's perfect for you! With your slender arms, you should never wear sleeves. The right shoes for the occasion, and you can go anywhere in it . . .' I add black palazzo pants and ballet flats, surely not what Catherine's personal shopper would deem the right shoes for the occasion, but right for an evening when my husband wants to make me happy by walking.

Settling into the reading chair in my office, I open *Mrs. Dalloway.* Clarissa is mending her green dress. 'Quiet descended on her, calm, content, as her needle, drawing the silk smoothly to its gentle pause, collected the green folds together and attached them, very lightly, to the belt.' The doorbell rings and the man Clarissa might have married arrives.

Might have. A phrase that reverberated in my mind for weeks after I opened a single sentence email: *I think you might have been a friend of my mother, LuAnn Wachowsky.*

My heart pounded seeing LuAnn's name. *Yes,* I wrote back immediately. *LuAnn was my best friend in high school.*

An hour later, a second email arrived. I reread it so many times, I can almost recite it now from memory.

Dear Ana (I hope it's okay if I use your first name),

I am very sorry to tell you that my mother passed away last March. Since you knew her, she got divorced, married my father, had me and my sister, and became a pediatric operating room nurse. Everyone said she was an amazing nurse. She was very soothing to the children. She always explained everything to them and how they might feel when they woke up. She made them laugh with her silly jokes.

Three years ago, my mom had a hysterectomy. There were a lot of complications and because she had severe abdominal pain, her doctor prescribed OxyContin. She knew about the risk of addiction, but she kept using it long after she should have stopped. When no one would write her any more prescriptions, she turned to any opiate she could find. We all begged her to get help but she refused. On March 17, she overdosed from heroin laced with fentanyl.

Over the summer, my dad decided to sell their house. While I was helping him clear out the attic, I found some letters you sent my mother during her first marriage and several she wrote you back but never mailed. That's how I learned your name. My sister didn't think I should bother you, but I could tell reading the letters that the two of you really loved each other. So I thought I should let you know.

My mother had a terrible last few years, but she was a wonderful mom when we were kids. She must have played Candy Land and Uno and Parcheesi with my sister and me a thousand times. She made the best Halloween costumes. On our birthdays, we had upside-down dinner with ice cream and cake first, and lots of our friends came to her with their problems. She always made everyone laugh. That's how I am trying to remember her.

Sincerely yours,
Sara Nessen
(LuAnn Wachowsky's daughter)

I wept after reading LuAnn's daughter's email: Sadness at how LuAnn had suffered, that I'd never known the woman or mother she'd become. Guilt that I'd let go of LuAnn. My best friend before Fiona.

That night, I emailed Sara back. I was so very sorry, I wrote, to learn about her mother's death and how much pain she was in during her final years. I added a few sentences about how smart and funny LuAnn had been when we were girls, and how good it is that Sara has been able to hold on to the memories of her mother from before her addiction. I wanted to tell Sara one of LuAnn's jokes, but the only one I remembered—*Why are there gates around cemeteries? Because people are dying to get in!*—was obviously off.

I debated suggesting to LuAnn's daughter that we meet, but I decided it would be a mistake. A mistake unless I was going to be truly available to Sara, who I sensed had fallen into a well of grief. She must have read between the lines that no door was being opened since she didn't write back.

I set my book on my lap. From the time I met LuAnn, we'd always spent our birthdays together. On my sixteenth, LuAnn insisted we play hooky. She pretended to be my mother, reporting to Sister Bernadette in the school office that Ana was seriously sick with spots all over her chest. She might be contagious! I then pretended to be LuAnn's mother, reporting that LuAnn had woken with swollen feet and green toenails. Throughout the day, while we tried on wigs and fur coats and wedding gowns at the Hutzler's department store and then gorged on fried clams and beer we were served after showing our fake IDs, we cracked up that Sister Bernadette had not questioned green toenails.

Not long ago, I listened to a radio interview with a writer who described her fictional characters as 'not *not* her.' Now on my sixtieth birthday, in my reading chair with *Mrs. Dalloway* in my lap and Central Park laid out before me, I would say the same about the girl I'd been with LuAnn: Catching LuAnn's eyes over the shoulder of a hand dryer salesman and then bursting, the two of us, into uncontrollable laughter. Bolting for the bathroom where we smoked a joint standing on opposite edges of the toilet seat, pretending to push each other in. Sneaking out through the bar's back entrance, running hand in hand for the first half mile, and then, once we were sure no one was following, walking the hour to my grandparents' house, where we agreed that we'd never go back to that bar and vowed not to sleep with another man until we were married—a vow only LuAnn kept.

That girl standing on the toilet seat across from LuAnn: She's not me, but she's not *not* me.

I READ ANOTHER FEW PAGES. CLARISSA DALLOWAY INVITES PETER, the man she might have married, to her party, while Peter thinks of his grief, 'which rose like a moon looked at from a terrace, ghastly beautiful with light from the sunken day.' I close the book and check the clock from my father: ten minutes before Henry and I should leave. When my father gave me this unexpected gift, I assumed he'd chosen the clock for its modernist design. Now I wonder if it was also an homage to his own father: the Swiss hotel general manager who'd insisted his employees be as punctual as the country's trains. My father had rebelled against his father's dictates, canceling appointments and—or so it had seemed—making a point of never being on time. And yet, his own work was premised on the precision his father had valued. He once told me he never needed a level; he could detect when a sconce was crooked by half a centimeter. His tyrannical sensitivity was part of what had made his marriage to my mother so doomed.

The lights from the buildings across the park are visible against the darkened sky, the swath of green like the Seine I'd been amazed at eleven, my first time in Paris, to learn sliced the city in half. It was George and my annual summer visit with our father, at work that year on the room renovations for the Hôtel de Crillon. Our first morning in the city, he handed us a map and some francs and told us we could explore on our own. George, too angry to enjoy anything offered or suggested by our father, would return to the hotel by five, but I would often walk along the bank of the river at this hour, the iron streetlamps casting slicks of light onto the water.

My mother never hid that she was glad to have the time without her children, and I once heard her arguing over the phone with my father when he told her he couldn't take us that year until mid-July. Still, my mother must have been envious that George and I were staying in magnificent hotels in glorious cities, while she sat after dinner on the stoop of her parents' house, the sounds of the baseball game her father would watch with the volume turned up high trailing her outside. During her two weeks of vacation, which she took to coincide with our Christmas and Easter school breaks, we never traveled aside from an occasional trip to New York, where we stayed with a friend from my mother's modeling days who'd married a fireman and moved back to Staten Island where she'd grown up. Seeing the city as I imagined my mother had when she'd first come to New York, I was aware of how disappointed she must feel about the way her life had turned out and how deeply she must resent my father for the years when she'd worked to support them as he launched a career that landed him such splendid adventures, whereas she had to return to her childhood bedroom in a row house in Baltimore.

I think now about my mother having said that if there was anything improper about my father's will, it was that he'd left nothing for her. My father had created a trust for Miko but overlooked the woman who'd funded his first architecture office. The woman who'd borne his children and then raised them while he worked on glorious hotels and shared his bed with countless others.

Moving to my desk, I reread my mother's 'Calculations' email. According to my mother, adjusting for inflation, it cost $85,000 to raise me. Assuming the price tag was the same for my brother, the sum for the two of us would be double. Is the $85,000 what my mother thinks my father, with his laggard or absent child support payments, owed her?

Henry and I put three-quarters of what I'd inherited from my father away for after Henry retires, but we've kept the rest—a tad more than my mother's tally—as cash we could access at any time. It's been my hope that one day we'd use that money to send Henry to a rehab clinic. Not soon, it seems, but not *not* soon.

Henry's day, though, is not here, whereas my mother's email is.

I've never thought of myself as an impulsive person—a person who on a whim would write a check for $85,000 with 'repayment' in the memo line. But this is not a whim. This, the check I'm writing, is what my mother must believe she is due. And if there is one thing I know about my mother, it's that if she, Jean, has done the calculations, she, Jean, is certain she is right.

10

ALICE

Nearly every week, someone calls Alice either an angel or a bitch. She's called an angel when she drives a four-year-old with a 106-degree fever and a terrified mother from the Harlem pediatrics clinic where she's the medical director to the hospital because the ambulances for the clinic's neighborhood will take too long to arrive. She's called a bitch when she raises her voice at the admitting clerk and says her patient must be seen immediately—before, not after, anyone tackles the clipboard of forms.

Angel or bitch, her staff tease that she has bionic immunity. Today, however, her T cells are on strike so that she's the one with the fever. Which is why she's approaching her Harlem brownstone two hours earlier than usual. Why she sees a tall, slender woman exiting the front door with a package under her arm.

Half running, gazelle-like, from Alice's stoop, the woman raises her hand for a cab and, of course, for this woman, one appears. As she approaches the cab, she turns her head and Alice sees white-blonde hair swept off an oval face—the face she studied on Ana Koehl's website when she researched the Koehl family after Rolf Koehl's obit had left her wondering if his father had been the man who wouldn't give her grandfather a job due to his being a Jew.

The package the woman is now lifting into the cab is wrapped in green and gold paper. Wrapping paper Alice bought last weekend.

Fuck you, Lance, Alice thinks about her husband. *Fuck you.*

ALICE AND LANCE PURCHASED THE BROWNSTONE ELEVEN YEARS ago by selling the stocks her grandfather had gifted her when she finished her pediatrics residency. They moved into the bottom three floors while she was pregnant with Zena, the top two set aside for rental income and Lance's office, and finished renovating three years later, just days before Wally was born.

From the foyer, Alice calls to their nanny, in the basement playroom with Zena and Wally. 'Marguerite, it's me. Can you keep the kids away? I'm coming down with something.'

Once in her bedroom, she strips off her work clothes and puts on a flannel nightgown she's had since her first year at Brandeis, a college she chose while an ardent Zionist following a summer on a kibbutz. When her roommates gave her the nightgown as a birthday present, she pasted on a pumpkin smile, doing her best to hide her dislike of the virginal bands of meadow flowers, which reminded her of her grandmother's stories of working alongside Swiss farm girls, churning butter and preserving whortleberries.

Alice had been a virgin then, but she didn't like wearing it on her sleeve. As for her Zionism, the last vestiges crumbled during medical school after her op-ed about Palestinian children with stunted growth from malnutrition spurred a torrent of angry letters, including one from a member of her parents' synagogue, who said Alice, not Anne Frank, should have died at Bergen-Belsen.

By the time she met Lance, at dusk on a beach in Kauai, she was resigned to being called a self-hating Jew. Lance had similarly been called an Osama bin Laden and an apologist for terrorism. On her worst days, Alice wonders if it is their shared experience of being reviled that brought them together.

HER HEAD IS THROBBING AND HER THOUGHTS TOO MUDDLED BY fever to confront Lance about Ana Koehl now. Still, she needs to let him know he'll have to handle their kids solo tonight. She calls his work line.

'I'm pretty sure I've got the flu. I saw half a dozen children with it this week.'

'That sucks. Do you need anything?'

'Another medical director to run the clinic while I'm out.'

'You're never sick. They'll have to manage for a few days without you.'

She sent in a prescription for Tamiflu, she tells Lance. The pharmacy will deliver it. Marguerite marinated chicken breasts and cut up broccoli. Zena has a math test tomorrow that she's worked up about. She should do the homework problems again. And Wally has to read for twenty minutes and then write three sentences in his journal. 'Put a timer on,' she instructs Lance. 'Otherwise twenty minutes will be six. And make sure he doesn't think three sentences means three lines of writing. Noun, verb, punctuation mark.'

'Wow. How'd I publish a book and no one ever told me that?'

'Don't forget to check his backpack to see what came home from school. Yesterday, I found half a sandwich smooshed in an outside pocket.'

'Al, I got it. Go to sleep.'

She pulls down the shades and climbs into bed. Over the years, she's seen photos in Lance's travel albums or stuck between the pages of a book of the women before her. The first time she saw a photo of her predecessor, Gina, with her long, smooth abdomen winnowed by lines of cocaine, she felt an unexpected sense of relief: there was no way she could compete physically, no reason to even try. What she offered was in a different phylum.

Lance has told her that on the day they met, it was the medical journal propped on her knees that caught his eye as he emerged with his surfboard under his arm from a navy sea. He asked her about the article she was reading and they chatted about New York, where Alice lived and he'd gone to college for a year. An hour later, sitting across from him at a picnic table at a take-out poke place, the sorrow at her childlessness burst like a buried cyst, mutating into a lust she'd not felt before. She'd never seduced anyone and she certainly wasn't going to try with this man with his loose stride and chiseled face. He was so clearly out of her league, she said it straight out: Did he want to have sex with her?

She'd not understood then but she does now that Lance looks at bodies the way an arborist does trees. His yes, she suspects, was largely because he was stunned by her boldness—but maybe also out of curiosity about what sex would be like with someone who experiences her real self as separate from her body, which she carts around like an overstuffed book bag.

When she called Lance to tell him that she was amazed and ecstatic to discover she was pregnant, she assured him that keeping the baby was her choice and he could be as involved or uninvolved as he wanted. She was shocked when Lance responded by saying they should get married and have the baby together.

At their wedding, Lance vowed to stand by her side, in sickness and health. What he did not promise is fidelity. The problem is not libido. Hers, she's learned with Lance, is as great as his. Rather, the issue is akin to what she recalls from a Brandeis philosophy class: a category error. For her, sex is fundamentally a physical act, whereas for Lance, as best as she can understand, it's something larger. Once he told her that for him, good sex is akin to the oneness he feels with the ocean when he rides a wave. Hearing this, she thought how sophomoric, how self-aggrandizing, how self-justifying. The truth, though, is she feels inadequate: She could no more experience a sexual interaction the way Lance describes than she could stay aloft on a surfboard.

Their arrangement remains unspoken. He doesn't expose her to his affairs, doesn't let them interfere with their family life. On her end, she's never pried or punished him for what she knows.

SHE WAS RELIEVED THAT HER GRANDPARENTS—BUBBE AND ZAYDE, she'd called them—were dead by the time she married Lance. Having fled Zagreb with Alice's infant mother after the Ustaše commenced their extermination of Yugoslavian Jews, they would have viewed her marrying a goy as even more heartbreaking than her not marrying at all.

In Zagreb, Zayde had been a prominent lawyer. He and Bubbe had lived in an Art Nouveau house with dining chairs from the workshop of Otto Wagner and a painting by Egon Schiele over the sofa and a Steinway grand piano on which Bubbe played Schumann and Debussy. In Sondrio, the Italian Alpine village where Zayde's cousin took them in, Bubbe and Zayde and Alice's infant mother lived in a lean-to behind Zayde's cousin's kitchen. Sixteen months later, Italy surrendered to the Allies. Fearing the Nazis would invade and his family would again be in danger, Alice's grandfather paid a guide to lead them over a mountain pass so they could enter Switzerland without going through a border station. Switzerland was officially a neutral country, but everyone knew there were unwritten agreements with the Germans. At the border station, they would have risked being turned away or having their passports marked with a red *J*.

The family was given shelter in a milking barn outside the village of Sils Maria, not far from St. Moritz, where Zayde hoped his fluency in six languages would help him get a job in one of the hotels that catered to winter skiers and summer hikers. When after a year no such job was forthcoming, they returned to Italy to board a boat from Naples for the sole refugee camp on American land. Alice's mother remembers Bubbe's tears of joy at the first sighting of the Statue of Liberty and then her tears of humiliation when on landing they were led to a tent on the dock and told to strip so they could be sprayed with disinfectant.

Arriving at the refugee camp, a former military base in Oswego, New York, Bubbe and Zayde saw the barbed wire fence and were terrified that they'd crossed a sea for a concentration camp. Their fears were assuaged when they were handed a key to their room: cold but clean. There was a school in the camp, and the camp children played in the courtyard with bicycles and balls the town children would pass through a hole in the fence. Now seventy-five, Alice's mother cherishes the memory of lining up with the other girls to meet the visiting Mrs. Eleanor Roosevelt, who handed out yellow pencils and copies of the Constitution bound in little red books.

Alice's mother says that with the war, Zayde stopped believing in the laws of man, which is why he never attempted to work as an attorney in America. Instead, after leaving Oswego, he moved the family to Hartford, where another Jewish family from Zagreb had settled. Together, the two men opened a kosher grocery store, which grew into a chain numbering two dozen. In Zagreb, Alice's grandparents had been secular Jews, but in Hartford they immersed themselves in the community of their orthodox synagogue, where Zayde eventually became the president.

ZENA CRACKS OPEN THE DOOR. 'MOMMY, MOMMY, CAN I COME IN?'

'Don't come closer.' Alice's voice sounds harsher than she intended.

'Daddy told me to bring you this.' She holds up a bag from the pharmacy.

'Thank you, Zeezee.' Alice's throat feels raw. She tries to gather her thoughts, but they're drawn like a magnet to the image of Ana Koehl's upturned face.

Zena's math test tomorrow. Percentages to fractions and decimals. 'How are you feeling about your test?'

Zena looks at the floor.

'You know how to do those conversions. Did you redo the practice problems?'

Zena nods miserably.

'Did Dad check the answers?'

'He said they're all right, but he does them in his head, so he couldn't check my steps.'

'He can convert percentages to fractions in his head?'

It's a bookie's trick his father taught him, Zena explains. He instructed Zena to tell her teacher that what matters is the answer, not how you get there.

When it came time to think about kindergarten for Zena, Lance had been in favor of the nearby public school. Alice was well aware that public schools suffer if affluent families don't send their kids, but with her own daughter, she couldn't get beyond the images of classroom windows that wouldn't open or science labs with broken microscopes. She'd had to accept her moral imperfections. As people would say now, her *privilege*. Accept that she was a mother bear with her kids, which meant she was determined Zena attend the best school for her.

Interviewing Ana Koehl about the school her kid attended was part of the research phase for finding the right kindergarten for Zena—a plan that was foiled when on the afternoon of their coffee date a screaming toddler with what looked like a fractured collarbone came through the clinic door as Alice was putting on her coat. 'Fuck,' she mumbled as she dropped to her knees to listen to the child's labored breathing. A pierced lung?

Jamie, the new doctor, could handle it. No, Jamie, the new doctor, could not. 'Fuck,' she repeated as she scrolled through her emails with Ana—no cell phone number—and realized she would have to ask Lance to go instead.

Alice's own children had eaten dinner by the time she arrived home after accompanying the screaming toddler and hysterical mother to the hospital. She propped her aching feet on a kitchen chair while Lance heated a plate of ravioli slathered with bottled red sauce. This was what he'd given Zena and Wally for dinner? No protein, no vegetables? The ER attending had controlled his anger, but it was clear he thought she was a bitch for insisting that a pediatric pulmonologist consult on her patient, who, as she'd suspected, did have a punctured lung. Don't act like one now, she told herself. Lance had covered for her. He'd left his racquetball game and gone to the diner to meet Ana Koehl.

Lance handed her the plate of ravioli. He took a beer from the refrigerator and sat across from her.

'How'd it go with the school lady?'

'No surprises. The place where her kid goes has all the bells and whistles. He's happy there.'

'I'll put your notes in the file.'

Lance raised an eyebrow.

'You didn't take notes?'

'Come on, Al. Give me a break. I wasn't interviewing a mullah. I can remember the details of a conversation about applying to kindergarten. Besides, you've already decided. It's gonna be private and all-girls.'

'The research shows that girls who attend single-sex schools are more likely to pursue math and science and to assume leadership positions.'

Alice put down her fork. She hated how pompous she sounded. 'Our public school doesn't even have a playground.'

'I'd take her to the park after school.'

'There's no enrichment program.'

'So she doesn't learn second-grade math in first grade. She'll learn it in second grade, which is probably better anyway.'

Now, seven years later, looking at Zena's anxious face as Wally bounds in, Alice wonders if Lance was right: if Zena would have been better off in public school, where no one would assume, as do too many of the girls at her current school, that everyone flies private to Aspen for winter break.

'Not fair!' Wally squeals. 'Marguerite said we couldn't come see you. Why does Zeezee get to be here?'

Wally's cheeks are red. Is he getting sick or is this indignation?

'You're right. But she came up anyway.' Alice holds up her hand like a crossing guard. 'Just don't get too close.'

She takes a long sip from her water. She's learned not to ask her kids dead-end questions: *What was the most interesting/fun/surprising thing that happened at school?* No child wants to decide. Instead, she asks Wally to tell her one thing about today. The first thought that pops into his mind.

'Pops like a balloon?'

'Mom means the first thing you think about,' Zena says in her older sister voice.

Wally stares at the ceiling, as though he might see the contents of his mind displayed there.

'We're doing a countries project. Everyone gets to pick a country and then we bring a food from that country for our class banquet. But it has to be nut free.'

'What did you pick?' Alice asks.

'Switzerland. Theo wanted Switzerland, too, but I told Ms. Murani that our family is Swiss so it's only fair that I get Switzerland.'

'We're not Swiss,' Alice says.

Wally looks alarmed. 'We're not?'

'What made you think we are?'

'Nana told me she lived there as a baby. In a hayloft. And she always gives us chocolate from Switzerland at Chanukah.'

Alice is racked with chills—her fever spiking. She loves her children, but she wants them to leave so she can burrow under the blankets and close her eyes. 'Nana was there for just a year, after her family left Za-greb, before they came here.'

Wally looks like he's about to cry. 'So we're Zagrebians? What foods do they eat?'

At Passover, she's told Zena and Wally about Jews being driven from country to country and then founding Israel on land occupied by Palestinians, but she's too sick now to explain how Nana went from Zagreb to Sondrio to Sils Maria to Naples to Oswego before arriving in Hartford at three years old.

'Zagreb isn't a country. It's a city. When Nana was born, it was part of Yugoslavia, but now it's part of Croatia.'

'So what country should I take?'

Zena is biting her lip. Of late, she's taken to also chewing her hair. The children in Gaza had seemed either profoundly disassociated from their circumstances or riddled with anxiety. There, the source of their distress was clear. With Zena, it's always been a mystery.

Alice's head is pounding. 'Wally, honey, I need to sleep. Tell Marguerite she can take you and Zena for ice cream.'

Zena stops biting her lip and stares at Alice. Usually, she and Wally have carrots and hummus or cheese cubes and apples for an after-school snack. Gross stuff, Wally complains, though he eats it all.

With Zena and Wally gone, Alice curls into a ball. She has no evidence that Ana Koehl has been to their house many times, but Alice is certain she has. Ana Koehl flew down the brownstone stairs as though she knew which step has a buckle and that the bottom one has a deeper drop. And if Alice, on the one afternoon when she came home unexpectedly early, saw Ana, surely Zena has too.

ALICE'S GRANDFATHER BEQUEATHED HER THE HABITS OF TAKING two tablespoons of apple cider vinegar in the morning, which he insisted aided digestion, and reading the obituaries. Every day, he read the obituaries in the *Hartford Courant* and then the ones in the *New York Times*, which he claimed were the best writing in the paper.

Alice's mother would smile when she saw her father reading the obits. He's looking for mention of his *lantzmen*, she told Alice. People he knew in Zagreb or in the refugee camp in Oswego. 'You'd be surprised,' Alice's mother said, 'how many names Zayde has recognized over the years.'

Now, Alice reads the *Times* obits herself. When she recognizes a name, it's usually a parent of someone she knows. Every once in a while,

though, a name rings a bell she can't locate. That's what happened a year
ago with the obituary for Rolf Koehl, an architect, she read, born in Sils
Maria, where his father had been the manager of a hotel that catered to the
European haute monde. Drawing on his childhood experiences, Koehl was
renowned for his renovations of historic hotels. 'Hotels,' he was quoted as
saying, 'should stimulate the imagination and comfort the body.' It hadn't
clicked why she recognized the name until she reached the last line of the
obit where the family members who survived the deceased were listed: the
architect's third wife, Miko; his two children, George and Ana; his three
grandchildren, Ella, Gemma, and Simon.

Ana. Ana Koehl. The wife of Gerry's colleague who Lance had talked
with about her kid's school.

At lunchtime, Alice called her mother. Sils Maria. Wasn't that where
she and Bubbe and Zayde lived before coming to America?

Yes, her mother said, they were in Sils Maria for nearly a year.

She told her mother the name of the architect. His father had worked
at a hotel in the town. 'Does the name sound familiar?' she asked.

Her mother paused. 'Darling, I was a baby. I didn't know anyone's
name.'

SHE FEELS CERTAIN SHE WON'T BE ABLE TO SLEEP, BUT SHE DOES.
When she wakes, Zena is cross-legged on the floor, crying softly.

Alarmed, Alice sits up. 'Honey, what's the matter?'

'You're going to die before me and then I'll have no mother.'

She hears Lance calling the kids for dinner.

'I had a dream last night that you were sick. And now you're sick.'

'Zena, how many times have you had a dream that didn't happen? It's
a coincidence. Or maybe I looked a little pale yesterday and you noticed
that.'

'And you died and Daddy married a witch like in Hansel and Gretel
and Wally and I had to run away.'

The truth is, were she not so wedded to science, she'd think Zena
has premonitions. She first had this thought the day Lance's mother had
her heart attack. Zena had woken that morning crying uncontrollably.

Something horrible, just horrible, was going to happen to Gran. She knew knew knew it. Alice was unable to contain her annoyance. Zena had a kindergarten interview that morning. She had to stop crying and blow her nose and eat her oatmeal so she'd be able in just ninety minutes to cheerfully respond to an admission counselor's directions that she draw a picture of her family. Alice was sitting on the sofa in the admissions office waiting for Zena when she got the call that Lance's mother was in the hospital.

Lance is hollering Zena's name.

'I'll be better in a few days. Go. Have your dinner.'

After Zena leaves, Alice lies back down. She stares at her trembling hands. It's hard to tell what is flu and what is smoldering anger and what is humiliation. Or is it simply sadness that she'll never ever be the one for her husband?

SHE AND LANCE HAD DOWNPLAYED FOR ZENA THE SEVERITY OF her grandmother's heart attack, which she luckily survived, but Zena still took it terribly. Alice blamed herself for having snapped at Zena that morning about her fears for Gran. She should have understood. She'd also adored her grandparents. As a child, she looked forward all year to the week she'd spend with them while her parents took their annual cruise. Every night, Bubbe would make Alice hot milk with honey and cherry syrup, which she'd drink in the leather club chair in Zayde's library while he had his evening pipe and told her about himself when he was her age. In those days, he explained, there'd been no bat mitzvahs, and bar mitzvahs hadn't been big parties the way they were now in Hartford. Bar mitzvahs had been religious occasions with a simple gathering afterward for the men to share a bottle of schnapps and the women and children to have a slice of honey cake. He spent the entire year he was twelve studying for his. The following day, he shocked his parents by announcing he no longer believed in God.

Alice was amazed. Amazed and confused. How could Zayde have ever said he didn't believe in God? He was the president of their synagogue.

Her grandfather took out his tobacco pouch and filled his pipe. For a while, he said, he'd stopped believing in anything he wanted to call God, but he never lost faith in there being a spiritual plane. 'If you lived through the war, the way Bubbe and I did, you understand that good and evil are on a continuum. You know what that means, right?'

Alice nodded. They'd studied continuums in science. Freezing to boiling.

'It's not an on/off switch. At one end were the Nazis, who denied the humanity of entire groups of people.' Zayde paused. 'And the Ustaše who killed my parents.'

Alice clutched the mug of cherry milk. She'd never heard of the Ustaše or that Zayde's parents had been killed.

'My parents and eighty percent of the Jews of Croatia. They're why your grandmother and I left.'

Zayde lit his pipe. For a moment, he looked away. 'I begged my parents to come with us, but they refused. They said they were too old, they'd rather die in their own home. I knew that wasn't the reason. They were afraid they'd slow us down and jeopardize our escape. Your mother was an infant. Your grandmother was still nursing her.'

Alice can no longer recall if it was on that visit or the next year when Zayde told her it was seeing the Alps that reopened his eyes to God. The Swiss mountains and valleys were so perfect, so majestic, they could only have been created by a divine hand. What was imperfect, what's always imperfect, Zayde said, were the people who inhabited those slopes and meadows.

She still remembers the pained look on her grandfather's face as he said that in Switzerland, with no army of their own, no way to protect themselves save with their wiles, nearly everyone was to some degree a collaborator. There were bankers who exchanged gold the Nazis had stolen for money, art dealers who bought paintings taken from Jewish homes, local officials who turned their backs when trains carrying German soldiers and weapons passed through. 'Don't get me wrong, bubbala,' her grandfather said. 'There were good people, just like there are everywhere.' People who went along but helped when they could— like the dairy farmer and his wife who let Bubbe and Zayde and Alice's mother stay in their barn. The night they arrived, Zayde said, the farmer had taken Alice's mother into his own house so Bubbe—she was half-dead after their four-day walk—could get some rest. The farmer's wife gave Alice's mother hot chocolate and cheese toast and bathed her and dressed her in clothes that had belonged to the farmer's own children.

Bubbe gave the farmer one of the pieces of gold jewelry she'd stitched inside their suitcase linings before they'd left Zagreb and, in an unspoken exchange, the farmer wrote an introduction for Zayde to the general manager of a nearby hotel. The farmer's son, a classmate of the general manager's son, escorted Zayde to the hotel, where the general manager handed him a stack of newspapers in different languages and asked him to read aloud various passages. The general manager was impressed with Zayde's command of English. His own English, the manager said, was not nearly as proficient—though it had allowed him to converse with the American playwright Thornton Wilder, who'd been a guest at the hotel.

'Everything changed after he asked for my passport. When he saw that there was no Swiss stamp, he knew I was a Jew. He'd been mistaken, he said. There were no positions open.'

Zayde knocked the ash from his pipe. 'I'll never forget what he said as he handed me back my passport. Sir, he said, I have my own children. My son is seventeen. He is taking his university exams in a month.'

Alice's grandfather clenched his leather tobacco pouch. 'I'd wanted to reply, Sir, I have a wife and baby living now in a barn, but in that moment I saw that in this man's moral universe, his responsibility for others stopped with his kin.'

ALICE WAKES AT THE TAIL END OF SUNSET. LOOKING OUT HER WIN-dow, she sees streaks of scarlet and tangerine. Her thoughts go to the green and gold wrapping paper. She bought it thinking it would work for birthday presents for any gender at the endless stream of skating, bowling, swimming, paintball, ceramic-making parties.

She remembers now that when she told Lance she'd read the obituary for the father of the woman he'd met years before while they were re-searching kindergartens, he didn't respond. Had Lance touched his scar?

It was his tell. At the time, she'd been too horrified at the thought that the woman might be the granddaughter of the man who wouldn't hire Zayde to pay attention to what Lance touched.

Zena was four when they were looking at kindergartens. Seven years ago. Has this—she can't even say the word to herself—been going on since then?

LANCE COMES IN TO ASK IF SHE'D LIKE HIM TO BRING HER A DINNER tray.

'No, don't bother. I'll come down soon.'

He approaches as though to give her a kiss, and she waves him away. 'I'm contagious.'

Lance steps back dramatically. Does he really think she's being overly cautious? The first time he teased that she leaves no stone unturned, she was confused. Was he criticizing her? She didn't understand, she said, why anyone would choose to do a half-assed job.

'You shouldn't sleep here tonight,' she says. 'You might catch what I have.' This afternoon, he sent her a text that Neil would be staying with them for a few days. 'Neil won't be here until tomorrow, right?'

'Right.'

'Maybe you can sleep in your office?'

So as not to get Lance's hackles up, Alice has learned to add the *maybe* when she announces her plans. The problem is never the plan itself, but that she always has a plan, and she always has it earlier than anyone else. Certainly, earlier than Lance, whose plans often seem impromptu, which, as far as Alice is concerned, is not a plan at all.

Lance picks up her water glass. 'I'll have one of the kids bring you a fresh one.'

'Are they doing their homework?'

'Wally has to fill out a worksheet about his countries project. He asked me how to spell *Zagrebians*—I couldn't figure out what the hell he was talking about. He got so frustrated he threw his backpack on the floor. And Zena says there's no point studying for her math test because she's going to fail it no matter what.'

'You were right. She would have been better off learning fifth grade math in fifth grade.'

'Did I say something as smart as that?'

'You did. You said it after you went to that coffee with the wife of Gerry's colleague.' She pauses before saying the name. 'Ana Koehl.'

From Alice's prone position, Lance appears to be looming over her. She's certain he's thinking, *Are you sure? Are you sure you want to open that door tonight?*

HALF AN HOUR LATER, SHE GOES DOWNSTAIRS. LANCE IS AT THE sink, loading the dishwasher. 'Ready to eat?' he asks over his shoulder.

The room is spinning and her flannel nightgown is sticking to her sweaty back. She leans against the refrigerator door. 'Maybe later. Where are the kids?'

'Downstairs. They finished their homework. I told them they could watch TV until shower time.'

She waits for the ceiling and walls to settle back into their corners before speaking again. 'I saw her. As she was getting into a cab.'

Lance shuts off the water. He wipes his hands on his jeans and turns to face her. She's grateful that he doesn't act dumb.

'I recognized her—from the photo on her website.' She clasps the refrigerator handle. 'Zena picks up everything. Tonight she was crying because she's worrying I'm going to die.' She doesn't add: *And you replace me with a witch.*

She crosses to the sink and takes a dishwasher soap pod from the cabinet underneath. She thinks about telling Lance that she wanted to run across the street and inform Ana Koehl that her grandfather was no better than a Nazi, maybe he was a Nazi, but her throat is raw and she's burning up and she fears her knees might buckle.

'It has to stop.' She hands Lance the dishwasher soap pod.

Back in bed, she pulls the covers up to her chin. Everyone had to collaborate to survive, Zayde said. Find their place on the continuum.

Switzerland, she thinks. That's where I am.

She closes her eyes. *Switzerland. That's who I am.*

11

ANA

'Happy birthday,' Carlos says as Henry and I exit the elevator.

'Thank you, Carlos. But how did you know?'

He points to a wrapped flower arrangement on the lobby console. I lean over to read the card:

"It was the moment between six and seven when every flower—roses, carnations, irises, lilac—glows; white, violet, red, deep orange; every flower seems to burn by itself, softly, purely in the misty beds; and how she loved the grey-white moths spinning in and out, over the cherry pie, over the evening primroses!"

Happy birthday, sister-friend. Love always, Fiona

I can hear Fiona reciting these lines to the florist with instructions on the precise punctuation. I look over at Henry, intending to joke that the flowers are from Clarissa, but there's a strained expression on his face.

The night after Henry gave my father some pot, I spotted Lance's book on our coffee table. With Henry having said nothing about the book, I put it back on the shelf in my office, pushing out of mind why Henry had been looking at it or what he'd made of the inscription Lance had written to me. Oh my God: Does Henry think—

'Fiona. A quote from Mrs. Dalloway.' Handing Henry the card, I tell Carlos I'll take the flowers upstairs when we return.

Outside, I inhale deeply. It is, indeed, the moment of the evening primroses: tree branches glowing, air balmy with the hint of the coming season. We cross the street and enter the park, joining young families en route to the playground, late-working nannies with toddlers in strollers, teenagers headed for trysts or smokes. It's Henry—even with his back injury, up every weekday at five—who has made it possible for us to live here, in this city that changes at a pace outstripping my rate of exploration so the sense of discovery is bottomless.

'You look lovely. Is that a new blouse?'

I'm embarrassed. Embarrassed that I'm more pleased by the compliment than I should be at sixty. Ashamed that it comes from a man I've treated so shabbily. 'My mother will disapprove of my not wearing heels, but I'm so happy you want to walk.' I hesitate, fearing an answer I don't want to hear. 'Are you sure?'

Henry looks warmly at me. Is he relieved that the flowers are from Fiona? 'We're not climbing Kilimanjaro. Just crossing Central Park.' He hasn't given me a birthday present, and for a moment, I worry it will be something extravagant—a trip to somewhere exotic or an expensive piece of art that if I give my mother the check in my bag, we will no longer be able to afford.

When we reach the reservoir, I ask, 'Should we circle north or south?'

'I think south,' Henry says, and I know that in his dependable but modest way—he always does the legwork, but does not view this as grounds for insisting—he's looked at a map and figured out our best route.

I wait until we're settled on our course before I begin. 'There's something I want to tell you.'

Henry listens, never interrupting, while I describe my mother's email with the accounting of what I cost her.

'I'm sorry,' he says when I finish. I imagine he's thinking that his mother, now gone, could never have treated her children in such an aggressive manner.

'In social work school, we learned about splitting: how certain fragile people can't tolerate ambivalence. They rope off their negative feelings and then direct them to one place. It made immediate sense to me. It's what happens with my mother: I get all her resentment and hostility and she's left with a clean slate of affection for George.'

'Are you sure you can still go through with tonight?'

I laughed when Fiona suggested bagging the dinner. Now, I seriously consider the idea. It's thrilling to know I'm free to choose. But what would I be choosing? As Gordon, with his never-cancel rule, would have said, I'd be choosing myself over everyone else arriving now to celebrate my birthday.

'I am. But there's something more I need to tell you.'

I search for the right words. There are none. I just have to say it in whatever clumsy way I can manage. 'Before we left, when I was alone in my office, I had this strange experience. It was as if a veil had been lifted and I could look through my mother's eyes. As if I were my mother, watching me. I could see how my attempts to get her to understand why I'm so upset about George not asking me before he gave Simon the money from my father feel to her like a slap in the face.'

I glance at Henry. He nods slightly.

'My father never asked her permission for anything. He cheated on her'—with *cheated*, my mouth turns dry— 'and then left her to take care of George and me on her own. What's on her mind is what should have gone to her.' There's the crunching of Henry's footsteps, the hum of distant traffic. 'It's sort of heartbreaking.'

I touch Henry's arm. 'I want to use the money I inherited from my father to give my mother what she calculated she spent on me. It would be as though he'd paid her back. But I won't do it if you object.'

Henry keeps his eyes on the gravel path. 'I brought a check with me, but I'll rip it up if you want me to.'

I count Henry's steps. Nine before he responds. 'You understand, don't you, your brother will never do the same?'

We've reached the southern edge of the reservoir and are walking east now, into the darkened sky. I haven't been here with Henry since Simon was a baby. Then, unable, either of us, to follow the pediatrician's advice that babies be left to cry in their cribs so they learn to put themselves to sleep, we'd circle the reservoir every night with Simon in his carriage. By the time we arrived home, Simon would be fast asleep, and we'd have a light dinner and a glass of wine and almost always make love.

We walk a few more paces before Henry continues. 'If it's important to you, you should do it.'

My eyes well with tears. That I've not been struck by lightning for deceiving this man is the strongest proof I have that the universe has no interest in me.

Henry's jaw is slightly clenched. For a few minutes, I've forgotten that he's what I still think of as the temporary Henry. Temporary even though it's been nearly a decade that he's been living inside the penumbra of pain. With the dimming light, I see the dark outline of that throbbing sensation, a tyrant that has silenced so much between us.

'Are you going to be okay without vaping?'

'I'll manage. If I seem reserved about your giving the money to your mother, it's because I'm preoccupied with the birthday present I planned for you.' Henry pauses. 'Can we sit while I tell you?'

I envision my mother's pinched look at our arriving late, then think, *Oh, Mom. You'll have to suck it up.* Or rather, I'll have to suck it up. Suck up my mother's disapproval.

Henry takes my arm and leads us to an alcove of benches. He presses the base of his spine against the back of the seat. 'I've come to a decision.' His voice is even and firm. 'I'm going to stop using pot.'

I've thought about this so very many times, just tonight as I was writing the check to my mother, but Henry's declaration still arrives as a shock. 'You'll go to a rehab?'

'No. The issue for me is more pain management than addiction. I've been researching new non-pharmaceutical methods. Neuro-stimulation, injection of fibrin into the discs. I'm going to consult with someone who's at the cutting edge of this work.'

Henry looks me straight in the eyes. 'The pot is destroying us. I'm losing you because of it.'

I wonder if now he'll bring up Lance, his having seen Lance's book, the *For everything.*

'Do you remember that series we read when Simon was little?' Henry asks. 'There was a volume for each year.'

'Louise Bates Ames. We still have them.'

'What she said about two-year-olds—they play side by side, in parallel, rather than together? That's how we've been living.'

Henry puts his arms around me. As he kisses me, the park lamps turn on. It's a real kiss, not a peck to the cheek, and my heart beats faster, as though he's a man I don't know.

When I look up, the path we've been walking on is illuminated—aglow like the sand under the feet of the boy and girl running arm in arm in Henry's *The Storm*.

THE DÉCOR OF THE RESTAURANT GEORGE, OR MORE LIKELY, CATHerine, has chosen seems intended to evoke a louche café in the days of colonial Saigon or Shanghai: a black and white mosaic floor, oxblood banquettes, banana leaves undulating under wooden ceiling fans. The sort of place where the fifteen-year-old girl in *The Lover* might have gone with the man who'd spotted her on a ferry crossing the Mekong river in a threadbare red silk dress and gold lamé shoes.

Following the hostess to our private room, I reel from the jasmine incense. LuAnn and I had wielded the same childish eroticism as the girl in threadbare red silk—LuAnn with her boobs showing above her sweetheart neckline, me in my Twiggy dresses. Not with a man waiting on a riverbank in a white limousine, but with salesmen in a Baltimore hotel bar. My breath catches as I see the room filled with so many people, none of whom ever saw my slutty getups: George supervising the sommelier's uncorking of bottles, Catherine laughing at something on Ella's boyfriend's phone, Fiona and Charlie talking with Gemma's husband, Simon and my nieces leaning into one another. Only my mother is seated, alone at the head of the table with an oversized glass of garnet wine.

Simon and my nieces swarm me, swallowing me in a group hug. Ella, an arm around Gemma, smiles at me, a telegram that she and her sister are okay now. 'I saw all of you earlier today,' I laugh as I extricate myself. 'Let me say hi to Nana.'

My mother regards me sternly as I cross the room, but instead of the usual sting of her judgment—My outfit, unlike Catherine's mint peplum suit and silver heels, is insufficient for the occasion? The ten minutes late? —I am amused. Sorry, Mom, I imagine saying: You would have been even more horrified if you'd seen how I dressed at sixteen. But now I'm sixty. I can wear whatever I want. I can sit on a park bench while my husband tells me he wants our marriage back.

Bending to kiss my mother's cheek, I'm more impressed than wounded by her extending her face while contracting her torso. Brava, Mom, I want to say. You could have been a Martha Graham dancer.

I touch the shoulder pad on the jacket of one of my mother's seven jelly bean–colored suits. 'You look very festive, Mom.'

'I told you I'd wear my suits.'

'And you were right.'

George clinks a glass with the flat edge of a butter knife and announces that everyone should take a seat.

'Did you read my email?' my mother asks.

'I did. Your calculations. Let's talk about it later.'

I can tell that she's about to object, but then Catherine calls out in the loudest version of her fluty voice, 'People! There are name cards!'

I catch Henry's eye, wondering if George or Catherine consulted with him—after all, he is the host—about the seating plan. He shrugs his shoulders and smiles. It's a trivial slight, I imagine him saying. Years ago, I would have taken offense on his behalf, but tonight I'm only grateful that Catherine, having placed her daughters on either side of their grandmother, has assured that my mother will be sufficiently doted upon.

Not until I'm seated, at the opposite end of the table from my mother, with Simon to my left and Henry and then George to my right, does it occur to me that I didn't tell Henry about Simon having set a date for their bottom surgery or their having a trans-mom who along with Ella will help them. Just thinking 'bottom surgery,' I'm flooded with gruesome images. I turn toward Simon so I won't have to look at my brother's face, which would only make it worse.

In the room's soft light, I see more clearly how Simon is feminizing. I think about the accounts I've read about little boys—four, five, six— who say they are girls, and little girls, the same age, who say they are boys, and what those parents confront as they decide how to respond. Remind myself, as Fiona has said, that I have no decision to make. It's Simon's, not my, bottom.

George again clinks the edge of his raised glass. He stands. 'To my sister. To another sixty years.'

Catherine beams at her husband. 'Hear, hear!' she adds.

Fiona rolls her eyes—in disbelief, I'm sure, that George can offer nothing more than that I survived six decades. So have the footed soup bowls stacked on the back burner of my mother's stove, I think. I remind myself what Fiona has said about George: he's just someone who shares half your genes. Not a brother. No brother would refuse a sister money for an abortion or leave her alone after her apartment was burglarized.

But then the thought comes to me: Fiona is wrong. George *is* my brother. Nothing he does or does not do can change that. He's the only other person who knows what it was like to live with our mother and grandparents in a decrepit Baltimore row house with the bathroom smelling of old people and dinners of sandwiches made from stale bread, and to then fly with placards around our necks to spend a few summer weeks with our father in rooms deemed too run-down for guests at a five-star hotel in a marvelous locale. He's the only other person who ate cereal in those footed bowls. That he doesn't match my idea of what a brother should be does not make him any less my brother.

HENRY AND SIMON AND MY NIECES AND FIONA GIVE REAL TOASTS. Henry talks about how he was raised in a happy home, already a high bar, but I created ours, he claims, with a level of kindness and beauty that surpassed anything he'd ever known and raised Simon to be an adult with the same fine qualities. I tear up from appreciation at being so appreciated.

When Simon stands, I see my mother peering at them. She reads the *New York Times* every morning, goes with her grandchildren to the movies. She knows about transgender people. Soon, Simon will have to tell her.

The greatest gift I gave them, Simon says, was to make clear that the only thing I want of them is to be well in the largest sense of the word—productive and healthy and ethically sound. 'This may seem like a modest thing,' Simon says, 'but it left me free.' They only now understand how very hard it is for parents to grant this space to a child.

Again, my eyes fill with tears. I wonder if anyone else hears what Simon is saying: that they believe I will continue to hold to that principle.

As they did for Simon's graduation, my nieces read a silly poem they've written, alternating stanzas between them, and reciting together the refrain:

> Sweet Aunt Ana was our babysitter
> So very kind and cool and super smart
> We were the pups of her cuddly litter
> We'll never ever—ever!—grow apart!

When they're done, Ella pats Gemma's belly and Simon cheers and everyone applauds.

Fiona stands next. She tells the story of how we met in grad school, before either of us even knew our husbands, how surprised she was when I asked to read her poems, and that we've been each other's confidante ever since. How we both abandoned English PhDs, but unlike her, I put what we'd learned to use, combining what I absorbed studying literature with what I mastered while in social work school about helping people. 'Ana's the unsung hero of so many fine works that would never have made it between two covers without her.'

Fiona leans over my chair to hug me, and we both whisper *love you*.

'Nana,' Simon says. 'It's your turn.'

'Nana! Nana!' Ella cheers. Gemma helps her grandmother to her feet.

My mother pulls back her still substantial shoulders. In my favorite photograph of her, she's modeling a bathing outfit: blue and white gingham with a halter top and a bottom that today would be called boy shorts. Now, in her jelly bean-colored suit with her box-blonde hair, she looks lumpy, more bag of flour than pinup girl.

'Thank you to our hosts, George and Catherine,' my mother says, 'for this magnificent meal. I'm sure it will cost a fortune.' She sweeps a regal hand in George's direction. He gives her a little salute while Catherine blows a kiss.

'And Henry!' Catherine calls out. 'Thank you to Henry too.'

My mother sits down.

For a split second, I think she's collapsed but then there's a squeak as she draws her chair in.

Henry reaches under the table for my hand. He traces small circles with his thumb on the inside of my wrist. Fiona mouths *What the fuck?*

George raises his glass again. 'Thank you, Mom. Without you, we wouldn't be here. Now, let's eat.'

WHILE THE WAITER BRINGS OUT THE SALADS, I EXCUSE MYSELF TO go to the restroom. I lock the door and stare at myself in the mirror. My face is drained of color, but composed. In her toast, my mother was unable to even say my name. I feel an ache in the spot where if someone were butterflying me for a roast, the knife tip would be inserted, but I am not obliterated. I am not wrecked. I am fully here.

On my mother's sixtieth birthday, she took the train from Baltimore, where she lived by then alone, staying, as usual, with George and Catherine. It was before Simon or Gemma were born. With Ella too young for a long restaurant meal, Henry had offered to cook: my mother's favorite beef tenderloin with a horseradish sauce. George brought the wine. I can't recall the cake. Probably Catherine organized it. It was a nice evening, but there was no husband to hold my mother's hand under the table. No friend to whisper *love you.*

I put on the coral lip gloss purchased to match my silk blouse, then check my phone. There's an email from Sara, LuAnn's daughter, with, to my surprise, *Happy Birthday Ana!* in the subject line.

After Sara's email informing me of LuAnn's death, I basically shut the door in her face. Politely, of course—the way earlier today I did with the man in the windbreaker on the museum bench. She'd asked nothing of me, but I sensed her anguish and what she yearned for from me, once her mother's best friend. Deemed what would be required to help her more than I wanted to do.

It was during my father's final days that my thoughts about Sara changed. I could tell he was burdened with regret and I didn't ever want to feel that way. 'It was the most important lesson he taught me,' I told Fiona. 'Not to put off doing the right thing because time really does run out and it really can be too late. With LuAnn's daughter, it dawned on me that accepting I wouldn't do everything for her didn't have to mean doing nothing.'

Fiona patted my hand. 'You're a good girl, Ana.'

Since then, Sara and I have been emailing and we've had a few video calls. The first time I saw her face, so like LuAnn's, I could hardly speak. But how does she know it's my birthday?

I open the email. Sara has attached a photo of one of the letters she found in her parents' attic. She thought I might want to read it today.

April 28, 1977

Dear Ana,

I woke up this morning and realized it's your birthday!!! Happy 20th Birthday!!! We're no longer teens. Before you know it, we'll be middle-aged ladies.

I haven't been able to mail my first two letters to you, but now I'm writing again because I'm hoping I can find a way to mail this one. I actually thought about standing on the road and waving someone down and asking them to put the letters in a mailbox in town, but Ron and his dad know everyone round here and I'm afraid they'd hear about it.

I miss you so much, it hurts.

Love,

LuAnn

LuAnn swims before me. Her gap-tooth smile, her auburn shag, the matching platform shoes we wore to the Hilton bar. Oh, LuAnn. How I would have loved to see you today.

WITH SIMON'S HELP, I BLOW OUT THE SIXTY CANDLES PLUS THE extra one for good luck on my birthday cake. My wish is that Simon will be well and safe as Simona. That's it, dear universe. Grant me that.

After the waiter has served cake to everyone, I carry my handbag to my mother's end of the table and ask Ella if we can switch places. 'Of course! I haven't started my piece yet. I'll eat yours and you can have mine!'

I take Ella's chair, and taste the cake. It's delicious: angel food with lemon preserves between the layers.

My mother pushes her plate an arm's length away. 'I'm going to take it home.' She points at the waiter, who's circling with a carafe of coffee. 'Tell him to wrap it for me.'

'I will. When he's done serving the coffee.'

'I want him to do it now.'

I cover my mother's hand with my own. 'It won't be but another few minutes, Mom. Don't worry. You'll get to take your cake home.' With my hand atop my mother's, we're like the trunk of a tree, its history inscribed in concentric rings. At the innermost ring, I'm still the four-year-old terrified when I'm left alone in the children's room of the library that my mother will never return. At the outer ring, I'm the adult reassuring my now eighty-eight-year-old mother that her cake will be packed up, in just a few minutes, and that she'll be able to eat it later in her robe and slippers with some milk in one of her thrift store glasses and the eleven o'clock news turned up high.

My mother purses her lips. 'I watch my figure. There's not an actuary alive who doesn't know that maintaining a proper weight is one of the most powerful predictors of life span—but also so I don't have to purchase new clothes.'

'You're very disciplined.'

I open my bag and take out the envelope with the check inside. I hand it to my mother. 'Don't open this until you get home.'

My mother holds the envelope between her thumb and forefinger. She looks curiously at me.

'It's from me, but it's also from my father.' I touch my mother's arm. 'And thank you, Mom. I mean it. Truly.'

I pick up the plate with my mother's slice of cake. 'I'll get it wrapped for you.'

'Ana,' my mother says, her usual booming tone now soft.

I lean closer so I can hear her over the din. 'You're my only daughter.' My mother's voice cracks.

In my sixty years, I've never heard my mother's voice crack. Never heard her say anything that suggested I was special to her. I kiss her forehead and whisper in her ear, 'You can say it, Mom. You can say you love me.'

My mother looks down at the table. She nods. It's the best, I know, she can do.

'I'm so old now. I feel so very lonely.'

'I'll come see you tomorrow.'

She grips my arm with her free hand. 'Do you promise?'

'I do, Mom. I promise.'

MIDNIGHT

I STAND OUTSIDE THE CLOSED DOOR OF THE TV ROOM, LISTENING to the whir of the fan, holding at bay my disappointment that Henry is vaping the marijuana he missed while we were out. Chastising myself for thinking that his announcement that he's going to stop using pot meant he would stop tonight.

I forgot to ask Henry if he's been following the story about Kayla Greenwood and Kenneth Williams—how, as an anesthesiologist, he views the race to use the expiring midazolam, the accusation that the execution was unnecessarily cruel. Now, though, what I want to know is how Kayla Greenwood, only twenty-two, just a girl really, moved beyond opposing the death penalty. Moved beyond punishment and justice to pure forgiveness.

In truth, I can't envision what my life will be like if Henry stops using pot. He's right: we've been like children in parallel play, even more so since Simon left for college. We've been sharing a roof and bank accounts and meals in the way of married couples, but I've been living like a single person—alone in the apartment while Henry is at work; alone, too, when he's home, behind closed doors in his vaping den.

What I really don't know is if Henry will be able to forgive me. Or, Fiona would say, if I'll be able to forgive him.

CHANGED INTO PAJAMAS, I GO TO MY OFFICE. THE PHOTO OF THE Buddha Vairochana is on my desk, still covered with the green and gold paper. A year ago, I would have thought Henry never comes in here. I would have unwrapped it, leaned it against the wall. Now I put the wrapped photo in my office closet.

For seven years, I've betrayed my husband. That remains despite my certainty now that Henry knows about Lance. Knows, all the while, perhaps thinking I know that he knows and I think that he does not want me to acknowledge that I know that he knows. It's such a twisted upside-down inside-out idea, even I can't completely untangle it.

Perhaps this is part of loving someone—letting certain things live underground. The communication unspoken but still there, like the fungal networks between trees Simon has told me about. Isn't the subterranean the foundation for great art? Isn't seduction dependent on what is not shown: a woman who reveals a wrist beneath the cuff of her tightly buttoned sleeve more alluring than the one with her breasts exposed? The spaces left for the viewer or reader or lover to fill in.

WHEN THE PHONE RINGS, I SEE FROM THE CALLER ID IT'S FIONA.

'Your mother! What a piece of work. The toast she gave. Oh my God. She looked like someone who hasn't taken a shit in five days. Even on your sixtieth birthday, it has to be about fucking George.'

'I went to the bathroom, thinking I was going to cry, but by the time I got there, all I felt was sadness for her.'

'I saw you talking with her afterward.'

'It was kind of amazing. She couldn't come out and say it, but I was certain she was thinking that she doesn't want to die with us so distant from each other. I'd be devastated if I ever felt with Simon the way she must feel with me.'

'That's like comparing a Motel Six with a Four Seasons. Just think about how you hug Simon and how she hugs, or more accurately, doesn't hug you.'

'Before we left for the dinner, I reread her birthday email, her accounting of what she'd spent on me, and for a moment, I had that experience you and I used to talk about with Virginia Woolf of being catapulted between minds. I felt like I could see myself as my mother sees me.'

It's quiet on the other end of the line, Fiona having stopped her puttering.

'Here she'd worked herself to the bone to raise George and me after she threw out her philandering husband—if you think about it, for her time, a pretty brave thing to do. And now George and I are both living so well and she's left still counting her pennies. Then there's this windfall we both get from her ex-husband. Money George doesn't need—for him, it's chump change—but she's too cowed by his wealth to get angry with him, so it's me who gets the brunt of her resentment.'

'She's a fighter. More battleship than mum, but a fighter. You have to give her that.'

I hesitate. Can I tell Fiona what I did?

'I decided to pay her back. I wrote her a check for the $85,000 she calculated it cost to raise me.'

'You're kidding.'

'I used the money I inherited from my father.' I exhale loudly. 'It felt right, like a sort of poetic justice.'

I hear a drawer opening, picture Fiona retrieving her hidden cigarette pack. 'Poetic justice makes it sound as if you got that money because of a crime you committed.'

'Well, maybe it was poetic justice for my father—that some of his money went to my mother. Either way, I feel lighter. Liberated.'

Fiona is quiet for a moment before she asks, 'How'd your mother react?'

'I gave her an envelope and told her not to open it until she got home. But I think she knew it had something to do with her calculations email because that's when she told me that I'm her only daughter.' My voice falters, the way my mother's had. 'She told me she's lonely.'

'Oh, love.'

'It's taken me sixty years to see it, but the reality is that neither she nor my brother signed on to be anyone's emotional handmaiden.'

'That's part of the job of being a parent.'

'For us it is. But it wasn't for her or most parents of that generation.

Her definition of her job was to make sure we were fed and clothed and reached eighteen still alive.'

There's the sound of Fiona opening the slider doors to her deck. I glance at the clock my father gave me. In another forty-five minutes, my birthday will be over. 'Your mom,' I continue, 'the way she wanted to understand you and be close to you, that wasn't the norm and probably still isn't the norm in most of the world. If it didn't make me so sad, I'd be amused by the irony—all those years when I hungered for my moth-er's tenderness, only to now have her hunger for mine. We've turned into the garden variety of an elderly parent's longing for their adult child outstripping the child's longing for the parent.'

I feel a twinge of anxiety. For Fiona, nothing with Nick has ever been or ever will be garden variety. Fiona knows I understand this, but I don't want her to wonder if I've even momentarily forgotten. 'You're probably thinking you'd jump with joy if Nick was independent enough from you that you'd be counting the days until you see him.'

Fiona laughs. 'With a son like Nick, there are no separation pains.' Fiona would never say, it's the consolation prize. For Fiona, Nick is simply Nick, a child who like all children brings joy and grief. She's unwavering in her refusal to let her dramas upstage anyone else's, in her belief that we all have painful experiences and they don't have numbers attached indicating whose is worse. 'Do you think your mother will cash the check?'

'She'll view it as my having won the volley, advantage Ana, but she'll cash it. I'm sure of that.'

'I wonder what she'll say to you.'

'If I know her, not a word.'

AFTER FIONA HANGS UP, I REALIZE THAT I'VE BEEN WAITING FOR Lance, who's never, save for his trips to far-flung time zones or off-the-grid locales, missed a night texting or calling since our first afternoon together at his studio. I check my email. Maybe he's written, thinking I'm still at the party? Or maybe what I said to Fiona about my mother is wrong. Maybe she's sent a thank-you for the check.

The only new email is from Bettina. She wants me to know how much better she feels since our meeting. A great fog of confusion has lifted. She can now see the road ahead.

I look out my window. My own fog of confusion hovers over Central Park: a tattooed man punching a trans woman in a Zagreb bar, the cover of one of the Louise Bates Ames books Henry and I would read, an image from a YouTube video about male to female 'bottom' surgery. I shudder imagining Simon on an operating table. With or without the money from their grandfather and (although they would never say this) with or without their parents' blessing, Simon has made it clear that for them, this next step is inexorable. As surely as my hands will line and gnarl, as my bones will grow porous, my muscles weak, my vision dim, Simon will become Simona.

On more than one occasion, Fiona has said that the most important thing she's learned with Nick is that the kindest act is to see people as they are. To want from others only that which they require to be themselves. I thought about this when Henry and I watched the Werner Herzog documentary about the young man who'd lived for years with grizzly bears, filming them in their extraordinary grandeur, his footage accompanied by a running monologue about how he'd crossed into a realm of empathic understanding with the animals such that they knew and accepted him as the protector he'd assigned himself to be. His project ended when one of the bears attacked and ate him. In the utmost expression of the horror and folly of his failure to recognize the animals for the wild beasts they are, his death was captured by the video camera he'd set up to film them.

For grizzlies, attacking when they feel hunger pangs is instinctual. There is no morality involved. The same is true for my mother. Being right, whether about the proper clothing for the day or the debt she's owed, is for my mother a necessity: her way of keeping herself intact. For George—the once pimply kid with every report card a litany of his failures and a father he believed forgot about him eleven months a year and then, during the weeks the three of us were together, still kept his mind on his work—reinventing himself as a rich patriarch who takes his family on fire and ice vacations has been his way of healing himself.

I move to my reading chair and spread the throw blanket folded atop the ottoman over my legs. Toothpicks, George teased when I was a girl, jeering until I would cry. It has taken two-thirds of a lifetime to understand how impersonal his taunts really were. How little the desire to hurt me had to do with anything about me, but rather with his having never wanted a sibling and most definitely not a younger sister who he was expected to walk to school and deliver to her classroom.

I didn't ask Henry how he paid for the dinner, but I'm certain that either Catherine arranged payment in advance or George insisted when the bill arrived that he and Henry put down two credit cards. How strange that I'm certain my brother—who handled our father's will, Fiona says, like a bagman and shifted the shares, she pointed out, to his family's favor—would not stick Henry with a bill from a more expensive restaurant than he would have chosen himself. I'm certain because my brother does not see himself as a bagman or a thief. Because he believes what he did with our father's will was simply a sound financial decision. He's probably now in bed, plowing through a political biography and thinking he did the right thing again tonight.

HENRY IS ASLEEP ON HIS BACK ON THE TV ROOM FLOOR. I SHUT off the fan and the television, remove the bolster from under his knees, and lie next to him.

I wait a few minutes, listening to his breathing, then gently shake his shoulder.

He moans. Can I infiltrate his pain? An ambush while the despot is off guard?

I move onto my side and unfasten his trousers. Put my hand inside his briefs and touch his warm, flaccid penis.

I cannot remember the last time I touched my husband's penis.

I hold his cock from the shaft and slowly move my hand up and down.

Henry opens his eyes. 'It's you,' he whispers.

When he flinches, I worry his back is spasming. But before I can ask if he's okay, he shifts so he's facing me.

'Ana,' he murmurs in a husky voice. He touches my lips and presses against me. 'Ana turns sixty.'

AFTERWARD, I GO BACK TO MY OFFICE TO SHUT THE LIGHTS. WITH the room dark, the trees in the park look like ghost dancers, their branches raised limbs. They seem to be waving at me. Waving goodbye. With a crush of pain, it strikes me that the goodbye is to Lance. Or maybe, with Lance not having called tonight, the goodbye is from him.

I hug my arms. Perhaps Lance and I have reached the end in tandem. If so, we'll be spared the anguish of one pleading with the other to be let go or to stay, though there'll be a different anguish: the decision not fully belonging to either of us, the fresh ache of our remaining even in our last moments in sync, aligned, attuned.

The iron lamps in the park are now yellow globes surrounded by a milky halo. It dawns on me that what I know, I know in the way a gopher can detect an approaching tornado or my starchitect father could see that a door frame was a quarter-inch askew. In the way I could smell when my child would in an hour spike a fever, that my neck prickled as I examined the androgynous dervish at the Rubin Museum and the man who would soon be my lover studied me from behind. In the way I can sense Henry knows about Lance and that my mother wants me near. It's far from everything, but it's more than I've ever let myself know that I know.

The clock my father gave me reads nearly midnight. For all the occasions he'd missed, he said when he gave it to me. I'm glad he didn't enumerate since no list would have sufficed. Had I learned before he died what Lance told me—Alice believed my grandfather might have refused to hire her grandfather because he was a Jew—I would have asked my father if he thought this could be true. Perhaps it was a gift that we were spared that conversation. One more item on his balance sheet.

With the hands aligning now at the twelve, heralding a new day, I hear the *n* my father took from my name. *An-na.*

I feel the three syllables of Simona form in my mouth. *Si-moan-uh.* Henry touching my lips.

I see my mother holding my check in her hand, Lance riding a motorcycle from Haifa to Kabul and a camel into Bamiyan. The years stretching before me, a field of wheat, the slender stems cast gold by the sun, the feathery leaves fluttering in the breeze.

What next? What next in this blink of a life?

ACKNOWLEDGMENTS

THIS NOVEL TOOK A LONG TIME TO WRITE. IT WOULD NEVER HAVE found its final shape without the help of many early readers, who put aside their own work to inhabit mine—an act of tremendous generosity. My heartfelt thanks to Alice Dark, Angie Kim, Sally Koslow, Margo LaPierre, Jane Pollock, Helen Simonson, Jill Smolowe, Nancy Star, Barbara Weisberg, and Mary Kay Zuravleff.

I am forever grateful to Geri Thoma, my agent at Writers House, who championed *Ana Turns* in its embryonic stages and, with her retirement, shepherded me into the sensitive hands of the dazzlingly smart Stacy Testa. My team at Turner Publishing—Ryan Smernoff, Amanda Chiu Krohn, and Makala Marsee—have been superb: devoted, meticulous, and kind, with an unwavering conviction that the words on the page belong to their author. On the publicity front, I've been lucky to have the help of the sage and patient Suzanne Williams during the nervous months leading up to the launch of the book—a span that eerily matches a pregnancy!

Three memoirs by trans women were profoundly helpful to me in learning about the varied experiences of trans women with their families of origin—experiences that range from extreme cruelty to, as Torrey Peters puts it in her remarkable novel *Detransition, Baby,* loving parents who 'make all the classic parents-of-a-trans mistakes': Sarah McBride's

Tomorrow Will Be Different: Love, Loss, and the Fight for Trans Equality, Janet Mock's *Redefining Realness: My Path to Womanhood, Identity, Love & So Much More*, and Meredith Talusan's *Fairest: A Memoir*.

Finally, as always, my gratitude to my husband, Ken, fact-checker extraordinaire, and my sons, Zack and Damon. My world turns because of you.

ABOUT THE AUTHOR

LISA GORNICK has been hailed by NPR as "one of the most perceptive, compassionate writers of fiction in America . . . immensely talented and brave." She is the author of four previous novels: *The Peacock Feast* (FSG), *Louisa Meets Bear* (FSG), *Tinderbox* (FSG), and *A Private Sorcery* (Algonquin). Her essays have appeared widely, including in the *New York Times*, the *Paris Review*, *Real Simple*, and the *Wall Street Journal*. A graduate of the Yale clinical psychology program and the psychoanalytic training program at Columbia, where she is on the faculty, she was for many years a practicing psychotherapist and psychoanalyst. She lives in New York City with her family. You can learn more about Lisa and her work at lisagornickauthor.com.